THE PYTHAGOREAN PATH

An Enneagram Tale

D1569900

The Pythagorean Path
An Enneagram Tale

Copyright 2021 © Julia Twomey

Cover design: Madeline K. Davy
Photograph: Peter Schuette
Shift & Shadow sculpture/ back cover: Gabriel Twomey
Interior book designer: Olivier Darbonville

The

PYTHAGOREAN PATH

AN ENNEAGRAM TALE

Julia A. Twomey, Psy.D.

Dedicated to Owen, Aden, Sam,
Luca, and Gabriel

Much thanks to the Off Campus Writer's Workshop,
and to Fred Shafer.
Thanks also to many friends who made suggestions.
And to my editor, Goldie Goldbloom

Contents

CHAPTER ONE

News!

TWO HUNDRED MILES ABOVE THE EARTH, the satellite cruised over the 66th Parallel. The camera on board focused on an ice cliff hanging above the Arctic Ocean. Images flew down an invisible beam, landing in NASA's Jet Propulsion Lab in Pasadena, California.

The lab assistant stirred her morning coffee as she watched the video fill her screen. Suddenly, she sat forward, spilling the hot drink over the desk. Grabbing the phone, she pushed the extension number.

"Come on, come on, pick up!" she said to the phone.

"Yeah . . . What's going on?" a weary voice asked.

"Something is very wrong. The ice cliff is gone."

The supervisor's eyes widened as she watched the disaster replay on her screen. A giant wall of ice crashing into the sea was a catastrophe they had all feared.

By noon, the scientists had gathered. They understood the danger heading toward the Atlantic Gulf Stream. A rush of icy water from the melted cliff meant drastic changes for weather patterns. There would be hurricanes, flooding of coastal regions, and crop failures. Homeland Security, and FEMA mobilized their agencies.

* * *

Two Thousand Miles East: Evanston, Illinois

The baby crawled quickly across the bedroom rug, grabbing the TV remote, and pushing the volume up to the max.

"WGN Chicago morning news at seven am. Today we have word that a major blow to the earth's climate happened overnight in the Arctic Ocean. We will bring you an update as the facts become available. Turning to local news. A prominent Chicagoan passed away this week. Joseph Spencer, a world-renowned engineer, died suddenly at the age of sixty-seven. Spencer's legacy included scores of patents aimed at reducing carbon emissions."

In the next room, Jack opened his eyes, awakened by the blaring TV, so loud he didn't make out the news report, or hear his dad running to grab the baby. Seeing the clock, he rolled out of bed. A moment later, he stood in the doorway, frowning at his baby brother, Charlie. Now in his dad's arms, the baby still held the remote.

"Sorry to wake you. He does love that gadget."

Charlie grinned and reached for his big brother.

"Not now Bub, I have to meet Grace and Mike in twenty minutes."

Howling at Jack's rebuff, the baby squirmed in his dad's arms. Jack grabbed a stuffed rabbit off the floor and handed it to Charlie, snagging the remote while the baby was busy with the bunny. The child stopped screaming, struggling to get down. As soon as he landed, he crawled off, dragging the rabbit. They both knew what was coming, however, when the baby discovered the prized TV control was now out of reach.

Jack's dad said, "There's an envelope addressed to you that arrived this morning. From a law firm. You better not be in trouble again."

Jack felt a shot of fear.

"I'm sure it's nothing. Maybe an ad for legal services after all the fuss last year. You always overreact. Don't you trust me? That mess was a bunch of government hacks throwing their weight around."

"Government hacks! Fuss! Really? You and your friends could have gone to jail."

"And… here you go again." Jack said, flipping his fear into anger at his dad.

"You know Mike and Grace's parents don't bring this up all the time. But you can't let it go. Can you?"

"You can bet we're going to take this up tonight," said his dad.

"Great. *More* quality time at the Abernault house. Can't wait," said Jack. Hoping to get his father off his back, Jack added, "Talk tonight."

His dad waved him off. But then called after him, "Tonight. I mean it!"

Prickling heat flushed up Jack's back. "Yeah, yeah. Whatever," he said under his breath.

Jack pulled on some jeans, and went down the stairs. The white envelope sat on the hall table, and he pushed down a wave of apprehension as he tore it open. Scanning the cover letter, he didn't find the word "lawsuit" on the paper, so he stuffed it in his backpack. The angry words with his dad still weighed on him. It felt like too much and too early to read the rest of the document. He needed to get out of the house. Closing the front door behind him, he tried to shut down his growing anxiety while he walked to the garage. He hopped on his bike.

A beautiful March morning, Jack breathed in the fresh air. The end of the long Chicago winter should have been enough to boost his mood. But thoughts of the lawsuit last fall swirled like a flock of angry starlings, and his mind refused to take in the hopefulness of spring.

All he could think about was his arrest. The federal agents at his door. Jack gripped the handlebars of his bike, trying to dispel the nightmare. The lawyers filing in. The court bailiff announcing the call to order. The bike wobbled. Pedaling faster, he pushed on. The sound of the judge's gavel cracked in his ears. And, always, last and worst, the look of disappointment on his dad's face.

It was a shock that a few wrong keyboard strokes on a computer could result in such swift reaction from law enforcement. Jack and his friends felt ambushed. They protested, not understanding what was happening. After their arrests that autumn afternoon, they sat in separate glass cubicles in the Federal building, waiting for their parents. Mike's dad, who served as their attorney, told them the charge was hacking into classified Defense Department files.

Shock registered on their parents' faces, followed by confusion. This was a preposterous accusation. These were good kids, they coded video games about sustainable living. Certainly, this was a mistake.

However, the evidence showed that on that fateful afternoon, the three friends had been skirting a game company's security wall, seeking a shortcut for their coding process. Mike had been distracted by something on Tik-Tok, and Grace had her hand resting on Jack's shoulder. Her touch had unsettled him, and he tapped into an anomaly in the code. This miss step flipped his search into a secure portion of the web site. At the time, they were unaware the same company that designed game platforms also held defense contracts with the federal government. When the screen signaled the breech, sounding an alarm, Jack immediately shut down the program, slamming the laptop shut.

"What the hell?"

A bolt of terror hit Jack. He lifted the lid of the laptop briefly, and the alarm screeched again.

"What have we done?' Jack said.

"Tripped over a code error, opening a backdoor?" Grace said.

"But a backdoor to what?" Jack asked. He felt stupid, careless.

They opened the laptop several more times, and now in addition to the alarm, there were big letters across the screen, announcing that they had invaded a government system, and were liable to prosecution. Nothing they tried would undo the slip up.

The next day, the three were hustled off in an unmarked federal van. Jack looked through the heavily tinted window and saw the brilliant orange autumn leaves now seemed withered.

Five months had passed, but the sting of humiliation was still raw. Jack turned the corner, gliding up to Grace's house. He found his two friends sitting on the porch. After the three had bonded over a decade ago, they had spent pretty much all their free time together. However, they often wondered about how different they were, almost like they hailed from alien planets. Typically, in a situation, Grace moved to take control, assuming the role of boss. Mike, on the other hand, looked for ways to blend into the mix, and to avoid any conflict. Jack was the careful one, the one who followed the rules. Not someone who hacked into government sites.

They shared interests: camping, math, and coding games. But, as close as Jack felt to these friends, recently he'd been hiding his worries, fearing they would see him as a wuss. Ever since the arrest he had been jumpier and more on edge. And, to complicate matters, Jack had found a shift in his feelings toward Grace.

He saw her now, sitting on the porch. Her deep blue eyes looked up at him, and strands of blonde fell out of her carelessly clipped hair. Why did these simple things make him feel so nervous?

"Hey," said Grace.

"Hey," said Jack, his voice squeaking.

He dropped into a chair, feeling his face flush.

"There's a glitch with the code," said Mike.

Grace and Jack shared a look. "I'll look at it, but, I gotta tell you. We can't get involved in any more legal messes."

"Wuss," said Grace.

"Thanks Grace. Just what I needed first thing in the morning," said Jack. Why didn't she worry?

"Geeze . . . One wrong key stroke, and the feds were all up in our grill. It's not like that company lost any money. Or that we were security threats," said Mike.

"Tell that to my dad." Jack said.

"He keeps asking why we didn't hack Dunkin' Donuts instead of the Feds."

Jack struggled to keep his comments upbeat, however something was gnawing at the edge of his thoughts.

"That company should have thanked us for pointing out their seriously defective security. How could we have known they stored defense department stuff?"

"I'm toast, if we get caught again," Jack said, because he couldn't help saying it, even though Grace would think he was even a bigger wuss, and not boyfriend material.

"Anyhow, I'm starving. Grace, do you have any cereal, or . . . toast?"

He grinned and pushed his wavy brown hair off his forehead . . . the move he'd practiced in front of his mirror.

"Get it yourself. I'm not your mom." Grace rolled her eyes.

"Nope, much cuter," he said to Mike's hoots, while he headed into the kitchen.

He returned a few minutes later with a bowl of steaming oatmeal.

"Mommm!" Grace yelled. "How come you cook for this yokel but not for me?"

"*She* loves me," Jack smirked.

"It's those weird green eyes of yours," Mike said.

"No, mate. It's my incredible physique, and sheer genius."

Grace threw a magazine at Jack, barely missing the cereal.

"My mom *does* think you guys are cute," she said with disgust.

"Hey, what can I say?" he said, as he scooped up another spoonful. He glanced at her. Her cheeks were red. A tiny kernel of satisfaction registered inside him.

Grace changed the subject back again to his least favorite topic.

"Our little walk on the dark side last fall was for a *good* reason. That shortcut would have saved us so much time. Gotten kids involved with climate issues. That company with their government connection just likes to hassle people."

Jack was losing his appetite. He stared at his cereal. Why couldn't she shut up? She just couldn't let it go. Give it a rest. So impossible. Everything was a big drama with her. If things were going smoothly, Grace found a way to upend it.

"Lucky my dad got them to settle for some community service," said Mike.

"Didn't hurt my uncle made a few calls," Grace said.

She was always bringing up her uncle, the detective. Weird, because Grace liked to break rules. Then his dad's face rose in his mind. The way he looked in the courtroom.

"Shut up," he said.

"You guys just won't let this stuff go. You're both complete losers. If anyone should go to jail, it's you two."

Grace glared at him, got up, and went into the house. Mike looked away.

Jack fumed. He knew his face was red. But Grace kept harping. It was clear that she didn't seemed bothered by the arrest the way he was. And, if it hadn't been for her, the whole thing might not have happened. Her presence had unsettled him. That day five months ago, she had been looking over his shoulder, one hand resting on him. He'd been the one to push the keys. But he probably wouldn't have done it on his own. In the back of his mind, he'd wanted to impress her.

Grace came back with her own bowl of oatmeal.

"My mom says she has to feed *all* the poor little clowns that I drag around with me, but . . ."

"I'm sorry," Jack said. "When we talk about the court case, it makes me crazy."

"I know," said Grace. She touched his arm. "I'm sorry too. Let's change the subject."

"All that fuss last fall seems like nothing compared to the *really* big disaster going on in the Arctic. Did you hear about the ice cliff that's now floating toward the Gulf Stream?"

"I saw it on the news this morning. I don't understand why nobody can stop this climate mess. It's not like any of us can escape. Don't those old guys in Washington have grandkids?" Mike said from behind his open laptop.

The collapsed ice wall was news to Jack, so he scanned the report on his phone.

"Everything is going to be floating or burning up in the heat," Jack said.

"Sound like the Bahamas," Grace said. "Not the worst thing in the world."

"Grace!" both boys said, tossing pillows at her.

Even after all their work on the climate game, researching the issues, Grace had no respect. Nothing was sacred with her. Anything to get everybody riled up. Stirring the pot is what his grandmother called it.

It was then Jack remembered the papers in his backpack. If not a new lawsuit, what could be in the letter? He pulled out the crumpled stack of pages and began to read.

When Grace saw concern grow on Jack's face.

"Read it out loud," Grace said.

"This has got to be some kind of scam, or a joke," said Jack.

"Let me see." Grace pulled the papers out of his hand.

Confused, Jack sat back, trying to put together his thoughts, and make sense of what he had read.

Grace scanned the page.

"You need to show this to your dad, Mike," and she handed the sheets over to him.

After reading a few minutes, eyebrows raised, he agreed.

"Oh yeah, dude. You need a lawyer. Big time."

"Yeah, I better check this out," said Jack.

The day that had started with a screaming TV and a crabby baby did not seem to be settling down. Anything but.

Mike pulled out his cell phone and in moments his dad picked up.

"Hey, can we come over now to talk with you? See there's this legal thing that Jack got in the mail."

Ten minutes later they threw their bikes on the lawn of Mike's house on Lincoln Street, and walked up the stone path to the door.

* * *

Dr. Vincent Marcov's Compound

Humming, Vincent Marcov twirled around his living room, dipping up and down with an imaginary dance partner. Then he landed in his armchair and reached for the brandy, pouring himself a drink. A contented look settled on his face as he thought about the progress made by his satellite's strike above the arctic that morning. Won't be long now, he thought.

The rogue scientist's goal of obliterating the earth's environment was a step closer. His thoughts took a victory lap, and the faces of taunting children from long ago rose in his mind. *Now* they would rue the day they had messed with him. Those kids, their kids and their grandkids would suffer the long overdue consequences.

He had warned them that they would be sorry. They probably had thought he would forget. But on that day, he had taken a vow. They all would pay. And now that he had an escape route, he was ready to take out the whole planet. That morning, with a simple push of a button, Dr. Marcov had cut a sizable ice cliff, dropping it into the sea. He had watched the huge mass bob to the surface and begin the journey south toward the Atlantic Gulf Stream. The icy water would create conditions ideal for a record devastating hurricane season.

Marcov planned to track the cold water as it entered the patch of ocean off the west coast of Africa. This breeding ground for tropical storms would send hurricanes dancing across the Atlantic, spinning into the Caribbean and Gulf of Mexico. His only disappointment was that someone else would get to name the tropical storms. That didn't seem fair.

* * *

Evanston, Illinois

Jack, Mike and Grace kicked off their shoes inside the front door of the Farrell's house. Usually, Mr. Farrell would be downtown by this time, so it was lucky that Mike's dad was free on such short notice to look over the letter from the law firm.

The lawyer sighed and looked concerned as he wondered what these kids had gotten themselves into this time. The three teenagers sat on the edge of their seats in front of his desk. Jack handed over the sheath of legal documents and waited.

An unsettled feeling rocked Jack's stomach. He liked routine, and this letter certainly was not that.

Mr. Farrell took his chair, sat back, and began to read, raising his eyebrows as the contents of the letter began to register.

After a few minutes, he took off his glasses and turned to Jack.

"Well, young man, this is quite a surprise, I'm sure."

Jack cut him off. "It's a scam, right? Has to be."

"Nope, not a scam. I know this law firm well. Bottom line, you have been named the heir to the Joseph Spencer Estate. A trust is set up to manage the property and business interests. It's all yours."

"That's impossible, I barely knew the guy."

Memories of last summer flooded his mind. An invitation to a family reunion. Based on DNA his mother had submitted to trace their genealogy tree. His protest at spending an afternoon with a group of random folks who happened to be third and fourth cousins. His mom prevailing. The event in Barrington. Hundreds of people from fourteen states. A meeting with an older man. Joseph Spencer.

"I heard on the news this morning that Spencer had passed away. He spoke once at the Chicago Bar Association, and I remember his message on climate issues. He must have raised tens of thousands of dollars for his foundation during that single lunch hour. What a legacy," said Mr. Farrell.

Grace leaned over and gave Jack a hug. Any other day he would have loved this closeness, maybe touching her hair. But today? Now? It all seemed unreal.

"This has got to be a mistake," Jack said.

He felt faint. He could see Mr. Farrell's mouth moving, but the words no longer registered. The office seemed to be tilting. Grace's hand was still on his arm, but he viewed it all outside himself. Gripping the wooden arms on his chair, he forced himself back into his body. Jack looked at Grace, seeing admiration, which for the moment, anyway, overshadowed any inheritance. "You must have *really* impressed this man, Spencer." Grace said.

"I only talked to the guy for a while." Jack heard his voice but felt detached from the words.

"Did you mention coding the climate video game?" Mike asked.

"Maybe, I don't remember," said Jack.

This all sounded too good to be true. What had he ever done to deserve an inheritance? Somebody was going to find out this all was a big mistake. Some relative would show up. Maybe Spencer was crazy when he wrote that will. None of this made any sense. His mind refused to accept this was really happening. Grace would find out he was a fraud. A bead of perspiration rolled down his temples, soaking into his collar. The chill settled around his neck, like a noose. Like he was guilty.

"This doesn't make any sense," Jack said, trying to dismiss the matter.

"Dude. Couldn't happen to a better guy," said Mike, punching Jack's shoulder.

"We should call your parents. Stay for lunch because this calls for a celebration," said Mike's dad.

* * *

Several Weeks Later . . . Lake Forest, Illinois

The navigation on the car's dashboard led them around curving streets lined by tall hedges and ivy-covered stone walls. Charlie was now awake from his nap, and fussed in his car seat. Over the back seat, his mom gave him a cracker. The baby reached for the snack, his cheeks flushed, and eyelashes tipped in blonde.

"What a slob. Charlie eats like a flock of pigeons." Despite the mess, it was clear, Jack felt a special bond with Charlie.

The baby took a bite then scattered the crumbled cracker with delight.

"Charlie, you little rascal. You did that on purpose. I'm on to you, hiding behind those sweet cheeks." Grace said.

The baby responded by batting her face playfully, sending more crumbs her way. Grace smiled. Then her gaze shifted out of the car window.

Jack stared at her profile for a moment. The pale-yellow curls falling on her cheek. He quickly looked away before Mike noticed the object of his attention. If his friend figured it out, it would mess everything up. Mike would be mad. It would change the friendship. He'd have to be careful. Moments like these tangled his feelings with his loyalties.

Oblivious, Grace said, "Wow, that house has a tennis court."

"Look at that campus," Mike said. They rounded a bend circling Lake Forest College.

"We should have dressed up."

Jack tossed his cap at Mike's head. The three fifteen-year-olds firmly embraced the fashion code of bus station at midnight. Grateful for this distraction, Jack punched and dodged Mike, the boys wrestling in the back seat like two bear cubs.

"Stop it." Grace and Jack's mother both snapped at the same time, sharing an exasperated look.

"You guys are clowns," said Grace.

"It never ceases to amaze me how in a flash these two can regress to the third grade," said his mom.

The commotion stopped as they passed a Tudor clock tower, the car coasting to a slow roll at Lake Forest's Market Square. Boutiques with awnings and heritage-colored doors bordered a lawn. Tips of green peeked from woody buds on pruned tree branches. Under a colonnade, a string of sparkling windows displayed eighteen carat gold jewelry, imported ceramics, and. highend housewares. In the last window, a mannequin glared at would be shoppers, daring them to enter her exclusive shop. An oversized scarf of Italian silk draped over her shoulder.

In contrast, the car his dad was driving was old and dusty, a pale brown minivan. There was duct tape holding the bumper to the car's frame. Jack squirmed in his seat. Everyone they passed turned and frowned at the van. He felt embarrassed. They didn't belong. The shoppers on the sidewalk all seemed dressed for brunch, wearing tweed jackets, or wrapped in handwoven shawls. Nobody wore jeans, sweatshirts, or old sweaters with stretched out sleeves.

Then, pulling up on the side of their car, a black SUV with tinted windows stopped long enough for a shadowy figure to check them out. The driver made an abrupt U turn, speeding off in the opposite direction.

"Well now that was totally weird. Are the paparazzi following you already?" said Grace.

"Yeah, totally creepy. Haven't you noticed the National Inquirer tailing us two cars back?" said Jack sarcastically.

Despite his joke, Jack sensed trouble. Maybe that driver was a detective. Hunting him down. Hired by one of Spencer's disgruntled relatives.

The Abernault's car turned toward the road leading down to the Lake. Sitting in the back seat, Jack had a sense that the life he had known was driving off a cliff. The faint smell of applesauce wafted up from Charlie's jacket. He noticed the frayed sleeves on the baby's hand me down. Clearly, they were misfits in this fancy village.

As his friends talked, Jack felt Grace's jeans brush next to his legs. The scent of lilac wafted off her curls. Sitting this close usually would have excited him, but he felt too anxious to relax. Everything seemed off, and all these sensations unsettled him. In the car, in his body, in this unfamiliar town. It was all uncomfortable.

Mr. Abernault swerved around a bend, almost missing the entrance tucked in a tall hedge of arborvitae. Putting the car in reverse, he backed up and they made their way under a wrought iron arch that read "*Morningside.*"

"Woah," said Jack's dad, "This is a *huge* estate."

"Jack, you're going to love mowing all that grass," said Grace.

"Hey, Grace . . . chill," said Mike.

"That's right. You guys need to take it down a notch," said Jack's mom who maybe also was feeling unsettled.

However, Jack was hardly listening. He felt he was spiraling into an alternate reality.

"Crap. It's a freaking castle. Is there gonna be a drawbridge, too? Just call me Richie Rich," said Jack under his breath.

His friends were silent. The worst possible reaction. At that moment, he felt alone. As if he had been pushed out on an ice flow. Life as he knew it, was floating away.

While the attorneys had assured him that the property transfer to his name remained all in order, he still worried that there was something they had not told him. His parents only had rattled on about how this was an astonishing turn of events. But Jack, a doubter by nature, began to look for a downside. He figured there had to be a catch.

This inheritance was nuts. After all, he had only met the guy once.

And why him? Maybe Spencer was mad at his legitimate heir, and so had left it to him out of spite? He had seemed a nice old man. With green eyes, like his. The guy hadn't acted crazy. But maybe the he had a stroke or something. Started doing wacky things?

Their van pulled up in front of a 1920's mansion with a slate roof, and walnut front door. The house, built of field stone, blended into the landscape. It evoked a sense of quietness. Despite his anxiety, Jack found the surroundings calming. His dad parked the van and then the group stood on the gravel, taking in the house.

"Holy Cow," said his dad.

"This is gorgeous," said his mom.

"At least it's peaceful. And no drawbridge," said Jack.

His friends laughed.

"You're going to need some Dobermans for security," said Mike.

The thought of himself walking two shiny black animals made Jack smile.

"Maybe I'll get a smoking jacket and silk scarf," he said.

"And a man servant named Rodney," Grace said.

"Can I apply for that job?" asked Mike.

"Sure, but you better have references," Jack said.

His friends laughed.

High above their heads, heavy branches shifted in the breeze, casting a shady maze on the lawn. A blast of cold wind came off the Lake, quickening their steps as the group walked around the exterior. Jack's parents said they would let him and his friends take the first look inside the house. They would follow when Charlie had a chance to move around for a bit.

"Remember. Meet us at noon in the front hall," his mom said.

"OK, twelve noon," Jack said.

Fishing the key out of his pocket, Jack turned the lock, and with Mike and Grace following, they entered. The three teenagers found themselves in a large hall with a wrought iron railing curving up a wide staircase. Walnut paneling covered the walls and coffered ceiling. The richness of the interior was interrupted by an unexpected modern light fixture glowing above their heads. A thick oriental carpet cushioned the floors under their feet, and the smell of polished old wood filled the air. Jack turned to see Mike staring at a painting in a burnished gold frame. It looked like a Georges Braque.

Jack could almost feel the house breathing.

Grace, let out a slow "Woah!"

Jack felt a flood of hope. With all this money now, Grace was impressed.

However, it occurred to him that now he would never know if she liked him for himself.

The craftsmanship, the art, and items most likely brought back from Spencer's travels ... this was the real deal. Like a museum ... but, nice, like a home. Jack tried to process this beautiful interior, thinking about how this house would alter his future, create a detour in his path. However, his fate had been thrust upon him. The unexpectedness of all this bothered him.

Wonder if the family would move up here? Sell the house in Evanston? Would he switch schools? Eat lunch with new kids? It would be hard to leave Evanston. There would be the weekends. But Grace might meet somebody. Couldn't stand that. And this place was huge. Charlie could get lost in here. Have to child proof all these rooms. On the other hand. The resources. Could go to any college. Just write a big check. All the doors would fly open. What a short cut. He'd be important. His dad would have to forget the arrest.

Jack felt the earth shift, his sense of time evaporating.

It was hard not to feel the presence of Joseph Spencer and his extraordinary achievements within these walls. However, he couldn't shake off his discomfort. There remained too many unknowns. His mind struggled to put this house in the context of the pleasant man he had met just that once. Maybe it was the responsibility that bothered him. Because Jack now sensed an obligation, a burden, resting on his shoulders. Could he live up to everyone's expectations? Follow in the footsteps of a great man's legacy? When he felt so unprepared? Mike brought him back to the moment.

"Wow. This place is awesome."

Grace was quiet. Usually never at a loss for words, she looked overwhelmed by her surroundings. Jack wondered what she was thinking. Maybe that he would turn into a jerk. Now that he was rich. He didn't know how to act. Then he thought about Joseph Spencer's will. How it had been clear that Jack was *to do the next right thing* with Morningside. Those words in the legal documents posed both a challenge, and a promise of unlimited opportunity. It seemed like a windfall, but was it really?

He saw Grace watching him.

"This is too much. I don't need all this pressure. Everyone is making a big fuss. And for what? Yeah, this house is great, but I have enough going on, without dealing with all this stuff," said Jack.

She took his hand.

"Hey, the house is *beautiful*. And Mike's dad said the foundation will manage it. It's not like you're all alone," she said.

They continued walking through the house while he thought about the choices that lay ahead. Jack caught a thin whiff of something burning, but he shook it off. Probably only embers from one of the fireplaces.

Swigging a gulp from his water bottle, he looked around. On the walls of a long hall, murals with mythological creatures looked back at him, seeming to confirm his unworthiness.

"You don't deserve all this. What have *you* ever done?"

Jack looked down to avoid their gaze. When he looked up, he was confronted with ancient deities on a ceiling, covered in shimmering mosaic. The images pressed down on him as he craned his neck. It was impossible to tell how far away the tiles were. One minute, the glistening figures seemed distant. In the next, they felt close in, accusing and judging him. Ready to smite him with a bolt of lightning.

"Fine," he said, talking to the walls and startling Grace. "I'm not worthy of *any* of this. I don't belong here."

"Uh, no kidding," she said. Then seeing the look on his face, she said. "It really *is* yours, Jack. *Calm down*."

Jack let out a sigh. They sat for a moment on a bench in a hall.

"Hey, I'd live here. Think of all the stray animals I could take care of. Maybe start a little zoo," she said.

"You don't even feed your cat," said Mike.

"Snickers doesn't like me, so I let the boys handle him," said Grace.

"Does his dislike have anything to do with the costumes you forced him to wear?" asked Mike.

"There weren't *that* many," said Grace. "And, as I recall. I didn't hear any complaints from you guys. You both loved it."

"Ah yes. The memory of Snickers, stuffed in red satin briefs, a matching cape tied around his neck." brought a smile to Jack's face. "You *are* bad, Grace."

"Yeah, and you love it," she said.

"I must," and he hugged her playfully.

Jack caught a look on Mike's face. Uh oh, he thought, Mike maybe was picking up on something. Better reign in the hugs. Wanting to escape, he said,

"Where's a washroom in this place?"

Ten minutes later, Jack heard the faint voices of his friends now coming from another floor. He moved on quickly at first, but found more frescoed walls. The scene on his right side showed scientists with test tubes. On his left, images of engineers working on machines brought on another rush of shame as it reminded him of an upcoming robotics competition. Again, he had put off completing the application, feeling he wasn't quite ready to make a commitment. As usual, his struggle with doubt had stopped him. Then Jack reminded himself that when he was involved in the actual work on the robot, he enjoyed himself.

On a table, a photo of Joseph Spencer receiving the Medal of Freedom at the White House caught Jack's eye. That could be him. Honored for engineering or physics. Wearing a tux. Walking the red carpet. Maybe win a Nobel Prize? Shaking hands with uniformed officials. A sash filled with medals. Grace at his side.

Then Jack's thoughts returned to the day he had met Spencer, recalling the well-attended family reunion. Finding the older man at the buffet table. Trying to decide between a chocolate torte or a slice of apple pie. Jack had waited. Spencer had looked up, asking which piece looked better. And, he had responded without hesitation that apple pie never disappoints. Spencer had served them both a slice. As they ate, they had talked about how the turn out for the event had been great, but that the crowd was a bit over-whelming. Jack had noticed the elderly man looked tired, so he had pulled up a chair for him. And had fetched him a bottle of water. It was then Spencer had confided that his wife had passed away, and that she generally was the one who enjoyed these big shindigs. Jack had admitted that he and his dad had been less than enthusiastic about the reunion, sharing they preferred smaller gatherings.

"My mother insisted. She wanted to meet people that our DNA turned up."

"DNA can hold some interesting surprises . . . about how we're all con-nected," said Spencer, his eyes twinkling.

"I guess," Jack had said.

That man had also been a good listener. Spencer had asked several inter-esting questions. One, in particular, had stuck in Jack's mind: *What activity allowed him to lose track of time?*

Without hesitation, he'd responded.

"I tinker with machines and computer programs. Hours fly by when I have a problem to solve. Must be following in my dad's footsteps. He's a mechanical engineer."

The older man had smiled, had taken a sip of water, and then had leaned back in his chair. At the time, Jack thought Spencer looked contented. Seem-ing to relax, the man gazed up into the branches of the massive oak tree.

Now, apparently, because of that single conversation, he was the owner of Morningside. Most people might have felt they had won the lottery. But Jack couldn't shake the nagging feeling that the attorneys had withheld something else about the estate. Jack asked himself, why hadn't Spencer left the fortune to some environmental group? It didn't make sense that he would sign over the whole deal to a fifteen-year-old. Only thing he had in common with the man was green eyes and the family DNA.

Lost in his thoughts, Jack suddenly noticed that burning smell again. He'd have somebody check the wiring in the house. A few minutes later, he found his friends on the second floor. They were pretty much coasting through the rooms, eager to see everything.

"Here he is. Master of the manor. Can you believe this place?" Mike said. "Man! The parties we can throw. There's an indoor, *and* an outdoor pool."

"Better keep the parties outside," Grace said. "This is no place for a bunch of rowdy kids."

"Pool parties outside all summer then," Mike said.

"This isn't a frat house, you know. No pool parties," said Jack.

"Yeah, this place *is* kind of magical. Not a place for horsing around," said Grace.

"Oh, so now your friends aren't fancy enough," said Mike.

"Look, you guys can swim. But I can't have a big free for all," said Jack.

"Whatever," said Mike, annoyed.

They walked back into the hall, but Jack again fell behind. Moving at a slower pace, he wished he knew more about his benefactor's early life, and what led him to study engineering. All he knew was that Spencer was a self-made man. He had grown up in a working-class family in Chicago, and a scholarship offered him a way to attend university.

It was incredible that someone with so few resources could build up this kind of legacy in one lifetime. Jack's parents, on the other hand, were educated, with professional careers. But they still drove a crummy van. How had Spencer managed to claw his way through a city high school and into an estate on a Lake Forest bluff?

Jack found his friends in the library, a room filled with leather volumes. In the center of a paneled wall, a portrait of a kind looking young woman in a black gown hung over the fireplace. Jack moved closer to view the engraved plate ... *Elinor Kaye Spencer-1982.* Joseph's wife, he knew.

"Aw, she's pretty," said Grace.

"Yeah, definitely a babe," Mike said.

"I think she looks serious. They must have been quite the couple," said Grace.

Jack thought of a portrait of him and Grace hanging in the room. But Grace, he knew, would never sit still long enough for an artist. It would have to be a photograph.

Jack surveyed the collection of ticking antique clocks.

"Wow, this is amazing," Jack said.

Making a mental note to return later, he knew these time pieces were early machines that had led to the industrial age. Mike, on the other hand, was content to get lost in the moment, seldom pressured by deadlines, or demands. Jack looked at his friend standing mesmerized in front of a glass clock that displayed the turning of gears, and the ticking of time.

"Earth to Mike," Grace said sharply.

Jack snickered at the clueless, but classic, expression on Mike's face.

"What? Isn't this cool?" Mike said.

But Grace had moved on, efficiently checking out each clock.

She *was* something else. Seemed determined to plough through this place. Jack again found himself stealing glances at her as she worked her way around the room.

But, as it turned out, Jack was not the only one sneaking a peek. Because, as the three friends took in the clock collection, they couldn't have known that at that moment, they were being observed. Behind the west wall a tall slender figure wearing a maroon bow tie peered through a peep hole hidden between the books. His gaze rested on Jack, sizing up this kid who seemed tall for his fifteen years.

When Jack moved to get a closer look at something on the shelf, Marcov's skin paled, registering the youth's serious green eyes.

Unaware of the intruder, but suddenly feeling unsettled, Grace called out, pointing to her watch.

The rogue scientist backed away from the peephole. Fleeing through a hidden passageway between the walls, he exited through a back hall. His black SUV with tinted windows was soon driving away from the rear of the coach house.

Back in the library, Grace was impatient.

"Come on. We need to move on," said Grace.

Mike groaned, but she shot him a look. Ignoring the rebuff, he turned to follow her out the door. Once they were in the hallway, Mike looked around.

"So where's a rest room?"

Jack pointed the way, and Mike started down the steps.

"Hey, so feeling better?" Grace asked Jack while they waited for Mike.

"This is a lot to take in," he said.

"Stop worrying," she said.

He wished she wouldn't use the word *worry*. Made him sound like a nervous old lady. He shifted his weight, wanting to change the subject.

"Look, this place is amazing. Things will work out. And you have a lot of help," said Grace.

Drawing in a deep breath, Jack switched gears, trying to appear cool.

"Yeah. Think I'll hire a bunch of hot assistants to whip this place into shape."

"I bet you will." Grace shoved him, laughing.

Jack smiled, and playfully pushed her back. Happiness flooded him, enjoying the body contact with this girl. Suddenly the room felt hot. Surprising her, and himself, he landed a kiss on her cheek.

"Oh, OK," and she returned the kiss on his cheek.

Mike caught up just in time to see Jack pull in Grace, kissing her on the lips.

"So, I leave you two alone for *five* minutes, and this is what you get up to," Mike said. There was an unmistakable edge to his voice.

"Oops, Grace can't keep her hands off me," Jack said.

"Very funny," said Grace sarcastically.

"I know what I saw," said Mike.

"Oooooo the hall police, are we now," said Jack, hoping to deflect.

"Whatever," said Mike. But his tone was irritated.

Jack started to howl like a wolf at the moon. And Mike chased him down the hall. They were eight years old again.

Grace smiled at her two idiot friends. Their childish behavior seemed to push the reset button on the three of them. The boys, with their horsing around antics, and Grace with her sarcasm, returned them to a simpler time before the pressures of high school, interest in romance, and now this inheritance. A less complicated existence, these playful moments reloaded their trust in each other. After ten minutes of chasing, and Grace's eye rolling, they were ready to continue exploring the house.

It was then they arrived at a hall with a gold leaf ceiling. A line of chandeliers hung like crystal jewelry over a polished floor that gleamed below their feet.

"And just when I thought we had covered the first floor. There's more," Mike said with some frustration.

"This place only keeps on going. Looks like a whole new wing," said Grace

"Sorry, if this is wearing you out, Mike," Jack said, detecting some envy in his friend. Maybe Mike was still annoyed about the kiss he interrupted.

"No, only I've never been inside a house this big," Mike said, trying to walk back his comment.

Jack knew Mike was ticked off. But about what exactly? He had never mentioned any interest in Grace. But neither had he, come to think of it. A pairing with Grace likely would mess up the friendship. On top of having this big house, now he might also have a girlfriend. Mike couldn't be pleased with all the change. He'd be odd man out.

In a flash, the sunlight blasted into the hall, igniting the gold leaf ceiling, beckoning them forward. Grace and Mike, drawn into the gilded hall, quickly walked on. But Jack paused, noticing another door . . . with simple grey stonework. On a whim, and maybe partly to process the tension with his friends, he called after them.

"Hey, go on ahead. I want to check out this side door. I'll meet you at noon in the front hall."

Mike gave a thumbs up, and Grace nodded. Jack couldn't have known that the next time he saw them, things would be exceedingly different.

*　*　*

Planet Sophia

At that moment above the Morningside estate . . . up in the sky . . . way, way up in the sky . . . and through a space/time portal . . . in another galaxy, on the planet Sophia, the Council assembled. Rushing into the gallery and dressed in brown robes, they took their places around an ancient oak table. The chairman banged his gavel and called the meeting to order. He told the group that Vincent Marcov had struck again. This time, the Council's arch enemy had launched a second attack on the earth's polar ice cap with his laser equipped satellite. Alarm filled the room, as the members pounded their fists on the table. These direct attacks on the arctic pole marked an escalation in Marcov's campaign to ruin Gaia's environment. And what happened on earth, eventually would impact Sophia, as earth's population would rush to leave their dying planet. Already, Marcov's space vehicle had managed to travel to Sophia. And, now that the rogue scientist had secured his escape route from earth, there was nothing to stop him from destroying the climate on his home planet. "The time has come to entrust Earth's people with the ancient book of wisdom, the Anamchara Text," said the chairman.

The council broke out in debate.

"It's about time," said an elderly man who was known as the Philosopher.

"I worry the book will be used to manipulate the population," said a member with wild curly hair.

"Things are too far gone. We must take the risk. They can't seem to fix their environment," said a young woman, with a baby on her lap.

"Marcov has sleeper cells who stand ready to block any progress with green technology," said the man sitting to the chairman's left.

The chairman's gavel banged.

"We know that in the hands of a fiend, the Anamchara Text could be weaponized. Centuries ago, it was decided that only special masters would have access to the knoweldge. They feared the wisdom would be misused. If Marcov gets his hands on the ancient text, he will suppress it, or twist it for his own purposes. Because the wisdom could end his influence. With the destruction escalating, we must act."

"Joseph Spencer's heir has the potential to save the earth's climate. If he learns the Anamchara Text, and teaches it to the people on earth, there is a chance. If he fails, it seems all is lost."

"Why is it a fifteen-year-old?" objected a thin man with a balding head. He looked around to see others agreeing with his objection.

"Because he has the hallmarks of a champion. Even if he doesn't know it yet," boomed a voice.

The council turned to look at the newest member, Joseph Spencer. His serious green eyes scanned the assembly, quieting the complaints. They all knew the exceptional circumstances that had brought Joseph and his wife to live on Sophia.

The gavel sounded again.

The room hushed, and the chairman's eyes rested on the table's carved inscription, "*For the Good of Humanity.*" This manifesto, cut into the oak, memorialized the founding charter that had ignited an enlightenment on Sophia, much like earth's Renaissance. Sophia's awakening had also been seeded by the writings of Pythagoras, Greek manuscripts, a newly diverse population, and trade connections.

"We know Marcov has used nanobots to coerce others to do his bidding. But, the effects of these devices wear off. If Vincent Marcov got his hands on the Anamchara Text, he could twist the knowledge into the ultimate weapon. So, we need to act first."

"Discussion is closed. The matter is decided. Two agents will meet Spencer's heir this morning at Morningside. This young man, Jack Abernault, is in imminent danger, because it's only a matter of time before he's attacked. Marcov is unpredictable, sometimes performing malicious pranks to terrorize, while other times his acts are deadly. It remains imperative that this Abernault youth accepts our challenge."

The Council nodded, and pounded on the table, signaling the group's consensus.

Then one voice spoke up.

"So which two agents did you send to deliver the letter to Jack Abernault?"

"I sent Max and Izzy," he said. His his eyes lowered, as he shuffled papers in front of him.

A massive groan erupted in the assembly.

"I know, I know . . . but they have to start taking on some responsibility. And, they were running around here this morning, making a ruckus. I was afraid they would wake up the old Man. And we *certainly* don't want that."

The grumbling abruptly subsided. They certainly did *not* want that.

Children had been taught from the time they could walk, never to open the large door with the letter carved into the surface. The old man had left specific instructions that he did not want to be disturbed.

But, it was clear, the Council members thought the chairman should have sent more experienced apprentices.

CHAPTER TWO

The Choice

As Mike and Grace walked down the gold leaf hall at Morningside, they wondered about their friend.

"I wish Jack would stop worrying about this inheritance. All this is amazing," said Mike.

"I know . . . right? He overthinks everything. It's good that he's careful, but geez. Sometimes I want to shake him," said Grace.

"He could retire when he finishes school. Coast for the rest of his life." Mike sighed wistfully.

"He'd never not work. Knowing Jack, he would start building something. Or think of how many polar bears he could save," said Grace.

"His money should help our video game. Now we can hire some top PR firm to promote it when it's finished," Mike said.

"Good point," said Grace.

"So, Grace. What's with you and Jack?"

"Don't know. Only fooling around," she said, twirling a strand of blonde hair.

"But Jack's not a fooling around kind of guy," said Mike.

"Maybe he is," said Grace.

Then she pointed out the tennis court visible through a window, changing the subject. The two friends continued down the hall, coming up with more and more ways for Jack to spend his money. Ducking into rooms, they took photos of cool items they found, including a meteor fragment and a model of a Japanese tea house.

Meanwhile, on the other side of the mansion, Jack was investigating on his own. After entering the simple stone passageway, he saw a stenciled triangle with an eye in the middle. This painted eye seemed to look toward a section of wall. He moved closer. To his surprise, he found a door camouflaged by a mural of tall ships. Tentatively, he opened it, and crossed the threshold.

He found himself in a small chamber, and there, before him, were two strange little boys sitting on a rug. Silver and moss green curls framed their faces. Jack assumed they must be the groundkeeper's kids. But what was with the hair?

The older boy smiled and jumped up.

"Hello, sir. I'm Max, and this is my little brother, Izzy."

The boy's speech had a strange mechanical cadence, with an overlay of high-pitched clicks and chirps.

The younger one whispered in his brother's ear, "Aren't we supposed to call him Master Champion?"

Max quieted him, "Not yet. He has to . . . you know."

Izzy's face brightened, "Oh, I forgot."

"So, hello," said Jack. "Are you hiding in here?"

"Noooo . . . we were *hoping to* meet you," said Izzy. He chirped and clicked out the words.

"Did you know I was coming up to Morningside today?" asked Jack.

"Uh huh," said Izzy in a somewhat sinister tone, staring at Jack.

Jack assumed he had stumbled upon a game of Star Wars in progress. He used to act out these scenes with Mike and Grace when they were in second grade. These boys looked to be about nine and seven years old, dressed in crisp white tunics. The speech pattern, he thought, was downright impressive. These kids had skills.

"I'm hungry. Do you have any food?" Max looked hopeful.

Jack pulled some granola bars out of his pocket, and their eyes lit up. He handed them over and greedily, the boys ate the bars. Jack stuffed the empty wrappers in his pocket. When he looked up, he was surprised to see a most serious look on Max's face.

"O.K., Good. You passed the first test. Sharing, you know, is the sign of a hero," Max said.

"We hoped you would take the stone hall, because we have been expecting you," said Izzy.

"What do you mean - expecting me?"

Jack wondered how the boys would weave him into their play scheme. He was surprised that these kids could keep up the pretense, not breaking character, but maintaining the weird talking pattern.

Max told him to sit down.

After Jack complied, the two little boys explained that they had come from the planet Sophia and that they needed his help. These boys sure had lively imaginations, going off script from Star War. Intrigued, he decided to play along with their game.

"Tell me more," said Jack.

The older boy said Morningside estate rested under a small sliver in the space-time fabric. As a result, a porthole existed directly above the mansion that allowed passage, outside the galaxy, to neighboring planets . . . that is, if you had the right vehicle. Max smiled tentatively. Then he admitted that he knew it sounded crazy. But he told Jack, that they had a way to move through great distances.

"Say what?" said Jack.

These kids were *amazing*.

Then, to humor them, he said, "No way." He wished Grace was here to see this.

39

"Who is Grace?" asked Izzy, pulling Max's sleeve.

Had he said that out loud? Jack didn't think so.

"Be quiet, Izzy," his brother said.

"Again, we have a special space vehicle."

These little guys were too much ... maintaining the clicks and chirps in their speech. Maybe they took acting lessons? Jack thought.

Max looked at his brother, raised his eyebrows, and countered, "Well, we'll show you how we travel. We can even have you back by noon."

Jack smiled. "Sure you will. Ok. Let's go."

As soon as the words were out of his mouth, Jack noticed the little boys' silver and moss green hair had soft tendrils around their faces, not like wigs from the Party Store.

"Come on. Follow us," Max said

They led Jack out a door where he noticed the sky had changed with heavy grey clouds now bearing down on the estate. Jack shivered as the fog's dampness landed like icy fingers. The chill traveled up his spine, and he wrapped his jacket tighter around his middle. Jack considered turning back, but then the boys entered a maze with eight-foot high hedges of boxwood. Spurred on, he followed them. They giggled, zipping through the turns and curves. Jack saw little stone faces peeking out of the shrubbery.

"Here he comes?" Jack heard in a raspy whisper.

Jack whipped around to see who was speaking. Did that stone head turn? No, of course not. Must be the younger boy messing with him.

"Shh ... Don't move. We don't want to scare him off."

"Get a grip," Jack whispered to himself. He took a deep breath.

Jack moved on, but Max and Izzy had disappeared again around a bend. He heard them rustling somewhere ahead in the maze. Their muffled voices punctuated with the high-pitched chirps. Jack paused a moment, noticing everything seemed kind of other worldly. Snow began to fall on the mossy path.

"Here we go again. It's supposed to be spring," said Jack.

Oddly, in spite of the falling snowflakes, the air suddenly seemed warm-er. The boxwood that brushed the back of his hand had a feathery feel, like a bird's wing grazing his fingers. Jack noticed the scent of blossoms filling the air. A silvery haze settled in his path.

"Max? Izzy? Where are you guys?" said Jack.

All he could hear was a whooshing sound, like a strong wind.

What was going on? Was he losing his mind? Where were those kids? They were here a minute ago.

Then, startling him, an old woman with kind eyes emerged from the mist. She looked like the portrait of Elinor Spencer that he had seen in the library, but decades older. She wore a simple black gown with a shawl and a veiled hat.

"Hello, young man. I am Elinor. I see you have met Max and Izzy. Darling boys when they aren't getting into mischief." Her eyes sparkled with amusement.

Her unexpected appearance should have rattled him; however, she had a calming effect on him once she began to speak. He began to introduce himself. But she hushed him.

"Oh, I know who you are. Joseph was so delighted to make the connection. You two have so much in common. As time goes on, you will see. You would do well to keep an open mind."

"So I'm kind of confused . . . ," said Jack.

"Be patient. Over time, you'll get your answers. You know, you're on the hero's journey, after all. It's a process that cannot be hurried. You're doing fine, choosing the stone hallway, avoiding the flash of the golden corridor. Keeping it simple is always a good idea."

Jack realized he wasn't going to get any answers beyond what she wished to tell him. He wondered how she knew what had happened in the house. Maybe this was all a dream. He recalled a cold breeze, then snow, then warm again. Surely, he'd wake up soon.

So, resigned, he listened as the woman continued.

"I used to tell my darling Joe, do the next right thing, and you will be fine."

Then, as quickly as she had appeared . . . she vanished, gracefully stepping back into the heavy mist that magically evaporated like a page had been turned.

"Ok, now. That was totally weird," he spoke to the air.

Was a theater company putting on a performance at Morningside? Maybe they didn't get the memo that there was a new owner. But then how had the woman quoted Spencer's will, to *do the next right thing.* Jack looked around, but the two little boys were nowhere to be seen. Checking his phone, the time showed 9:30 am. He was not sure if Elinor Spencer, Max, and Izzy were actors or odd hallucinations. Or a delusion due to dehydration, or a funky vitamin pill. Then he felt the empty granola wrappers in his pocket. Bewildered, he thought, no, they were real.

Well then, where were they? He looked around.

Exiting the maze a few moments later, Jack looked up and saw a huge glass cube resting in a low branch of a massive oak tree. A rope ladder dangled from the lower limb. While his instincts told him to hesitate because it didn't look too secure, his curiosity took over, and he climbed up to the tree house. It seemed odd that he could not see through the glass structure, so he moved closer, and his hand found an indentation that responded to his touch. A panel slid open, and there, smiling from ear to ear, stood Max and Izzy.

These kids certainly had a kick ass tree house at their disposal. Jack acted against his usual tendency to pause and leaped in to join them. Rocking in response to his added weight, the glass cube moved up and then down. The boys laughed, but with a staccato quality that sounded chirpy, and a little creepy. He was about to ask where their dad was, assuming the groundskeeper must be somewhere around the property.

But before he could get the words out, spinning, and rising, the cube began to fly!

Jack screamed as a swirl of mist encircled the cube. They jetted straight up like a rocket so that he could see Morningside, and Lake Michigan recede in the distance below him. Jack and the boys blasted through the clouds.

"Help! Stop! Nooooo!" Jack yelled.

Moments later, the cube floated through the sliver of a space/time portal. Jack's stomach had flipped over at least six times. The pressure in his head was massive. He could hear himself screaming. His body was in full on revolution.

Overwhelmed, he tried to grasp his predicament. Where was he going? And why?

Max reassured him, trying to deal with Jack's panic.

"We will have you back by noon."

"You're safe!" said Izzy. "Don't worry,"

But Jack's eyes were wide with fear as he yelled even louder.

"Make him stop screaming," said Izzy.

Max waved his hand in front of Jack's terrified eyes. But there was no calming their captive.

Their little faces hovering over him were the last things Jack registered . . . before passing out on the silver cushions.

CHAPTER THREE

The Challenge

WHEN JACK CAME TO, IZZY STOOD ready with a tall glass of water. As he took a sip, the boys reassured him that they flew this cube all the time and it had a perfect safety record.

"There really is nothing to worry about. You're safe with us," said Izzy.

"What the hell!" Jack said.

"We will explain, but you need to stay calm. Let your body adjust to the flight," Max chirped.

Jack's heartrate settled, perhaps due to his hope that this was only a bizarro dream sequence. He would awaken any moment now and laugh about his crazy nightmare. His mind could not accept what he was seeing. Assuring himself that the flight wasn't happening, he let his curiosity take over as he watched them move through space.

The view was dazzling . . . amazing, with planets and constellations blinking like jewels tossed against a velvet backdrop.

The beauty of the universe seemed to settle the reluctant passenger. His senses now seemed to click into their typical connections, doing a sytem's check of some kind. He was hearing a humming sound. There was the smell of ozone. The sense of propulsion through space. He could see light flashing. He began to accept that he was, in fact, not asleep. What to do? Pretend to be asleep and then pounce? Wrestle them? There're is two of them. But he was bigger. Then again, he didn't know how to control the flying cube . . . so, basically, he was screwed. The motion sickness returned, flipping his stomach. Weakened, he begged.

"Look, what's going on? Where are you taking me?"

"You'll get some answers. But, right now, you need to settle down."

"Settle down? Are you kidding? I've been abducted by two little kids in a flying treehouse. Going who the hell knows where!"

"Did he say a swear?" Izzy cried, almost bird-like. Tears dropped on the child's cheeks.

Max turned and frowned at Jack,.

"See what you've done? Izzy is not used to yelling. Who raised you?"

Surprised by the reprimand, Jack felt bad. Tears always had this effect on him. Izzy reminded him of Charlie.

But he quickly shook off this thought. *Wait* a minute. These kids were criminals. They had abducted him. He would *not* feel bad for them.

Izzy blew his nose, sniffing back more tears. Max now seemed ready to talk.

"Look, we've been sent by a Council commission to enlist your help. Turns out you were correct when you thought there might be something more to Morningside than just a big house."

"I *knew* it!" Jack said.

Then the little space boys boys shared a glance, concluding that Jack had recovered his senses. Max passed him a large envelope with *Jack Abernault*, written in silver ink. Jack noticed the unusual paper texture. Opening the letter, he read.

Max and Izzy hail from the planet, Sophia, beyond the Milky Way galaxy. We are an evolved population of homo sapiens, with advanced science that has resolved the issues around climate. Our world has a similar atmosphere to earth, and it supports human life.

Trying to process this incredible information, Jack looked up into the faces of the two little boys. They grinned, showing too many teeth to look totally innocent.

"This has to do with earth's environment?" Jack asked.

"It's not that simple," said Max. He gestured to keep reading.

Jack returned his attention to the letter.

But our planet now shares a serious problem with your people. A rogue scientist, Dr. Vincent Marcov, discovered the space/time portal that allows him to travel to Sophia. For decades, this troubled genius has blocked attempts to fix climate problems in your world. Sometimes his attacks directly poison the air and water, but often, he sabotages climate agreements and green policies.

"Dr. Vincent Marcov?"

He could see the fear in Izzy's eyes.

"One sick dude," said Max.

"*So* mean," chirped Izzy.

Jack read on.

In order to repair the climate, your people must evolve . . . and do it fast. As it stands now, your population remains stuck by Marcov and his collaborators who block environmental reforms. We need to boost the awareness of your people . . . to raise their consciousness . . . We will give you a teaching that lies within the pages of a special wisdom book, the Anamchara Text. The writings hold a powerful, ancient formula to help individuals evolve. While there remain many avenues to enlightenment, this book holds a special set of insights . . . like yeast that leavens the bread of consciousness.

Not everyone will be able to absorb this knowledge, but if a large enough number of people take the teachings to heart, they will move to heal the climate. Sophia wishes to help the earth's population, because we fear, that if your environment collapses, we will be overrun with earth's people fleeing your dead planet. As it stands now, a number of your great minds and hearts live with us, and their gifts continue to bloom under our care. Your planet will become uninhabitable very soon, unless your population has a change of heart.

If you accept this challenge, it will entail three tasks:

First, go on a quest where you will meet certain individuals. Observe them, and listen closely, not only with your ears, but with your head, with your heart and with your gut.

Second, learn the teachings of the Anamchara, and explain the book's contents to your people.

And then, lastly, neutralize Vincent Marcov.

The path, dangerous and demanding, requires courage and cleverness. Our future and yours remain bound together in this endeavor. We await your response.

The Council . . . Sector 41 . . . Planet Sophia

Dropping the letter on his lap, Jack stared at the brothers.
Finally, he spoke.
"Why me?"
Max reached over, placed his hand on Jack's shoulder.
"Hell, if I know."
Jack fell back on the cushions. He couldn't believe this was happening.
Izzy handed over a carbonated drink, and Jack chugged the liquid. Closing his eyes, he wished, if only the cube would just stop spinning. Maybe, if he kept his eyes shut, and one foot on the floor. He curled into a ball.
Max and Izzy watched him, and waited. They chirped and clicked in their strange language, a chatter that sounded like the bird house at Lincoln Park Zoo. Exotic birds shrieking. Wings flapping too close to his ears. Reaching out his hand, Jack signaled for quiet. His insides roller coasted up

and around, and back and forth. Thankfully, the boys stopped talking. Jack tried to shut down his senses, gripping his knees, trying to anchor himself. The carbonation settled his stomach. Jack picked up the letter, re-reading it.

"This is nuts," said Jack.

"Look, Vincent Marcov has a laser capable satellite that is cutting off ice, causing the sea to rise, and hurricanes to form. The guy has hacked into water filtration systems, and sabotaged climate treaties. If you don't help, it's only a matter of time. Everything is going to be burning up or floating."

Jack thought he had used those exact words. Sitting on Grace's porch? The day he had gotten the inheritance letter. Pretty weird. Were these kids psychic or something? He was well aware that the earth was running out of time, however, he was fifteen fricking years old. A champion? He'd thought of himself as a worrier, not a warrior? What was this Council thinking?

But at least he was right about something. He *had known* something was very fishy about Morningside.

Jack wished that he could get up and leave this cube that reminded him of a food storage container. He sat slumped, a pile of sour insides, and hurling through space. Everything felt upside down, flipped from a gravity respecting world to a wild and wooly universe that spun his guts in a cosmic blender.

"Home. I wanna go home," said Jack. Pleading now.

"Not yet. We have to show you something," said Max.

Jack moaned.

The image of an incoming missile flashed in his mind with Dr. Vincent Marcov and his advanced technologies targeting him and his family. If he accepted the Council's challenge, they would all be in peril. It felt as if some menacing tattoo artist was busy with a hot needle searing his back with an indelible bullseye.

Jack squeezed his eyes shut, hoping to erase all of it. But when he opened them again, nothing had changed. The strange children, in their white tunics, and unsettling chirping, stood in front of him. Looking expectant.

How was he even supposed to find Marcov much less neutralize him? And what did that word *neutralize* even mean? Did they expect him to kill the guy? Why didn't they pick someone else? Reading his mind, Max responded.

"Well, we don't know, but Joseph Spencer found you full of potential. And you chose the stone passageway, resisting the golden hallway. Or, it has something to do with your green eyes, maybe your temperament, and your talents in problem solving. You need to know the Council, and all of us, are depending on you. Izzy and I are only apprentices, not privy to the decisions made by our Council."

"Just take me home. I can't help you," Jack said.

"We will, just not yet," said Max.

Cold sweat rolled down Jack's temples. How could he possibly trust these children who had lured him into this flying glass jail? Were they even human with the green and silver hair? The avian voices? If he said no, would they toss him out of this cube, leaving him to die, his body floating until it burned up in space? Jack tried to calm himself, but these dark thoughts collided with his mounting fear. It seemed like an internal circuit board was overloading and sparking.

After some extremely disturbing minutes, the maelstrom in his body seemed to slow . . . seemed to pause.

Then gradually, bubbling up from the depths of his being, rose his sense of responsibility. *This* core value had always served as his dependable rudder.

He recalled the veterans in his family, and how they had stepped up. Jack remembered the photos in the family album. The Civil War Pennsylvania enlistment records for his great-great-grand father, Francis Xavier McGlohin. The photo of Joseph, his great grandfather, dressed in the white uniform of a First Lieutenant Naval Officer in World War Two. Jack imagined the prospect of entering a battlefield. Images of Gettysburg came to mind. He'd seen the photos. But they had served, despite their fear.

Now, the planet was at stake. And it was *his* turn.

Jack understood climate was the world war of his generation. This battlefield looked different from other conflicts. No foxholes or conventional weapons. Rather, the instigators remained hidden in their offices, up in silvery skyscrapers. Battle plans filled their computers designed to dismantle environmental regulations . . . extracting natural resources to maximize profits for a select few.

Jack knew the average citizen was also to blame, ignoring conservation and recycling. Wasn't this *exactly* why he and his friends started working on the video game with the climate theme? He thought of Charlie and Grace, and the air they would all breathe.

Then the fear returned.

"How am I supposed to do any of the things in that letter? In case you haven't noticed, I'm fifteen years old!" He said to the strange kids.

"You got me. All I know is we have this old book to give you that supposedly has some answers. We tried to read it, but it won't open. You'll have to figure that out for yourself. But first, we need to show you where we live, so you can see how different life can be, compared with your soon to be gasping planet."

Max's chirping and clicking now seemed less prominent. Jack wondered if they were doing it less, or if he was getting used to their weird speech.

"Oh great, the book won't open."

Jack now knew how Houdini felt, under water and locked in chains. Next, he thought, they would be telling him about three fire branding dragons he would have to slay.

"So, explain how I'm supposed to neutralize this space traveling engineering genius, Dr. Marcov?"

"Look, we keep telling you, the Council made the choice. They didn't pick a karate black belt, or an army general. Personally, my choice would have been one of those Nobel Prize winners. But they chose YOU. You'll have the Anamchara Text. You'll meet some key people on your quest. We don't have the answers. We only have a single question.

Will you step up?"

Jack considered his predicament.

A brief thought crossed his mind.

If he *could* muster the courage to accept this challenge, he'd be a hero. He might be a dead one. But he'd be remembered. For a moment he pictured his flag draped coffin. Surrounded by Grace and his family weeping. Sad, but proud of their patriot. Then he became aware that Izzy was reading his thoughts.

Izzy frowned, his cheeks now reddened.

Jack tried to erase his dreams of glory and focus on his decision. Could he accept this challenge? It all boiled down to overcoming his doubt and building up his courage.

Fears had always haunted him. Been his *classic* nightmare.

Could he see this through? Sign on to a commitment of this magnitude? Could he honor his word? This was a pivotal moment that touched all his vulnerabilities. Pushed all his buttons.

Then, he recalled Joseph Spencer, and how this man's life had mattered. The engineer had set up an environmental foundation, and left scores of patents. Jack couldn't deny he had given plenty of lip service to saving the climate by creating a video game. He *wanted* to help . . . but without the danger part.

So, bottom line, the question . . .

Would he live a consequential life?

Meanwhile, Max and Izzy waited anxiously as he considered his answer to the Council. Jack sensed their agitation.

Izzy whispered to Max in a worried tone.

"What if he says no?"

The whispering sounded to Jack like the plaintive peeps from a nest of baby chicks.

Max squeezed his little brother's hand, trying to reassure the child.

Jack would say later that it was loyalty, buried deep in his core, that finally tipped the scales. He realized that in little ways, he had been preparing for this moment all his life. Practicing simple habits. Like being on time, putting in the work, taking on challenging tasks.

A look of resolve settled in Jack's eyes, as he thought of Joseph Spencer's words to *do the next right thing*. It felt like he was jumping off a cliff.

"Fine, I'll do it," said Jack.

The two little boys stood erect, saluting him.

But as soon as these words determining his future were out of Jack's mouth, a tiny part of him began to waffle. There remained too many unknowns. So, while Max and Izzy remained confident that they had their guy, Jack held back a tiny sliver of doubt. He worried that Izzy might sense his hesitation, but the boy looked overjoyed.

This scrap of reluctance bothered Jack as not following through with an undertaking violated his core sense of responsibility. But, he drew a deep breath, realizing that for now, anyway, he would have to live with this tension. He would see how far he could go.

It wasn't long after he gave his answer to the boys when the glass cube slowed. Ahead, floating in space, he saw a gorgeous blue and green planet. The north and south poles of the sphere glowed with a rosy light. Shades of green formed the land masses.

"Wow. I've never seen colors like that . . . like a halo pulsing around the whole planet."

"We wanted to give you a tour of Sophia so you can appreciate what sustainable life looks like," Max said.

Within minutes the craft floated over miles and miles of rolling hills covered with fruit trees. Jack had never seen so many kinds of vegetation growing together on American farms.

"What about pest control?" Jack asked.

"A planned ecosystem self-sustains. So minimal issues with pests," said Izzy.

"You mean natural ways to maintain animals and plants together?" asked Jack.

"Yup . . . the geese eat the snails. And the goose poop feeds the soil."

"That's great. I wish we planned farms this way," said Jack.

A large mountain range loomed ahead, and Max explained this formation was made from composted materials. The peaks were beautiful with snow frosting the tops like a series of whipped cream cakes in a bakery window.

"Is that a ski resort?" Jack asked, his eyes widening.

"It is. Sophians vacation up there most of the year," said Max.

Then he steered the craft, veering around the left side of the mountain. Jack's stomach flipped. A glistening body of water rose on the horizon.

"See how we treat salt water from the ocean. Sea water is sent up the mountain top with those pumps," said Max.

He pointed at a silver tangle of pipes.

"Then it's released off that cliff. Looks like your Niagara Falls. The force of gravity desalinates the water, and then the water irrigates the crops. Nice, right?" Izzy said.

"What powers the pumps?" asked Jack.

"Would you believe, squirrels, and rabbits? We harness the energy of all kinds of forest animals to power the desalination contraption."

"What? That's like from a cartoon," said Jack.

"Yeah, well, it works. The woodland creatures are moving around anyway. Better to put them to good use. And we made this huge habitat designed for their pleasure. The abundance of water, planting soil enhancing vegetation, and animal manure all contribute to a rich topsoil for farming," Max said.

"Also, we use solar, hydrogen power and wind. All with the help from the woodland creatures. And, pipelines transport flood water to areas low on rainfall thousands of miles away," said Izzy, proudly.

Jack was impressed. He'd never imagined a world where the population embraced sustainable living to this extent. He thought of the Chicago skies that often looked bruised with clouds harboring troublesome particulates.

"What are the asthma rates here?" Jack asked.

"Almost nonexistent. And no more cancer," said Max.

"Wow," said Jack, considering all his relatives who had died of the disease.

Jack now understood why the boys had insisted on this tour. Sophia was amazing. Could earth ever look like this wonderful place?

Within minutes, the glass cube landed with a soft thump. The panel opened, and the boys jumped out. Jack found himself in a huge garden with unfamiliar plants.

"Watch your step, the lawn is still damp."

Jack shoes were soaked.

"Too late," he said as an icy chill raced up his body.

Izzy quickly produced a canister that looked like a giant saltshaker.

"Here, shake some of this over your shoes and socks."

Jack took the container and followed Izzy's directive. In moments, his feet were dry and toasty warm.

"Wow, that's good stuff. What's in there?"

"Don't know . . . but my mom makes me carry it with me as I tend to find all the puddles," said Izzy.

"So, you guys have parents?" Jack said with surprise.

It seemed hard to imagine these independent beings belonging to a regular family.

"Of course, we do, dummy," sassed Izzy.

"Hey, don't say *dummy*," Max said, "Not nice, remember?"

Izzy looked at his shoes.

But Jack's attention had shifted. He stood mesmerized by this place that looked as if a botanical garden had exploded with giant tree-sized versions of flowers. Ornamental shrubs, the branches heavy with blossoms, strained in the breeze. Trees, as tall as sequoias, towered over him, making him feel like a tiny being in a magical forest. A Lilliputian, right out of Gulliver's Travels.

He looked up through the umbrella sized petals that filtered the sunlight, casting shapes on the ground around his feet. Fragrant scents of pine wafted in the breeze. The light from the sky seemed off, but in a good way. Beams from another sun must hit this place at a different angle. Everything around him seemed to glow like the soft illumination before sunset. He couldn't be sure of the season.

"I'm amazed!" Jack said.

Max nodded, "This way, master champion."

The older boy led them over to a café, choosing a table with a view of the water. Robots glided through the diners, serving meals prepared from fruits and vegetables. Sauces flavored the dishes that tasted better than any burger and fries.

For the first time in his life, Jack understood the word *ambrosia*. He would weigh a thousand pounds if he lived here. Sweet and savory didn't begin to cover it.

As they finished their meal, Jack noticed only lush vegetation around the restaurant. Apparently, on this planet, the vehicles hovered, with no need for cement or asphalt. Walkways were cobbled from fieldstone that blended into the greenery. The city appeared more as a garden with vine covered buildings. Jack recalled an illustration of the Hanging Gardens of Babylon in one of his school texts, an ancient wonder of the world.

Jack tried to take in the things he had seen. Mind bending, he thought. Space travel. Space/time portals. Bunny powered irrigation. Tree-sized flowers.

Izzy, mind reading again it seemed, responded to his thoughts.

"Yeah . . . space/time portals . . . it has something to do with parallel planes, but we haven't covered that yet in class, so I can't explain it," said Izzy.

Mike and Grace would be amazed. All this would be impossible to describe. Maybe in a poem? Or a song? Would his camera phone work?

But Izzy, reading his thought, shook his head.

"You are freaking me out, little boy," said Jack.

The corners of Izzy's mouth began to tense and droop. Tears welled up in his eyes.

"Oh no, don't cry," said Jack.

Too late, lines of tears streaked the little guy's face.

"Sorry, but it's weird to have someone reading your thoughts," said Jack.

But Izzy had already turned away, his shoulders heaving at the slight.

"Don't worry about him. He needs to toughen up. So sensitive," Max said.

"He reminds me a little of my brother. Charlie freaks out if he can't find his stuffed rabbit. Or if he needs a nap."

Max left to soothe Izzy with ice cream, which apparently also worked with kids here on Sophia.

As Jack waited for the boys to return, he stood and surveyed the landscape. He considered the logistics of his current location. While he knew physics allowed for parallel planes, the distance he had traveled by flying through the portal was impossible to process. Unable to wrap his head around this space/time leap, he thought of a Super Mario Game with the figure suddenly jumping up a level. His sense of stability, challenged, Jack felt disoriented and out of his body. Then he saw the boats, hovering over the water. Shimmering colors of blue greens. Oddities assaulting his senses. It left him reeling, with vertigo, like he was walking up walls and across ceilings.

"I'm sooo tired," said Jack when the boys returned with ice cream.

Max poured him an ice water, dumping an envelope of vitamin powder into the glass. Izzy whispered in Max's ear that their visitor required some down time. A nap.

Jack was massively jet lagged from the trip through the space/ time portal. Max said they all needed rest before returning to Lake Forest in time for Jack's family lunch with his friends. The boys explained that travel through the portal increased hunger tenfold and exhausted all the faculties. Biological stressors and mental disorientation caused a type of shock. So, Max and

Izzy took Jack to a small hotel, where they booked him a pleasant room.

Where were they taking him? His legs felt weak. But, too tired to protest, Jack followed along. He seemed to be having an out of body experience, swimming out of himself. Too exhausted to know what was real, and what might be a hallucination, he dragged his body along. So, when he saw the bed, he collapsed on the fresh sheets, passing out as soon as his head hit the pillow.

It was not long before a dream unfolded, like gossamer wings opening a magical portal. Through veils of white, Jack's body floated through space, until he found himself in a huge hall with a circular table. A carved inscription caught his eye on the oak surface, "*For the benefit of humanity.*"

Individuals materialized, and Jack recognized them from various portraits and photographs. They were dressed in brown robes: Winston Churchill, Harriot Tubman, John Lewis, Rumi, William Blake, George Washington, Ada Lovelace, Cezanne, Galileo, Rosalind Franklin, Marie Curie, Confucius, Albert Schweitzer, Alexander Hamilton, Siddhartha, Tesla, Sojourner Truth, Jonas Salk, Benjamin Franklin, Gutenberg, Francis of Assisi, Marconi, Abe Lincoln, Albert Einstein, Elinor Roosevelt, Hildegard of Bingen, and Leonardo Da Vinci were a few of those assembled.

Then his gaze met the serious green eyes of Joseph Spencer. Elinor sat next to her husband. She smiled at Jack, and his heart seized up with questions. The group began to speak with one voice, telling him that when the time was right, he would find the courage if he remained faithful to the quest. Along the way he would meet individuals who would advance his understanding.

"Why me?" asked Jack.

"Answers will come when the time is right. Trust the process, learn by listening and by doing the next right thing," said Spencer. A tall redheaded woman, wrapped in rose colored silk, stepped forward. Resting her green eyes on Jack, she extended her arms toward him. A small vial of oil appeared above his head, and she proceeded to pour something over his forehead.

Jack tasted the oil, feeling a warmth fill his body. At that moment, the delegation faded, and Izzy appeared in the dream. The child bowed and presented him with an engraved golden cylinder.

Jack noticed a quickening in his being that felt as if he was walking into his true self. A fortifying substance coursed through his veins. Then the dream faded away and, rolling over, he fell back into a deep, deep sleep.

Hours later, the sun came up, and Jack found he was holding the gold cylinder in his right hand. A series of engraved numbers on the metal surface caught his eye. Fragments of the dream returned, the anointing with the oil, and the advice from the green-eyed Council members. Shaking off his sleepiness, Jack noticed he felt different . . . maybe more solid? And he was hungry, famished really.

The boys sat around a table on the hotel's balcony for breakfast. An unusual woven mat rested under the plates. Izzy noticed Jack staring at the texture.

"So, do you like our table covering? It's modeled after shark skin so that it naturally repels germs and viruses. No need to launder," said Izzy.

The robot waiter appeared and served vegan sausages and pancakes. After they finished the meal, Max and Izzy escorted Jack to the glass cube. After they jumped aboard, the panel closed with a hiss. The cube levitated and then jetted up, leaving behind the beautiful planet of Sophia. They flew in darkness until they slipped through the space/time portal.

Jack tried to broach the topic of the dream and his anointing by the woman in rose silk.

"Oh, yeah, she's the Druid Prophetess who sometimes serves as a muse," said Max.

Jack wondered for an instant if the boys were related to her. However, it seemed clear they had said all they were going to reveal. Jack showed the gold cylinder to the boys, but they only smiled, their eyes twinkling.

"What do the numbers mean?" asked Jack.

"Your first task, I guess," said Max. Then he picked up a huge book.

"Ok, one more thing. The Anamchara Text. It should fit in your back-pack. But good luck with opening it," he said. And, with that, Max handed over the weighty looking volume.

Jack prepared to recieve a heavy book. But shock registered when the massive volume weighed less than a lettuce leaf.

"What the . . . !"

"It's a surprise, isn't it? Something odd to remember us by. You see our periodic table is expanded . . . lots of cool materials with interesting prop-erties."

"Look there's earth," said Izzy, pointing down through the cube's glass floor.

Jack looked out and tears filled his eyes as he got an astronaut's view of his home planet. From this vantage point, the earth looked so gentle, so peaceful.

Then he worried. What if we land in a hostile country?

Izzy caught his eye, and he was shaking his head.

"We'll land in the old tree. You'll see."

Jack shivered. That mind reading was so weird, so unsettling. Even creep-ier than the chirpy talking.

Izzy frowned.

Sorry, Jack thought. The emoji with the sheepish smile flashed in his mind.

Then he put the Anamchara Text and golden cylinder, in his backpack, taking extra care to zip the bag.

"There's Morningside. Prepare for landing," said Izzy.

Jack wrapped his arms around his center, hoping to stabilize his sloshing breakfast. The cube dropped like a duck shot out of the sky. Jack's stomach plummeted, but before landing, he sensed some flaps engage that slowed the final descent.

The glass vehicle fell into the old tree, with the larger branches rocking them back and forth in a tug of war to contain the cube. Finally, the rolling ceased. Jack's head was spinning, his middle section flipping. Max slid open the panel, and the boys climbed down the ladder. Jack marveled that the boys seemed fine, moving steadily as if they had just flown business class. Jack hauled his backpack, following them down the rope ladder. Immediately he dropped to the ground, curled up on the grass, hugged his knees and closed his eyes. Thank God. It's over. Balled up, his body seemed to be running a system's check to see if he really was all there. After a few minutes, Jack got to his feet and looked around, but Max and Izzy had vanished. The glass cube, gone.

Jack wobbled over to the house, trying to adjust his legs that felt jelly filled. He entered a porch door, making his way down a side hallway. A window was open, and he drew in a deep breath of air.

Turning the corner, Jack found his mom, dad, Mike, and Grace. They had just finished looking around the estate. Charlie smiled sweetly from his stroller.

The large clock in the hall dinged the noon hour.

"Oh, there you are! Grace told us you went down a different hall, but that you'd find us . . . and here you are. Right on time. Anyone hungry?" Mr. Abernault smiled.

"Yeah . . . *here* I am," said Jack, reassuring himself, as much as to greet them.

His dad led them out to the driveway. They piled in the car and drove a short distance to the Deerpath Inn. Jack, still in shock from his experience in the glass cube, followed along, feeling disoriented and weak. His dad requested a corner booth with a highchair, and they settled in, focusing on the menus. There was a pitcher of ice water the waitress had left on the table. Jack drank it down, filling his glass multiple times. He noticed he was also famished. The friendly waitress returned with her order pad ready.

"I'll have a Caesar salad," said Grace.

"Make that two, please," said his mom.

"Hmm . . . I could really go for a grilled cheese, and add some tomatoes," said Mr. Abernault.

"Yeah, same here, thanks," said Mike.

"Rice and vegetable bowl, with a side of potatoes," Jack said, closing his menu.

His mom gave him a look, but withheld commenting on his unusual choice.

The waitress smiled, taking their menus.

"Looks like somebody was thirsty," and she walked off with the empty water pitcher.

Grace and Mike went on for a full hour about all the amazing rooms at Morningside, giving him cover so he could fade into the booth. Jack didn't think he could put a single sentence together as his body was still pretty checked out. Only Charlie seemed to notice his older brother seemed different, because he gave Jack a quizzical look. But his parents and friends left him alone. Maybe they figured he was overwhelmed by the visit to the estate. But he couldn't muster the energy to care what they thought.

Mike, oblivious to his friend's mood, now was talking about his sisters, a pair of scrappy girls. He described how dinner time served as a stage for their nightly dramas. Jack thought this sounded awful, getting an inkling of how his friend felt. After all, he only had this cute baby in his house. Grace, not to be outdone, complained about her two younger brothers who spent a sizable amount of time looking for ways to bother her. But to Jack, because their problems took a different shape, his friend's lives sometimes looked easier. It could be annoying to be on alert for small items that Charlie might choke on. Gates and doors needed to be secured, and Jack found it tiresome to keep the noise down in case his brother was napping. Just in the past week, a text alert on his phone had awakened Charlie a number of times.

As the others talked, Jack barely listened to the conversation. He shoveled in the rice dish, sloshing it down with more water. He hoped to bury the whole flying cube odyssey under a mountain of food. He started in on the loaf of bread. Suddenly the hastily eaten meal revolted.

He found the restroom in the back and pushed open the door. Dabbing his face with wet paper towels, he looked in the mirror and saw his pale face. He needed to get a grip. Pull it together. If he started talking about the ride in the glass cube, his parents would take him to the closest emergency room for a psych evaluation. He splashed more water on his face. Right now, he needed to get through this meal. He took a deep breath, plastered a neutral look on his face and willed himself back to the table. His dad signed the tab and then slid his credit card into his wallet.

"All set?" Mr. Abernault asked the group.

They gathered their stuff, and filed out, wading through the tables filled with diners.

During the car ride home, Jack dropped off to sleep, exhausted, and overwhelmed.

"I think he's coming down with something," his mom said.

"There's a bug going around. My sister had it last week," said Mike.

"Yeah, maybe. But what's with that bowl of green beans and rice?" Grace asked.

Charlie's eyes closed, and the car quieted for the remainder of the ride. The Abernaults dropped off Grace, and then took Mike home. When the car rounded the corner at Orrington Avenue Jack awoke with a start.

"What a nice day," said his mom.

"Yeah, great," said Jack, but his voice didn't sound convincing even to his own ears.

They entered the house. Jack admitted he was bushed and took the steps two at a time up to his room. Soon he slept, dead to the world, as his body continued to adjust after the shock of space travel.

Four hours later, Jack awoke. He drank a glass of water and descended the stairs, intending to tell his parents about his wild adventure. Hoping that unloading the odyssey would relieve some of the pressure, he found his parents in the family room. However, Charlie was making headway in his efforts to stand.

"Oh my gosh. Get a photo of this. Is this cute or what?" said his mom.

His dad moved closer with the phone, clicking the shot, and then start-ing the video.

Clearly, this was not the time. Sometimes it was hard to be a big brother. Turning around, he walked into the kitchen and made himself a sandwich. Then, as if an invisible linebacker had taken him down, fatigue struck him again. His body craved his bed. So quickly he washed down the food with milk. From the other room, he could still hear them fussing over Charlie.

Jack called out that he was going up to bed, but he didn't think his par-ents even heard him. He grabbed some crackers and returned to his room. Flopping on his bed, he screamed into his pillow. His body felt heavy, as though he was still hurling through space. How long would he experience the physical after-effects from the space travel? He pulled the covers over his head and dropped again into unconsciousness.

CHAPTER FOUR

Numbers

A T SEVEN THE NEXT MORNING, JACK awoke to the sounds of a crying baby. Flipping over in bed, his eyes landed on the golden cylinder. He stared at it for a moment in confusion. Then, like an out-of-control eighteen-wheeler, the shock of the previous day hit him. Vertigo returned with a vengeance as Jack gripped the bed, reliving his jet propulsion through the universe.

"Make it stop," he begged his pillow.

However, the memory of Max and Izzy, and the Council's challenge dropped on him like a colossal anvil. His body felt caught in a speed trap, his insides moving at a cruising speed. Overwhelmed, he pulled his pillow around his head. Why can't it all go away? Drawing up his knees, he curled up. Exhaustion took over. An hour and a half later, Jack yawned and sat up in bed. The feelings of traveling through space had passed. The house was quiet now. He knew it was time for a serious talk.

Pulling on a sweatshirt he went down the stairs, hauling the backpack with the items from Sophia. His parents were in the kitchen, and with the baby down for his morning nap, Jack had their undivided attention.

"So, I have some disturbing news. Can you promise me you will just listen?"

"So you ARE getting sued again?" His dad looked angry.

"I wish," said Jack.

"WHAT!" said his dad.

His mother touched her husband's arm.

"Let the boy speak."

"Can you keep quiet while I try to get this out? I'm freaked out enough," said Jack.

"This better not be you and your friends breaking the law again," said his dad.

"It's not. Ok?" Jack said.

"What then?" said Mr. Abernault, "You're scaring your mother."

"I'm fine. You're the one who needs to settle down. Go ahead, honey. Just tell us."

Her face, however, indicated she was running through all the possible troubles a teen age boy might be having.

"Yesterday morning, I had the most unbelievable, crazy, experience that I'm still trying to process. First, I'm going to tell you in a few sentences, and then I'll go back and explain the whole thing. And I don't expect you to believe this until you hear me out. . . . but after I left Mike and Grace in a hallway, I met two odd kids who I thought were playing Star Wars. I assumed they were the groundskeeper's kids. They talked funny, with clicks and chirps, and they claimed to be from another planet. They reminded me of when Grace and Mike and I would act out Star Wars all day long. So, of course, I played along. Anyway, I followed them outside. They were hiding in what seemed to be a glass tree house, but when I entered, it jetted up millions of feet in the air, through a space/time portal."

Jack's dad slammed his fist on the counter, his face flashed with anger.

"Ok, right there! Stop! It's clear you ARE being sued again, and you're afraid to tell us. You're grounded for a month. Get out of my face and go to your room."

"No, I *swear* I am not being sued. I *knew* you couldn't just listen. Don't you think I *know* this sounds crazy? Do you think I haven't questioned my sanity? But here's the thing, I was given two items that will prove what I'm saying is true. The fact is . . . Jack drew in a deep breath. I visited the planet, Sophia."

Lifting his backpack off the floor, he unzipped it, pulling out the gold engraved cylinder, and the large volume. It was the unexpected weight of the Anamchara Text he knew provided evidence of his bizarre story.

"Here, take this," and he handed the book to his dad.

"What the . . ." his dad's expression changing into disbelief.

Jack's mom took the text, and surprise flooded her face.

"Whatever is this made from?"

"Sophia has new materials . . . an expanded periodic table."

"I told you. I went to another planet. *Now* do you believe me?" Jack asked.

They were quiet.

Finally, his mother sat down to get her bearings.

"What in the world happened to you?" said his dad.

"I'll tell you the whole story. But look at this other thing I got," said Jack.

They examined the gold cylinder.

"This looks like solid gold. What do those numbers mean?" asked his dad.

"I don't know . . . yet," said Jack.

He felt he was finally gaining the upper hand in the conversation.

"So NOW. Can you two just listen?" he said.

"I have to say this reminds me of that incident at O'Hare airport back in 2006. Remember,those airline pilots witnessed a flying disc that jetted up, punching a hole in the clouds. It happened right above one of the terminal gates. People reported seeing a circle of blue sky left in its wake. CNN and NPR covered it," said his mom.

Jack's dad lifted the Anamchara Text again, too confused to comment.

His parents sat dumbfounded as Jack described the encounter with Max and Izzy, meeting the old woman in the maze, the ride in the glass cube to Sophia, the Council's challenge, the Anamchara Text, and the engraved golden cylinder.

Jack hesitated now. Afraid of confessing the most disturbing part.

About Vincent Marcov.

His parents would freak out hearing about a genius rogue scientist who used high tech methods.

Jack drew in another deep breath and the words rushed out of him, as if he was being exorcised. He knew Marcov, hell bent on destroying earth's environment, sounded terrifying. A man capable of building a laser capable satellite, and a space vehicle for himself so he could escape from a dying planet to safety on Sophia. In the back of his mind, Jack kind of hoped his parents would forbid him from leaving the house. That his story was mind blowing seemed a massive understatement.

Jack finished the highlights of his bizarre experience that had begun at Morningside the previous day. His parents slumped on the sofa, trying to process the threat. His dad finally rose and walked over to his desk. Shuffling papers in the drawer, he pulled out a document from Spencer's law firm.

"We got this letter after you signed the estate documents," said his dad. "The letter predicted that you might find yourself in the center of major advances in the social sciences, and in a big demand for green technology."

"We certainly had no idea about space travel, or a dangerous scientist," said his dad, his voice choking up.

"What you're telling us changes everything. Spencer should have left his estate to a government agency, or someone with a security detail like Elon Musk who actually owns a space craft!"

This was bad. They're feeling guilty now for not being more suspicious. But they should've listened to him. Hadn't he questioned the inheritance? Repeatedly? The challenge was enormous. Totally beyond him. He would fail. Everyone would hate him. Or they'd say he made up the whole thing. Wanted attention. Grace and Mike wouldn't be allowed to hang out with a crazy kid. He'd never be normal. Too anxious. Too weird. And a liar.

Jack could see his parents felt hoodwinked, wishing they had been more diligent. He couldn't help but feel sorry for them.

"So," Jack summed up weakly, "*not* a lawsuit."

His parents moved in, wrapping their arms around him, like a cocoon. He wished he could stay in this moment and closed his eyes. Even if their power to shield him was an illusion, a happy lie was better than the harsh truth. When his parents finally released him, he could see the worry in their eyes, for him, for Charlie, and for the family. This was devastating news.

For the next few hours, Jack and his parents sat on the sofa while they asked all kinds of questions. His mom seemed most worried about the challenge he had accepted, under what his parents saw as duress. His dad started taking notes, considering what options lay open to them. Could federal laws have been broken? Who was this Spencer, really? And, surely, a federal agency or airport traffic towers must track flying vehicles that enter American air space.

"You can sue away, but this challenge I accepted is a done deal. I said *yes*." Jack said, a few tears dropping on his sweatshirt.

"Look, I can't say I don't know about the seriousness of the climate problem. Coding that game was *supposed* to be my big contribution. Now, it seems, I need to man up, and actually *do* something about it," Jack said.

The ceramic globe sat in the corner, a birthday present to Jack from his grandparents. Was it glaring at him?

The Abernaults understood the crisis. There even had been talk in the news about space exploration in case earth needed to be abandoned. Most people considered this option far-fetched and not even feasible. However, venture capitalists eyed the valuable minerals on other planets. And Hollywood screen writers spun science fiction scripts about such an exodus. Most of the world's population though ignored the danger. Acting like the proverbial grasshopper, fiddling as winter approached.

Mr. Abernault, however, had spent a decade working at the Argonne National Laboratory, The scientific community knew that a clock was ticking on their planet. Some said the earth had twenty years, others ten, but if the polar ice cap melted, all bets were off.

Jack's dad also knew about dark matter, likely filled with undiscovered subatomic particles. And he was aware of growing evidence that the universe was not a closed box. Parallel universes were possible according to string theory. Lurking in these corners of the universe could be pretty much anything.

The news of Dr. Marcov's sabotage, also explained factions at work who ignored science, in favor of spin and greed. This rogue scientist, maybe the most powerful man on the planet, sounded downright terrifying. Now that Marcov could escape to Sophia, there was nothing to stop him. And the rogue scientist had satellites and the latest technologies at his disposal.

Jack looked at his own arsenal, a fat book that weighed next to nothing, and a golden trinket with some numbers. And the stupid book wouldn't even open.

Jack placed the AnamcharaText and gold cylinder on the table.

"I'm screwed. I'm supposed to figure out how to open the text, and to find out what the numbers mean. Not exactly what I had planned to do over Spring Break."

Jack had hoped to get some relief by telling his parents. However, sharing it had only made his mission even *more* real, adding a deeper and darker weight . . . his family's safety. And, seemingly on cue, Charlie howled. Nap was over. Moving toward the steps to scoop up the baby, his dad loped up the stairs.

The next morning, Jack sat on the edge of his bed, examining the numbers engraved on the golden cylinder. What could they mean? Maybe a bike ride would help clear his mind. He went out to the garage and got on his bike.

But dark thoughts rode alongside him, like a demon on a speed racer. Jack hated the position he was in. And his parents probably blamed him. The inheritance had put the family in danger. He felt tricked. First, by

Spencer. Then by the two bird like kids. It was all too much.

And then there was his father's reaction. Did his dad think *he* could have handled the pressure? In high school? Well, that Council should have picked his dad. After all, he was the grown up. He had degrees under his belt.

Jack felt a rush of anger. Then guilt. he was ready to throw his own dad under the bus. He was a horrible son. A terrible person.

Jack pedaled, hoping to put some miles between himself and these dark, shadowy feelings. The sign for the Skokie Lagoons loomed ahead. This collection of ponds, northwest of town, was created in the 1930's to drain swamp land. Following the bike path, Jack breathed a little easier as he rode into the forest, the foliage muffling the sounds of civilization. But soon the chirping of the birds brought back the memory of Max and Izzy's weird talk. And the line of trees along the shoreline reflected an upside-down version in the water, mirroring his distorted reality. The sensations flipped him back to the space ride and to the oddities on Sophia that made him want to flee. Everything was setting him off. So, when Jack encountered an unfamiliar bend in the waterway's trail, confused, he switched directions. Pedaling now, wanting to escape what was inside him, he rode deeper into the forest. Finally, he stopped to check his phone. There were no service bars. He was lost.

Unincorporated Cook County

Through the open window, Margaret Mason felt the sun's warmth as she scrubbed the sink for a second time. A line of glasses sat on the sideboard waiting for the dishtowel that hung on the hook. Her jaw set, Margaret briskly scoured the counters and back splash. She pulled open a drawer, frowning at two wayward spoons that she straightened. Then she lined up the cookbooks. After they looked satisfactory, she grabbed the mop, thrusting it like a bayonet, attacking an invisible film of dirt on the kitchen floor. Margaret surveyed her work, training her eye on the windowpane. A smudge now highlighted by the sun's rays caught her eye. She sprayed and polished the glass and stepped back to check her work. Now there was another unruly fleck that required her attention.

While she worked, she noticed someone approaching the house at the edge of the forest. This must be the postman, *finally*. She wiped her hands on her apron, feeling her irritation rise.

* * *

Walking his bike to the edge of the tall grass, Jack found a red brick walk. A gate led to a patch of freshly plowed soil ready for a future vegetable garden. It was far too early in the season for this. Who planned this far in advance? And who lived in such a remote area in the middle of the woods? Then Jack saw a house that reminded him of an illustration of a cottage inhabited by a dozen industrious elves.

What if he met an elf this morning? After his recent encounter with Max and Izzy there was no telling what might await him. And how had he gotten lost? And in a forest? This couldn't be good. But the choice now was getting more lost in the woods or trusting that he might find help from the people who lived here.

Jack walked his bike slowly toward the cottage, still considering if he should turn back. Then he saw a girl about his age in a checked apron standing in an open door. He was taken aback when she yelled at him.

"You're late again! Every time we have a substitute, the schedule is off. Don't you know I've got chores. This poor service just won't do. I require punctuality," she sniffed.

Then the girl seemed to settle down.

"Oh, I see you're a kid, like me, so YOU can't be the mailman."

Surprised by the scolding from this bossy girl, Jack said hesitantly, "Uh ... Hi?"

"What are you doing way out here?" asked the girl.

"I guess I'm lost. I was trying to make a call, but there's no cell service in the lagoons."

"I see," said Margaret Mason. But then she scolded, "You *should* have thought of that possibility before you came traipsing up the lagoon trail."

He thought, what a nag. He didn't need this. He'd turn around and leave.

However, Margaret Mason relented and told him that he could stand in the yard and try for cell service.

Jack pulled out his phone. Nothing . . . maybe a dead zone in the cell network?

Margaret's dad walked in the garden.

"Who do we have here?" asked the man, carrying an armful of books.

Margaret explained about the cell phone, but Mr. Mason looked suspicious.

"How did you get way out here?" he asked.

Didn't these people ever go on a bike ride? At least they weren't elves. And they didn't chirp. But what's the big deal? He wasn't trying to sell them anything. Not very nice. No wonder they live way out here in the sticks.

Jack said, "Well, that's the thing . . . . I was riding my bike, and then I got lost . . . so tried to make a call, but . . . no cell service, not even Google maps."

After faltering through this explanation, Jack's mouth was dry, and he tried to clear his throat.

"Let's get you some water. Come on in for a minute," said Mr. Mason.

They ushered him into the cottage and told him to sit on a wooden pew in the hall.

As he waited, Jack saw the living room through an arched doorway. It looked like the inside of an English cottage. An embroidered sampler hung prominently on the wall, with an inspirational message, *There must always be room for improvement.*

Linen covered the sofa armrests, and windows with starched curtains circled the room. A hint of vinegar hung in the air. Oak floors shined with a coat of wax. Not a speck of dust sat anywhere. Jack thought this orderly space, must be the cleanest house he had ever seen. He figured the Masons must not have any younger kids or sloppy pets. He wondered what Charlie and his crackers would do to this place in ten short minutes.

Margaret returned with a glass of ice water. Then Mr. Mason confirmed that he didn't have cell service either.

"I'll draw you a map so you can ride back out of the lagoons," said Mr. Mason.

"That would be great, thanks," said Jack.

Mr. Mason left to get paper. Jack drank his water.

To make small talk, he turned to Margaret.

"So where do you go to school?"

"I'm home schooled. Regular classes are too easy for me. I like math because there's a single correct answer. Subjects like English Lit have too many interpretations and I find that unacceptable. I require precision. My parents both teach math."

Mr. Mason returned, handing Jack a paper with a crudely drawn map.

"Here you go," said the father.

Then it dawned on Jack. This family, devoted to numbers, might solve his problem. So, he pulled out the gold engraved cylinder.

Showing it to the pair, he said, "Any idea what these numbers might mean?"

Mr. Mason and Margaret looked at the odd trinket, seeing eleven digits.

"Hmm . . . Now *this* is interesting," said Mr. Mason.

Margaret closed her eyes and seemed to be running through some possibilities in her head.

"Let's write them down." She handed Jack a pen and paper.

Jack scribbled them on the sheet.

"Could be a formula . . . a phone number? Or a lockbox at a bank . . . a combination to a storage unit . . . birthdays?"

Suddenly, Mr. Mason spoke. He sounded upset.

"I know what this means."

Alarmed, Margaret stood up. Jack felt afraid, regretting he had showed them the cylinder.

"So what do the numbers mean?" Margaret asked.

Her father looked at her, pointing to the map on the wall.

"Those numbers describe the coordinates, latitude and longitude, of OUR HOUSE!"

Jack looked at the father and daughter with confusion.

Just then they were startled by a large *bang!*

A giant book had fallen off the top shelf of a nearby bookcase. Margaret moved to pick it up. Embossed on the leather cover of the volume was the title, *Pythagoras*, and rolling out of the book's spine, a gold cylinder, identical to Jack's, landed beside his shoe.

"Now, how did that get there?" asked Margaret, astonished.

They examined the engraving on the new cylinder, finding a new set of numbers etched into the surface. More coordinates? Mr. Mason handed the gold trinket to Jack.

"It seems no mistake that you ended up at our door this morning."

Jack felt the cold metal of the cylinder. It now dawned on him that the Masons must be the first stop on his quest. He felt the hair on the nap of his neck stand on end.

Mr. Mason's phone rang. When he saw the caller's name on the display, worry crossed his face. He answered. Listening, he responded to the caller in a low voice.

"Yes sir, I understand. Right away, sir."

He put down the phone. After a moment, he turned to Jack.

"Can I look at those cylinders for a minute. I'll polish them up for you," said Mr. Mason.

The golden tubes looked fine to Jack. However, shining things up seened a high priority . . . a Mason family value. So, he handed them over. Then he checked his phone. Sill, no service bars. A few minutes later, Mr. Mason returned,.

"Here you go, no more *cosmic crud.*"

Jack put the two cylinders in his pocket.

Meanwhile, Margaret turned pages in the Pythagoras book. Jack looked over her shoulder and saw an interesting triangle, laced with dissecting lines, and contained in a circle. Somehow, it reminded Jack of a sand painting he'd seen at the Field Museum. He knew that for thousands of years, people fashioned circles, mandalas, to contemplate, and to open-up their minds,"said Mr. Mason.

"Can I take a photo of this diagram?" asked Jack.

They nodded, and he snapped a shot of the image with his phone. Then Mr. Mason's phone dinged with a message. He frowned.

"We have to go. There's a family issue. Margaret, in the car. Now."

Mason's voice was urgent and demanding. Margaret gave her father a concerned look and hurried out the door, followed by Jack.

Jack was rattled by their sudden departure. But, even more concerning, as the girl got into the car, he had overheard Margaret ask her dad if the buzzing had started again. Jack didn't hear much of his response, but he did catch the word, *nanobot.*

Father and daughter drove off, dust billowing down the lane. Jack got on his bike.

He felt shaky, but at least he'd made it out alive. And there had been no elves to deal with or time travel. However, the mention of nanobots. That was different. That was terrifying. He remembered an issue of *Scientific American* described how these miniscule capsules entered the bloodstream and delivered medicine to a specific body part. But in the wrong hands, they could re-program parts of the brain, turning functions on and off.

Jack had sensed something "off" about the Masons, so rigid, and obsessed. Their place reeked of perfectionism, but nanobots took his concerns to a whole new level.

However, right now, Jack needed to find his way out of this forest. He checked the hand drawn map from Mr. Mason that showed three pine trees with an arrow to the right. Jack scanned the forest and spotted the trio of giant evergreens. Riding toward them, he veered right, and the lagoon came into view. Soon he was on the main bike path.

Would all the people on his quest be as weird? Then his thoughts returned to the nanobots. Scary scenarios sped through his mind. What if he was attacked by them? Would he even know? Had it already happened? With worry threatening to overwhelm him, he pushed hard on the pedals. He needed to put some distance between himself and the freaky house in the woods.

Jack sped toward the edge of the forest. Soon he rode into familiar streets lined with mid-century homes and kids on bikes. He took in a deep breath, feeling safer in this neighborhood. He thought of the Council's instructions. Had he tuned in well enough to the Masons? Listening to them with his head? Listening to what they said with his heart? And paying attention to his own gut experience with them? Maybe, he thought, but maybe not. He had heard the words, but had he really processed the interaction with the Masons, registered their impression within him, "gotten their beat?" His gut intuition needed to develop as it still felt murky, still needed some work. The fear scampering around in his head, and the anxiety growing in his chest seemed to interfere with a complete picture.

He passed the signpost for Evanston. And as he rode down Lincoln Street, he had the uncomfortable feeling of being watched, sensing eyes on his back. However, when he looked around, he saw no one there. Pedaling faster, he fought off the paranoia.

Rounding the corner on to Orrington Avenue, he saw his mom unloading groceries. His dad appeared and Jack joined them, hauling a parade of brown bags into the house, and setting them on the counter. While his dad deposited the milk in the fridge, Jack grabbed a bag of chips, tearing open the top. The strangeness of the forest house had creeped him out, and it was a relief to be home. The salty chips crunching in his mouth somehow felt grounding.

"Well, it seems my quest has begun," he said, getting his parent's attention. "And I heard about nanobots."

Concern flooded their faces, and it pained Jack to see them worry.

"Space travel, aliens, rogue scientist, and now nanobots!" his mother said. She sat down.

"Yeah, I totally freaked," said Jack.

Jack's dad said,

"We need some answers. And protection. I'm looking into how to pull in the feds, but I must be careful. If I tell the wrong person, or go to the wrong agency, I could have my security clearance at work pulled, maybe lose my job, and in the end, not be believed by anyone. All we really have is the impossible weight of that book. For all we know, the government might have some new material, recently discovered, that could explain the book's weight. So that's not enough proof. Not yet."

A flush of guilt hit Jack. The realization that this situation could ruin their lives. The magnitude of all this was too much. Could destroy them. Put his parents out of work. No one would believe them. Could end up homeless. On the street. His dad pushing a grocery cart with all their belongings. Charlie in foster care.

Jack pushed these thoughts away. Focusing on worst-case scenarios was not helpful. He switched gears and began telling his parents about the Masons. Jack explained how Margaret's dad had recognized the numbers on the golden cylinder as location coordinates of their cottage. Then Jack showed them the image from the Pythagoras book on his phone and explained how the book just dropped out of the bookcase with the new cylinder rolling out of the spine. His parents looked at the photo from the old text, and at the new gold cylinder.

"The numbers give map coordinates?" his mom asked.

"Yup, seems so," said Jack. "Let's see what this new sequence brings up."

He pulled out his phone, typing in the coordinates. Google Maps zeroed in on a spot in the ocean off the coast of New Zealand.

"Well, *that's* not happening," said his dad. "That's the other side of the world. And under water."

"So strange that today you got lost right where you were supposed to go," said his mother. "Way beyond coincidence. But then, to get this new location that's impossible to access."

Jack felt confused. Not even the Council could expect a fifteen-year-old to take a journey to the southern hemisphere, and then explore under water. But then he wondered, might these new numbers refer to something other than a location?

Putting that thought aside, he explained how the design from the Pythagoras book, reminded him of sand paintings at the museum.

"Art often predicts advances in science. You know I always loved the idea of how cubism predicted the splitting of the atom in the *avant-garde* paintings," said his mom.

"One can't deny the artists have a special vision," his dad said.

"Remember Uncle Peter told us about attending a Big Sur conference, and how his group of experimental physicists overheard the Buddhist monks at the next lunch table talking about the same phenomenon . . . but in the form of poetry? That really blew my mind," Jack said.

"William Blake certainly was tuned in to something beyond the rational, with his poetry and mystical drawings," his mom said.

"Well, right now, I have to figure out how to open the Anamchara Text. I wonder what's the big secret." Jack said, looking at the enigmatic book.

He did a web search of Anamchara. It was a Gaelic term, sometimes appeared as *anam cara*, meaning *soul friend*. The phrase was derived from the Irish tongue. Jack knew the early alphabet, Ogham, carved on stones, developed into the language of the Ulster Cycle, myths from the first century. *Soul friend*, he repeated to himself, taking in a deep breath. He'd take one of those.

That night Jack had a dream. He saw a room with the Anamchara Text on a table. Then he saw his relatives, but as they looked as children.

"Look at this mess. Hand me a dust cloth." Aunt Betty glared at the text.

Great Grandma Louise served lemonade, making her rounds with the pitcher.

"Opening this book may take a while and I want everyone comfortable."

Uncle John consulted a manual for effective ways to open an old book without damaging the spine.

Uncle Francis worried that Dr. Marcov might find them, and so he wanted to call an adult for protection.

Amazed to see his relatives as children, Jack noticed they each offered a different approach for solving the problem of the sealed book.

"Prepare to be dazzled. Watch this!"

Uncle Tom jerked the tablecloth out from under the book with a flourish.

Amazed when the Anamchara Text remained on the table, the children clapped with delight. However, Aunt Betty snapped at their frivolity.

"Cut that out. This is serious business."

Grandfather Mike ignored Betty and prepared to hurl the book out the window to break the seal. But the kids intervened, blocking his path. Jack knew Mike eventually learned to control his temper, becoming a labor union leader who could stare down any team of adversaries.

After Mike settled down, Uncle Richard took a turn. He was known in the family for his low energy and calm personality. Sometimes he seemed a little lazy. Richard yawned and then suggested the kids all close their eyes, and just breathe for a few minutes. Nothing else had worked, and they knew Jack's dream was about to end, so they all closed their eyes. Taking in deep, slow breaths, they all slowly exhaled. Four long minutes passed.

Then, Richard opened his eyes, reached over, and lifted the book's cover.

The children clapped, looking impressed.

Richard tipped the volume forward, showing the text written in a strange language. Again, he closed his eyes, took in a deep breath, and the letters scrambled, settling in a fancy scroll of English. The pages looked as if they had been penned by a wizard with a quill feather dipped in ink.

Jolted out of his dream, Jack sat up in bed. Realizing it was still night, he rolled over and went back to sleep. Soon Grace, riding a chestnut horse, galloped into his dream. He climbed up behind her and they rode a short distance, into a forest. Jack pulled her gently off the horse, and took her hand, leading her behind a waterfall.

Hours later the morning sun blasted into his room. He awoke feeling groggy and descended the stairs. He was halfway down the steps when he looked in the dining room. Open on the table, sat the Anamchara Text.

"Hey, come down here. The old book is open!" He called up the stairwell.

His parents carried Charlie into the dining room, marveling at the open book. Jack described his dream. Not the one with Grace.

"That's incredible," said his mom.

"Yup, Cousin Richard, did it. After all the others tried," Jack said.

"Wonder why it was only your mom's side of the family?" asked his dad.

"Hmm ... that's odd, but they all had the green eyes," said Jack.

His mother, always one to find a teachable moment, shared that many scientific solutions happened because of clues that appeared in dreams, and in half awake states.

His parents watched as Jack carefully turned the first page. He noticed the paper had an oily parchment texture.

"Oh, no. Some of the text is faded."

He turned another page to find lots of torn or missing sections.

"Wonder if the space travel affected the book's material," said his dad.

"What can I learn from a damaged book?" asked Jack.

His disappointment overshadowed the awe of looking at what remained of the ancient book. Still, the family understood the secrets in the Anamchara Text had been guarded for millennia.

Jack began to read

"all people, by the age of seven . . ."

Then the text faded. On the next page, Jack saw the phrase, *acting like a taproot*. . . then more unreadable words, and then the word *overdo*.

"Wait. What?" said his dad, looking over his shoulder.

"There's more words, but I can't read them, they're too faded," said Jack.

Jack turned the next page, but most of the words were missing.

"Well, this is pretty useless," said Jack.

"It's going to take some time," said his mom. "This is what archeologists do with ancient texts. Patience and slow progress."

"I can't believe this. How am I supposed to learn this stuff if I can't even read the book?"

Charlie was getting impatient, and his dad had an appointment. The family ate breakfast.

After putting his cereal bowl in the dishwasher, Jack got on his bike. He knew he had something important he needed to do. It was time to tell Mike and Grace. To fill them in on what had begun after they left him at the entrance to Morningside's golden hallway.

CHAPTER FIVE

Say What?!

G RACE AND MIKE LAUGHED WHEN JACK began to share his experience
that had begun at Morningside.

"*Very* funny, Jack," said Grace. "What makes you think we need to hear
a stupid story like that?"

"Yeah. We're not eight years old anymore. And I thought Grace was the
one who made up stories to rile her parents," said Mike.

"OK . . . I don't blame you. Hold on a minute," Jack said.

He moved to the stair well. "Dad, can you come down here?" he yelled.

"And bring the book and the gold tubes."

"You've been spending too much time on our video game. I've heard of
things happening like this. A dude just gets sucked in. Too much screen
time. Next thing you know . . . delusional," Grace said, folding her arms
across her chest.

Mike knew his friend never made stuff up. However, the serious look on
his face suggested he was considering another option . . . maybe Jack had
snapped . . . had suffered a mental breakdown of some kind. Pressures of
the inheritance. The added responsibility and all the attention at the school.

"Did you maybe hit your head, have a concussion?" Mike asked.

"You'll see. I'm *not* crazy," said Jack. His eyes were gleaming. Too brightly maybe. Not really helping his argument.

Mr. Abernault entered the room, handing the old text to Grace. As expected, she prepared for a heavy volume.

"What the hell!" she said, handing it over to Mike.

"That's lighter than Styrofoam," he said.

"Jack isn't lying. Something very, very weird happened to him, and this feather lite book is evidence. He's trusting you with this information, but you must promise that all this stays in this room. If word gets out, we all could be targeted. For now, this *must* remain a secret. Understood?"

Mike and Grace had never seen Mr. Abernault address them in this tone. Not even during their arrest last fall.

The teens looked stunned. And afraid.

"Ok," said Mike slowly. You could almost see his heart pounding under his shirt..

"Yes," said Grace, her eyes widening.

Jack had never seen her this subdued.

"So, *no*, I didn't hit my head. Nor am I suffering a massive delusion. I'll tell you I wish that was the case. Because I'm totally freaked out. Feel trapped, like I'm in a science fiction film. But the movie won't end. Just keeps looping. So . . . definitely scared out of my mind."

"Are you at least OK *physically*?" asked Grace.

Jack said his body seemed Ok, but his emotions were all over the place.

"I keep trying to push the experience in the back of my mind. But the reality of what I went through is overwhelming. It's like I'm going about doing my everyday stuff. And then there's this other reality, like a parallel existence just beside me. Like I'm on a train, and another train is riding on another set of rails, but I'm on that train too. I can't make it go away. It happened. I'll never be the same."

Jack fought back the tears, brushing an escaped drop with the back of his hand.

Grace said, she had noticed his preoccupation. But she had chalked it up to his feelings about the inheritance. She could never have guessed the reason involved space travel in a glass cube.

"Explain it again . . . You kind of lost me with the flying cube, and the kids who click and chirp. Start over. We want to hear everything," Grace said, taking his hand.

"It's like my mind just shut down when I heard the paranormal stuff."

"We're here for you," said Mike.

Three hours later, his friends, in a state of bewilderment, tried to process Jack's meeting with the space kids, the Council's letter, and Vincent Marcov. It looked to Jack as if Mike and Grace felt circuits in their heads fizzling with the mind-blowing encounters. Astounded that this odyssey began moments after Jack turned into the plain doorway, they seemed to be trying to wrap their heads around this craziness. When their rational minds objected, they were left with the evidence of the book's impossible weight and Mr. Abernault's serious concerns. When Jack finished, Grace sat back.

"Wow. What an opportunity. After all the coding work on a game to *warn* people about the climate, your mission calls for *real* action. Any help you need, I'm *all* in."

To hear Grace, describe the Council's challenge as a *mission* surprised him. But it was, wasn't it? For an instant, the image of Grace and him dressed in tall boots and hero capes flashed in his mind. He blinked. He told himself, this was *not* Comic Con. He needed to stay cool. After all, Grace was *all in.*

Mike, however, hesitated, looking uncomfortable. Finally, he spoke up.

"See, I'd like to help, but this sounds *really* dangerous. We could all end up dead. Put our families at risk. My sisters are a pain, but I can't put them in the crosshairs of a crazy genius. I'll help you with logistics and computer stuff. But the dangerous parts, no way."

"Hey, we can't let Jack do this alone. And we're already in the climate crosshairs. Wake up, Mike. There's no place to hide," said Grace.

Jack saw the tension on Mike's face.

"Look, guys, I don't want to be in this mess either. And I don't expect you to put yourself in danger. But I really needed to tell you. And you *have* to keep this a secret," said Jack.

"Thanks for understanding. And, of course, I won't tell anyone. They wouldn't believe it anyway." said Mike.

Grace wrapped her arms around Jack, and he closed his eyes, recalling the dream under the waterfall. Her embrace seemed reason enough to continue with the challenge. Her awesomeness gave him hope. That there might be a path through.

The ticking of the mantel clock intervened, dinging ten o'clock. It was time for his friends to leave. It amazed Jack how Grace had reacted. Ready to take it all on on, not at all deterred by the danger. Mike, on the other hand, looked over his shoulder as he left the Abernault's home. Jack watched them walk down the sidewalk. He could only imagine what they were thinking.

* * *

Wednesday 9 am Chicago Loop

Sitting in his office overlooking Millennium Park, John Franklin shuffled his papers, confident that he would close a deal this morning that would make his career. The plan to marshal the central banks into green technology investments felt like nothing short of genius. His friend, Bob McCaffrey, had come up with this financial structure as the most effective way of linking parts of the market. As a result, a profitable transition from an oil-based system to a green economy seemed possible.

John wanted to purchase the outline, but his offer was a fraction of the idea's actual worth. He was amazed at McCaffrey's naivety when the friend accepted. This guy was clueless, so John went one step further, failing to pay several installments.

John set out to gather venture capitalists and environmental experts. The outline resolved the objections that had stalled reform for decades. This plan involved a cooperative of engineers, scientists, the Sierra Club, city planners, and bankers. A cascade of investments, cleverly situated to benefit the environment, moved money through a series of industries. John's only problem remained the worry that Bob McCaffrey might interfere if he got wind of the project's significant scope. Knowing he had failed to compensate his friend according to the terms of their original deal, he hoped that by the time Bob found out, it would be too late. He did stop to wonder now why he had chosen to cheat his friend over a relatively small sum of money.

At ten o'clock the board room filled with the businessmen and scientists. The meeting proceeded smoothly and by eleven o'clock, with the papers signed, they were about to adjourn. Just then, the board room doors flew open. Bob McCaffrey stormed in with his lawyer, slamming the cease-and-desist order on the table.

"Gotcha! You snake," hissed McCaffrey.

"There's been a misunderstanding here," said Franklin. However, his scarlet face said otherwise.

The individuals in the room expressed shock about the accusation of fraud. Then, members of the press arrived, and the businessmen and scientists scurried down a back staircase to avoid seeing their faces on the evening news.

Down in his SUV, Vincent Marcov snickered at the ease of derailing this project. All it had taken was a phone call to McCaffrey, and a tip slipped to the Sun Times. Marcov had also dispatched a few nanobots delivered to John Franklin's condo a few months back. The tiny robots, tucked into a pizza box, soon worked their magic on Franklin. The bots entered his bloodstream, turning on the greed and deceit in his brain that lay just under the talent for deal making. The environmental plan, now in ashes, would have changed the future, offering a road to a brighter, safer world. And Vincent Marcov knew he could not sit by and watch *that* happen.

* * *

The following Monday at lunch, Mike left the table to buy a bag of chips. Jack took the opportunity to ask Grace if wanted to take the train up to the Lake Forest house over the weekend.

"We should've gone last week, when we were on break, but the next few days are going to be warm. We can bring our bikes on the train. It'll be fun. We can look over some of Spencer's files. I've got the password for his computer. And we can swim after," said Jack, trying to keep his voice steady.

"I've got debate practice at 9:00, but then I guess I could go. Doesn't Mike have allergy appointments on Saturday?"

"I think he's got some family thing," Jack said, trying to sound casual.

"Ok, but I can't stay too long. I'm meeting up with Jimmy at seven."

"Oh sure, we can be back by five," his voice wavering.

What was this Jimmy thing? Never thought she'd go for that type. Not the brightest penny. Dopey grey eyes. Wonder if they've gone out before. She never said anything. Jealousy grew in Jack's heart.

"Alright, I'll meet you at the Davis Street station at ten o'clock," Grace said.

* * *

Saturday morning, they stood on the train platform with their bikes. Warm air blasted them as the giant engine glided into the station. After hauling the bikes up the steps, they found their seats and looked out the train window. Baby leaves popped with green as if an artist had dotted the branches with a paintbrush. The Midwest on a day like this was magical . . . fresh colors, gentle breezes, the air brimming with possibility.

Within the hour, Grace and Jack stood in the main hall at Morningside.

"This place is *so* amazing. I'd never get tired of this," said Grace.

"Come on, let's get to work," said Jack, thinking of his revised plan for the day based on the *Jimmy* information.

"Do you think we'll meet any little space boys?" Grace asked.

"I sure hope so. But if they take us for a spin, you might not make it back for Jimmy."

Grace laughed.

They headed up stairs. When they reached the second floor, they opened large double doors, and entered an office paneled in teak with a matching desk. White screens filtered the natural light, casting soft shadows that shifted gently on the carpet. A collection of Japanese ceramics glinted in the sunlight.

"Someday I want to go to Japan," said Grace.

"I'll take you," Jack said nonchalantly.

"That's a date, master of the manor," she said with enthusiasm.

Jack moved toward the desk with a ring of keys.

"Hopefully one of these is going to fit."

The second key turned in the lock, and Jack pulled a laptop out of the drawer.

Grace watched as he entered, *Smogdiamond1#*, the password provided by Spencer's attorney. In a flash, green leaves flooded the screen. A file labeled *Smog Diamond* rested in the center.

"This looks promising," Jack tapped the icon.

"Cool password but what's a *smogdiamond*? Sounds like the name of a band," said Grace.

"Here we go. Into the mind of Joseph Spencer," said Jack.

First up, he found a design for pulling carbon dioxide out of the air, showing a tower with propellers. Powered by solar and wind, the structure sucked carbon dioxide down a piping system, and into an underground facility. Pressurized air pollutants then transformed into smog diamonds. These stones then were fashioned into jewelry.

"Wow, that's so cool. I've never heard of that before."

"Look, there's an attachment," said Jack, clicking on the file. The pdf showed a necklace with a single diamond.

"That's gorgeous, so simple. Even I'd wear that."

"Well, maybe *Jimmy* will get you one," said Jack.

She swatted him.

"His mom hired me to tutor him in math, but maybe I can get her to pay me in diamonds," she said.

Jack felt a flood of relief, rebooting his original plan for the day.

Clicking on another file, he found other uses for captured CO_2, making soda carbonation, and gravel.

But Jack was finding it hard to pay attention. He sensed Grace leaning in to see the screen. He could smell the scent of lilies of the valley coming off her hair.

Grace seemed unaffected by their closeness as she clicked on an image. This file described the Mississippi delta with sea grass that functioned as a natural filter for CO_2. A second photo showed a coast set with millions of clams absorbing ocean pollution according to the caption.

"Look at all these inventions. There seems to be patents attached to each one," said Jack.

Grace pulled open a long narrow drawer that housed drawings of huge areas of land reforested with faux plants that behaved like trees.

"I've never heard of mechanical trees. They perform photosynthesis," said Grace.

"Here's a water conservation project. Giant ponds with floating balls reduce evaporation. And another design for harvesting heavy metals rocks from the ocean floor."

"I saw a TV show about how those rocks power electric car batteries," Grace said.

A satellite design tracked methane leaks from companies. That type of pollution accounted for twenty-five percent of total methane emissions.

Grace was so close. He wondered if he should make a move. Then he hesitated. What if she got mad? What if he'd only imagined her interest in him? He'd feel like a fool. He'd better wait.

Oblivious, Grace moved the mouse on the laptop, opening another file labeled "brightening."

"Look at this. A man-made cloud produced by spraying particles over the ocean above the coral reef. The design is based on jet printer technology," said Grace.

"The particulates capture the sun's light before it hits the ocean's surface. Like a giant marine umbrella protecting the reefs," said Jack.

"So amazing. A group of retired scientists in Palo Alto, California worked on this project, because they hoped to save the climate for their grandchildren," said Grace.

Jack pushed her hand aside, wondering if she sensed the tension. He took over the mouse.

But she was focused on reading about the Gates foundation. Their project used a field of mirrors trained on a point that heated materials to intense degrees. This produced a way to manufacture cement or steel in a carbon neutral process.

But maybe the most amazing discovery showed a fungus that consumed radioactivity. It seemed Spencer planned to add this fungus to clean up nuclear dump sites.

"Wow. Here's a special recipe for animal feed that reduces methane produced by cows."

"Look at this," Jack said.

She read over his shoulder.

"A super pact political group that lobbies for sustainable technologies . . ."

"I wonder if any of these designs were ever built?"

"Let's Google them."

They looked up, *smog tower, smog diamonds, mirror technology, cloud to protect the reef, harvesting seabed, diet for cows to reduce methane, radioactive eating fungus, satellite detecting methane,* and *seagrass riverbed.*

"*Woah.* They're *all* here," she said.

"They've all been used or built?" Jack sat, confused.

"Yup."

"Why haven't we heard of most of these projects? And why aren't they available in more places?"

"They threaten the fossil fuel industry," Grace said. Big energy companies don't want change. "Remember Greta Thunberg. The environmentalist from Sweden. She talked about this problem."

"She's amazing. Speaking truth to power," said Jack. "And so focused, the advantage of being neurodivergent."

"And what about that mess in Texas where the private companies charged high electric rates but then didn't invest in insulation for the equipment. Rich folks had private generators while regular people froze without water, heat, or lights for a week."

"Let's wind up in here. Enough to think about for one day," said Jack, checking his phone.

"We can swim, and then grab lunch near the train station afterwards."

"Great," she said.

They made their way to the wing that housed the pool. Jack pulled open the doors. Above them the vaulted ceiling shimmered with mosaic and mother of pearl designs. A dozen potted ferns added to the Moroccan vibe.

The sunlight hit the pool. Undulating shapes of silver, and star glints sparkled on the water's surface. An undercurrent sent another rush of geometric designs twirling in a stream, making the water appear to be dancing with the sunlight. Jack felt a rush of excitement, pulling his clothes off, down to his swim trunks.

Grace stripped down to a bikini that looked awfully like underwear and dove in the pool. It was most unlikely that Grace's mom had seen this skimpy swimwear.

"So Grace, are you *trying* to make a move on me?" Jack said.

"Oh yeah. That's it," she splashed him.

Jack dove in, and feeling encouraged, began to splash her, working his way closer.

Grabbing her playfully, his instincts took over. Her body pressed against him. His mouth found her lips. Embracing her tightly, he felt her return the kisses. Moving to the edge of the pool, they made out.

A door slammed. "Oh, sorry, sir. Didn't know anyone was here today."

The two looked up, and pulled apart, to see the groundskeeper backing away, his face reddened.

Grace laughed after the guy had gone, "Well we just made his day, I'm sure."

Why hadn't he messaged the groundskeeper? Should have seen that coming. *Bad,* bad planning. He was an idiot.

It was getting late and with the mood broken, they climbed out of the pool, toweling off with terrycloth robes. Thirty minutes later at the station, they climbed back on the train, hauling the bikes through the doors. They ate their sandwiches and Jack put his arm around Grace's shoulders as the train headed south. He wondered if Grace was thinking about their time in the pool.

When they arrived back in Evanston, they kissed and rolled their bikes off in different directions. Jack felt happy. And he hadn't given a thought to Vincent Marcov or the nanobots for at least a few hours.

* * *

A week later

Jack sat in his room trying to study, but he couldn't seem to focus. Between the New Zealand dead end location, and daydreaming about Grace, he felt spun around. He knew his grades were slipping, but he was preoccupied by a parade of characters. Vincent Marcov, Max, Izzy, the Masons, and memories of odd dreams led his thoughts marching off in unproductive directions.

Something else was troubling him. The words of the council haunted him. He sensed he had missed something. Was he *doing the next right thing?* Had he listened to the Masons, learning all he could from his visit.

His quest had ground to a halt. And he couldn't read much of the Anamchara Text. Laying on his bed, he closed his eyes, replaying the scene at the Mason's house. In the freakishly clean cottage. Reviewing the interactions. His thoughts were interrupted by a ringing phone in the hall.

Suddenly, Jack sat up. The ringing triggered a memory. Mr Mason had been upset by his phone call. Then even more agitated with the subsequent text. Jack recalled how a shift inside his body at that moment had signaled trouble. Was that his gut intuition?

The sun streamed through his window. He glanced over at the new cylinder now glistening in the shaft of light.

But something was off.

He picked it up and looked closely at the tube's surface. There was a distinct *difference* in the quality of the engraved numbers. Why hadn't he noticed this before? The first three numbers were sharply etched, however the next two digits had right angles that didn't match the others. These lines looked crudely scratched into the surface, turning number *ones* into number *fours*. Writing down the new sequence, he opened his laptop, entering the new coordinates. The map zeroed in. But not off the coast of New Zealand. Rather, the pin located a place in Rogers Park, a city neighborhood, south of Evanston, not far from Jack's house. Grabbing the cylinder and his laptop, Jack ran down the steps to show his parents the discovery. They were sitting in the kitchen.

"You're not going to believe this," he said.

Using the flashlight on his phone he highlighted the cylinder's surface.

"Altered?' said his mom.

"Yup. It seems so. Mr. Mason must have scratched in two new digits. Now that I think about it, I thought I saw some number ones in the surface when I first looked at this new cylinder after it rolled out of the book. Before he took it away to polish it."

"I wonder why the sabotage?' asked his mom.

"He got a phone call and a text message that rattled him," said Jack.

"That's unsettling. I thought you said they seemed excited to discover you had found their house based on the numbers," said his mom.

"It all changed with that phone call. It creeps me out, but at least now I won't have to feel bad about not going to New Zealand," said Jack.

"So where is the new destination?" said his mom warily.

"Only a few miles away. An animal clinic," said Jack.

His parents were quiet now.

"Look, I know this looks suspicious. But if I go in the morning. It's a busy neighborhood, lots of people around," Jack said.

"As weird as the Masons were, I came out OK, and I was deep into the forest. If they really wanted to hurt me, they could have."

"Well, be careful," said his mom. "I don't like this."

* * *

The Next Morning: Rogers Park Neighborhood

The tower of St. Ignatius Church cast a shadow on Glenwood Avenue. Lindy Simons passed storefronts as she made her way to the animal clinic. Fumbling with the keys, she juggled her handbag and shopping totes, and entered the vestibule. Phillip, the pet rabbit, hopped over and nuzzled her frizzy ankle socks. Lindy scooped up the angora bunny, planting a kiss on his head. Then she stashed her bags behind the counter and bustled around the clinic. First, she filled water bowls and pet dishes. Then she splashed water on the linoleum and threw down some rags to absorb the mess.

"I can't have customers slipping on a wet patch of floor," she said to the rabbit.

While she skated around on the soaked rags, she sang, belting out some energetic show tunes, as this always got her day off to a pleasant start. She knew the phone would be ringing soon, and that her assistant Jen would begin the routine of cleaning the cages. Unfortunately, Jen often arrived late, coming up with all kinds of excuses. In response, Lindy knew she would just smile, secretly hoping this employee would do better the next time.

After wiping off all the counters, Lindy looked through a growing stack of unpaid receipts. She didn't have it in her heart to say *no* when an animal was suffering. As usual, she pushed aside the thought that these clients took advantage of her sweet nature.

Suddenly, a heavy shadow crossed her face. Lindy grimaced, experiencing a whirring sound in her head. Something sinister now looked out of her eyes, rocking her head for a moment. Calmly, she turned, locked her gaze on the rabbit, and viciously kicked the bunny across the room. The animal hit the wall with a thud. A moment later, Lindy's eyes fluttered.

"Oh well," she said, "It's important to be kind," quoting the heart shaped decal on the glass door.

Then she frowned, wondering why the rabbit was cowering in the corner.

Just then, Jen ran in the door, apologizing at her lateness.

"My roommate used up all the coffee and I had to go the long way to get some caffeine in me. You know I'm useless without my Morning Joe."

Lindy smiled, continuing to polish the front counter. Jen picked up the hose, but Lindy stopped her.

"Oh I already did that. Can you check the backdoor for deliveries?"

Jen disappeared. Twenty minutes later Lindy found her on the phone with her boyfriend.

"So, I'm not sure I want Thai food again. How about the Lebanese place on Devon? We can ask Andrea and Pete to meet us there." Jen said, evenly making eye contact with Lindy.

"Are you going to text them? I can make the reservation."

Lindy asked Jen to straighten the waiting room.

Jen looked up, making eye contact again, but then, seeming in no hurry to comply, proceeded to discuss menu options.

Lindy retreated, reciting under her breath, "she only needs more positive reinforcement."

* * *

A few miles away, Jack hopped on the "L" train at Noyes Street. Twenty minutes later he got off near Glenwood Avenue and walked several blocks to the Burton Animal Clinic. He pulled open the glass door and a young woman with a flowered head band and matching apron smiled at him.

"Good morning. It's getting warm out there," she said brightly.

Jack asked if they could talk for a few minutes. The girl settled in a chair, saying her name was Lindy Simons. But before Jack could speak the girl suddenly hopped up again.

"Wait, I'll get us something to drink."

Minutes later she returned carrying a tray of triangle sandwiches without crusts, and a pitcher of lemonade. This spread reminded him of a baby shower his aunt had hosted before Charlie was born, but that had been catered. This seemed a bit much.

"I *love* cooking. Seems a lost art, with all the fast-food. Kind of a hobby of mine. Putting together these sandwiches, freezing them. Only need to pop them in the microwave."

Jack picked up a sandwich from the far side of the serving dish. Thinking this might be safer, he recalled the Masons' deception.

After taking a small bite, his eyes widened.

"This is amazing."

"The filling is an old family recipe," said Lindy, proudly.

He took another bite. After all, he had to trust some people. Right? Surely, not everyone was like the Mason's. And they *had* helped figure out the engraved numbers referred to a location.

Lindy changed the subject, asking if he had an animal that needed treatment. He shook his head.

"These numbers led me to this address."

He showed her the slip of paper where he had copied the street number.

Lindy seemed perplexed. Abruptly, she excused herself and left the room.

Jack looked around the waiting area. He heard the furnace kick on and the unmistakable sharp smell of animals filled the room from the vent over his head.

Then he saw a rabbit under a chair across from him. It hopped away with a limp, and Jack saw the animal had been resting on a gold cylinder. He reached over and quickly put it in his pocket. Lindy returned with a plate of cookies.

Jack explained he was following clues . . . on kind of a quest.

Then her assistant Jen, apparently listening behind the curtain, burst out like a demonic puppet.

"That sounds like one of those treasure hunts on TV."

Lindy ignored Jen's rudeness and launched into a list of all the supplies she could provide for his quest.

"I can loan you a waterproof tent, boots, blankets, flashlight, actually any kind of camping equipment. You know you will need lots of supplies. Better to have and not need, than to need and not have."

Jack stepped back, holding up his hands.

"Whoa, hold on," he said.

What was with her? Boundaries, girl. She was trying to help, but yikes. It felt smothering. Dejected now, Lindy admitted.

"I get that a lot. Honestly, I wear myself out. Trying to wait on everybody. And I know people avoid me. I'm just too needy. Have trouble being alone."

Jack cringed inside, hearing her pitiful confession. He couldn't help feeling sorry for her. Maybe he would end up like her, saying *yes* too often. Like when he accepted the Council's challenge. A knot tightened in his stomach. Grace would probably get sick of him too. It was hard to know. When to help, when to stand down. He didn't want to be a doormat. Girls would walk all over him.

"Don't go yet. I need to talk to you," said Lindy, grabbing his arm.

"All my trouble started years ago when a man brought in a pet rat who had swallowed a metal object. My dad asked about the animal's diet, and he determined that feeding grain to the pet would help pass the item that appeared on the x-ray. But this guy flew into a rage, demanding a prescription. When my dad explained the side effects of medicine, the man stormed out, leaving a bag on the floor. My dad picked it up to toss it in the trash. But, then these tiny metal bug like things ran up our arms and into our noses. It wasn't long before we started to feel this whirring in our heads. My mother fainted, and I felt dizzy."

Jack felt the hairs on the nap of his neck stand up when he heard the description of nanobots. The words, *nanobot, mind altering, brain eating functions* looped a repeating message.

Made his skin crawl. Could he get infected? Sitting here?

"His name was doctor something or other ... Vocram?" she said. "Something Russian sounding."

"Vincent Marcov?" Jack asked.

"Ugh ... That's it. I think I try to forget it, on some level."

"So, what happened after that? Did you all get better?"

Lindy continued, describing how, in the following weeks, it became apparent that they all had neurological issues. Within three months her parents had passed away.

So nanobots didn't only mess with your head. They could kill. They *had* killed. What if he was attacked? Then Charlie's face came to mind. What if his little brother was infested with nanobots? He'd never be able to forgive himself. For drawing this danger to his family.

"After their death, my aunt, who is a vet, moved to Chicago to manage the clinic. At first, friends tried to help because they could see I was sad. But, apparently, I wasn't easy to be around. I had to *one up* everyone with fetching and serving. The last time I saw one friend she told me to stop with the veneer of cheerfulness." Now Lindy was sobbing.

Jack didn't know what to say other than, he was sorry. He looked at her. She was a mess. Awful. Pitiful. Made him want to flee. Drove him crazy when girls cried, with the red and puffy faces. He had to get out of there..

Lindy noticed his discomfort and unable to resist, she asked him.

"Can I get you anything?" Smiling weakly, the irony was not lost on her.

Jack shook his head. How could that Marcov guy target her? She was pathetic.

"I'm sorry. I wish there was something I could do."

But inside, he recoiled. Lindy hugged him, grateful for his words. Jack left the clinic.

The girl watched him walk down the street. Then an odd look came over her eyes, like a slot machine hitting the jackpot. Giving a devilish little smile, she picked up her phone.

"Yeah, he totally bought it. Left here completely freaked out."

She pushed up the sleeves on her canary-colored cardigan, revealing Vincent Marcov's initials tattooed on her left arm. She smirked, knowing the bitcoin would appear in her account.

Jack slumped next to the window on the L train. Tears pricked the back of his eyes. Nanobots again. But now, *killing* nanobots. A grinning demon seemed crouched next to him, poking him with the words *Nanobots, Killing nanobots*.

He was losing it. He had to get a grip.

Jack found himself falling back on his thinking skills, rational logic. Data. Information. He needed to find out more. Learn if there was a way to counteract the nanobots. Some, he recalled, had a tiny metal component. Maybe that passed through the body after a time. Did they rust?

Jack drew in a breath, and then another.

What was that sensation now? A calmness? But something else, as well. An unfamiliar urge . . . to push back.

HMMM. This was new. He felt more put together somehow. Maybe more integrated?

Typically, he stayed in his head, with his worries looping on replay. Floundering in this pool of fear, his mind generally reached for strands of logic. This pattern had been his comfort zone, his wheelhouse. Obsessed with a threat, then grabbing for a logical solution.

It was as if his head sat on top of his shoes. But, as his worry built, overwhelming anxiety grew in his chest. His head spun with worries, over his chest loaded with anxiety, on top of a pair of shoes, like a two-part snowman . . . with no gut.

But as he rode in the train car, his worry loosened, dropping from his head, into his core. This sensation had an uncomfrotable fuzzy quality. Then the feelings morphed, landing in his belly, and changing into rage.

Jack felt himself light up with fury.

The unmistakable feeling of pure, unadulterated anger detonated in his body. The thought occurred to him that he actually could kill Vincent Marcov with his bare hands. That monster with his death dealing nanobots. The rage in him blasted like a rocket out of a silo. He wanted to kick, to punch. But he couldn't act out here, in a train car. *Breathe* . . . Breathe, he told himself.

Closing his eyes, he concentrated on holding the breath, then slowly releasing it. He opened his eyes.

Some kids a few seats away stared at him. His face must be flushed. He tried to look normal. They looked away, returning to their conversation. He wished he could be so easy and relaxed. But then these kids knew nothing about the climate threats from Vincent Marcov. And even if they did think about the state of the planet, they probably figured somebody would come to the rescue. Invent something. Bail everyone out.

Overloaded, now, Jack knew he had to switch gears. So, he tried to relive the time with Grace in the Morningside pool. However, his unrest resisted, camped out in his body. He could feel it coursing from his palms. They were hot. The kids across the train aisle now stared at him again. For sure, his face must be bright red. He looked out the window. When he got home, weary from the meeting in Rogers Park, he was surprised to find a puppy scampering in the hall. There had been talk of getting a dog, and more recently, a big one who could bark and protect. However, this little thing clearly belonged on a lap. What were his parents thinking? But Charlie was delighted with the fluffy playmate named Lad who brought ball rolling to a new level of fun.

* * *

Later that afternoon

Meanwhile, Mike was dealing with another chapter of teen war games, as he hid in his room. Anyone passing by the open windows could hear doors slamming and voices screaming. His sister had taken the car without permission, and his parents had had enough. Mike crouched on the floor on the far side of his bed, trying to lay low. He knew if they found him, he would end up arguing with them. Dinner would be miserable with his sisters, pouting and back talking. Mike wanted to crawl under his bed. Other kids considered him so relaxed, but underneath he was seething much of the time. His sisters accused him of being their parent's favorite. He thought, well, yeah. *He* was not sneaking out with the car keys. Secretly, he wished he could be more like Grace because no one gave her grief.

So Mike would have been surprised to find that several streets over, Grace was dealing with her own set of problems. For the umpteenth time, her mother complained in a deceptively sweet voice that she failed to understand why her daughter wanted to stop ballet lessons.

"Ballet is so graceful, and I always hoped you would dance," said her mother.

"When I was ten I liked the fun black swan costume. Now I want to take modern dance. The music and moves are so much cooler."

Exasperated, her mom left the room, defeated, again. Watching her mom retreat always brought Grace a sweet feeling of satisfaction, like a refreshing splash of water. But later, she felt bad that she seemed angry all the time, and maybe too ready for a fight.

CHAPTER SIX

Slick

So, while Grace steamrolled over her mother, Mike tinkered with the climate video game to avoid his crazy family.

The following Saturday, Jack checked the numbers on the new cylinder to find the map coordinates. As expected, when he entered the digits, a new location appeared, showing a sprawling house with too many arches, and pillars. A web search indicated that a business man had bought the property for two point three million dollars. Another article reported, the owner, Grainger, had been convicted of embezzlement, but had weaseled out of serving time.

* * *

Euclid Place, Evanston

Trip Grainger toweled off his shoulders after climbing out of the pool. He put on a terrycloth robe and picked up his phone that was vibrating on the table. It was his club.

"O.K ... Let me get back to you about the golf tournament?"

He ran his fingers through his blond waves, as he set the phone down.

Then the nineteen-year-old took a drink from a bottle of water. He began texting.

A moment later, the phone dinged. Looking at the response, he smiled. Entering the house, Trip stopped in the hall to check on a delivery, then started up the steps. The housekeeper called after him.

"Sir, will you be here for lunch?"

"Yeah, there will be three of us. And grill some burgers. It's going to get up to 80 degrees today."

Under his breath, to himself, he said. "Seems way early for this kind of heat."

A short time later, Jack's bike stopped at a house with a fountain spitting water in the air that matched the web photo. Parked in the circular drive, a copper-colored Nissan GT-R sat next to a black Range Rover that looked like a rhinoceros on wheels. Several men in overalls raked twigs off the lawn and loaded tarps with tree debris. The Grainger house aimed to inspire awe, however Jack thought it looked tacky, with a slew of materials competing for the eye. While Morningside's fountain blended into the landscape, the Grainger's water feature borrowed elements from several styles. As if details from palace facades from different centuries could grant respectability to the owner of this place.

Jack walked up to the entrance and pressed the bell. A uniformed housekeeper opened the door. He introduced himself, but the woman said in a somewhat disinterested voice.

"You can wait on the patio. The others will be here soon."

Showing him the way, she asked if he would like something to drink. "Sure, thank you."

Jack wondered if he had stumbled into a gathering. In the hallway, Jack passed a tall glass cabinet filled with trophies. The opposite wall was covered with photos of Grainger posing with various celebrities.

What a showoff, he thought. Wonder if one of these guys is the judge who let him off easy.

The housekeeper led him outside and gestured to a ring of cushioned chairs. Jack saw a shimmering infinity pool with blue glass tiles. A striped cabana stood in the corner, and stacks of terrycloth towels waited for a swimmer. He thought Grace and Mike would laugh at the pillars and fountain. Then again, they'd like this pool. He wished Grace was here.

The housekeeper returned with a pitcher of iced tea. A few minutes later, a tanned young man wearing aviator sunglasses, a pink polo shirt and khaki slacks walked down the steps to the patio. He looked perplexed when he saw Jack, but extended his hand, introducing himself.

"I'm Trip Grainger. What can I do you for?"

Trip, with his slicked back blonde hairdo, and professionally whitened teeth, gave a disingenuous smile.

Getting to his feet, Jack introduced himself.

"Hi, I'm Jack Abernault. It's nice to meet you. I'm here because your house came up on a Google map."

But before Jack could explain about the coordinates, Trip cut him off, sounding irritated.

"Look, we're not interested. The house was taken off the market. Did your parents send you over? Because we have a realtor if we ever wanted to sell. Blanca shouldn't have let you in here."

Jack noticed the guy kept steady eye contact, seldom blinking, intent on getting Jack to "buy" what he was saying. It reminded him of a used car salesman his dad knew.

"No, you have the wrong idea. No realtors in my family."

"Oh, so a reporter." Trip switched to an even more annoyed tone.

"Should have known. Look, the Graingers don't *give* interviews. You need to leave now. No story here."

"But I'm not a reporter."

Holy crap. What a piece of work. Maybe he'd gotten the address wrong?

"Out NOW," Trip said.

"Ok, Ok. Look at this." Jack pulled out the golden cylinder.

When Trip glanced at the trinket, Jack thought he saw a hint of recognition, but it was clear that his host wanted him gone.

"I'll show you to the door," said the young man.

Jack had no recourse but to leave.

Had he gone to the wrong place? Was this guy under the influence of nanobots? Trip Grainger was an idiot, either way. As he walked back down to the curb, he could hear Trip berating the housekeeper for letting this random person in the house.

What was he supposed to do now? He'd thought he'd get another golden cylinder. How would he continue the quest? What a big waste of time. And his stomach felt sour. A bitter aftertaste coated his tongue. He wondered about the flavoring in the iced tea. Or maybe he was reacting to being thrown out. That was a first.

As Jack rode home, he thought about the people he had met so far. Margaret Mason needed to be right. Irritated when things weren't perfect. It seemed the good became the enemy of the better. Lindy Simons, on the other hand, was a different story. She basked in the pride of her good works. However, she served, to the point of annoying others with her incessant fussing. The Graingers, talented in business, felt compelled to win. Even if it meant scamming the system. Maybe Jack had found the correct address, after all. What an *odd* group of people?

Then Jack recalled Mr. Mason's sabotage, the altering of the engraved numbers. Now that he had a few hours this morning, maybe he would scope out the Mason's cottage again. This time he would watch from the forest's edge to see what he could learn. He knew his parents would be upset that he was taking a risk. They would say he was tempting fate by returning there. He considered bringing Grace and Mike for the reconnaissance. Then he thought, no, three people would be easier to spot. Going alone was safer.

When he got home, he changed into his khaki shirt and taped his bike frame to camouflage his presence in the woods. Before he headed out toward the Skokie Lagoons, he left a note with his destination under his notebook. Jack knew all of this was risky, but his curiosity about the Masons trumped his worry.

Forty minutes later, he thought he was nearing the Mason's cottage. Getting off his bike, he wanted to find a safe place to observe the house. As he rolled his bike through the forest, he thought about what he'd do if he was discovered. Checking to see if he had cell phone service, he saw one bar. A moment later he checked again. Now there was no service. He was on his own, and probably close to the cottage.

Then he saw the property. Or, more accurately, what remained. Jack stood at the edge of a burned-out patch of dirt, a charred heap. Only the remnants of the fireplace and chimney remained. The smell of embers filled his nostrils. Jack could not believe his eyes. He wondered if the Masons had escaped, or if they had been killed in the fire? No trace of them was left.

Jack wanted to get out of there and he rode his bike as fast as he could. He wished he could move his family someplace out of Vincent Marcov's range. But where? He ruled out Alaska: not enough sun. Californians put up with earthquakes and fires, and the coast suffered hurricanes. While tornadoes battered the Midwest, the Southwest and Southeast harbored poisonous snakes . . . and it was all getting worse. The climate hammered people everywhere. There was no escaping it, and so apparently nowhere to hide from Dr. Marcov . . . even way out on the planet Sophia. And, each week, Jack heard reports of more ice cliffs melting into the Arctic Ocean. But most people still went about their business, ignoring the weather, and cranking up the air conditioning.

* * *

That evening Grace and Mike came over to play video games and eat pizza. For several hours, they sprawled on the sectional, tossing one of Charlie's soft toys back and forth. The cheesy slices landed inside Jack like a soft pillow. It felt like old times until Grace popped the bubble.

"So Jack, do you think Vincent Marcov is away on Sophia, or somewhere nearby?"

Immediately, the food in his stomach morphed into an indigestible lump.
"How should I know? And thanks for bringing him up," Jack said.

"You're welcome," she said, undeterred.

She could be such a pain. Why was he even attracted to her? She's annoying. If a thought crossed her mind, she just blurted it out. Absolutely no filter. Didn't matter how other people felt. She didn't *care* what other people thought.

But she did have courage. Was an unstoppable force. He couldn't deny that.

"Well, you can't pretend Marcov's not out there. When there's a showdown, just know I want to be there," she said, getting in the last word, as usual.

"Why would you bring up Marcov? Can't we have *one* evening?" Mike asked.

Plopped on the sofa, he was the flashcard for the *immovable object*.

"You just wanna stick your head in the sand," said Grace.

"It's stupid to ignore the threat," she added.

"Guys. FYI, Vincent Marcov is *always* on my mind. Those nanobots turn functions on and off in the brain. Changing people. So they act in ways they wouldn't choose. Like they're in a trance. And they can *kill*," Jack said grimly.

"And if that isn't enough to freak you out, the ice cap is melting as we speak."

"Time to get out the aluminum head gear," Mike said, trying to smooth over the tension in the room.

Grace threw Charlie's stuffed bear at his head.

Geeze, she doesn't know the meaning of letting it go. Always scanning for trouble. And, if she brings up her favorite Halloween costume. That stupid Viking helmet with the horns, from when she was five. Telling us again how it showed what she felt inside. He'd strangle her, right then and there. They all knew that if there was a line in the sand, Grace couldn't wait to cross it.

After a few minutes, Grace piped up again.

"Just tell me when and where."

"Enough!" The boys said, tossing toys and pillows at her.

"Grace, we get it. You want to be there when it happens." But now they were all in a state. No chilling out this night.

So Jack told his friends how he had gone back to the Mason's house. And that it had burned to the ground. And that there was no record of them on the web. The family had vanished into thin air.

"That's *very* weird," said Mike.

Jack could tell his friend was genuinely rattled.

"So, Mike, you're all ready for a showdown?" asked Grace, still unruffled by their rebuff.

Fuming now, Mike got up to leave. "You don't get it, Grace. This is life and death stuff. Not some Wonder Woman fantasy in your head. You need to grow up."

Mike turned and left the house.

"Happy now?" Jack asked.

"Yes, actually, I am. Mike needs to wake up," she said.

"Well, you want him to *wake* up. And he wants you to *grow* up. I want you *both* to *shut up!*"

And with that, Jack went upstairs, leaving Grace to let herself out.

As Jack heard the front door slam, it occurred to him that Grace should be impressed with the courage it took for him just to get up in the morning. Most of the time, these days, he wanted to curl up in a ball.

At that moment, he hated her.

* * *

That same night, two hundred miles above the earth, the stealth satellite hovered over another ice cliff. A flap opened and a laser beam appeared, slicing off another gigantic chunk of white. Shuddering for a moment, the glassy ice dropped, crashed, and then dipped below the water's surface. Popping up, the ice ominously floated south.

News reports covered these strikes, and governments around the globe attempted to stop the attacks. An iron dome project was begun to fortify the security at the top of the world. It was hoped that this technology could block the lasers, however the construction would take time. The deteriorating ice cap weighed heavily on Jack. The clock was ticking.

Part of him still wanted to run and hide, while another part hoped he could find a way to fight back. At these times, Jack remembered the words of Elinor Spencer and the Council. He would try to *do the next right thing*. Following the clues.

CHAPTER SEVEN

Achilles' Heel vs Kryptonite

Lake Geneva, Wisconsin

A TEENAGE GIRL STARED OUT AT THE LAKE; a small book of poetry rested in her lap. She reflected on the beautiful phrases she had just read. Strains of cello music wafted out of the windows, muted by the mist not yet cooked off by the sun. The screen door opened, and a woman wearing a turban and a silk caftan stepped out. She sighed deeply, taking in the view.

"Esme, dear, would you like to go into town so we can pick up some glazes for your ceramics?" asked the woman.

"That would be awesome. I'm hoping to find some shades that match the colors in the water."

"Capturing light and motion, and how they impact color variations remains an elusive aspiration," said the aunt, twirling a tendril of red hair that had escaped from her Gucci headgear.

"I'm so lucky to have you Aunt Lutetia. You just *get* me."

A mournful look crossed the aunt's face, knowing well the artist's way could be difficult.

Aunt and niece sat in silence, gazing at the interplay of light and colors, intermingling the sky and water.

* * *

Sunday morning, after the fight with Mike and Grace, Jack woke with a headache.

The decade long friendship was suffering stress fractures, and seemed to be falling apart. Maybe they were all just too different. Grace drove him nuts much of the time, and Mike could be so checked out and oblivious. Jack felt alone with his responsibilities. His temples were throbbing as his thoughts turned to the Council's challenge.

How would he continue his quest? Grainger was a dead end. He rolled over on his side.

Jack looked over at the golden cylinder sitting on his shelf.

Incredibly, a fresh set of numbers stared back at him.

What? Wait. He blinked.

Then he realized the first two cylinders, the one from Sophia and the one from the Mason's had vanished!

Jack leaped up. Just when he was ready to throw in the towel, a path seemed to light up ahead of him like emergency lights on the floor in an airplane's cabin. But who had taken the other two cylinders?

A chill of apprehension rushed up his spine. Someone had been here. In his room.

Quickly, he entered the new coordinates in his laptop. The pin zeroed in on a house in Lake Geneva . . . the home of a local artist, according to the web. Jack brought the cylinder into the kitchen. His parents were having coffee. In his highchair, Charlie played with his Cheerios.

"Any chance you guys want to drive up to Lake Geneva today? Look at these new coordinates."

His dad looked at the map.

"Hmm . . . I was going to take Charlie to get some new shoes. But a day trip might do us all good. Traffic won't be too bad if we head back before three o'clock. You know how congested the highway gets on Sunday afternoon," said his mom.

"But weren't you going to clean the garage today?" She asked her husband.

"Yeah, but Lake Geneva sounds like a good idea. For all of us. The garage isn't going anywhere."

"Great. Last night, Mike, and Grace got into it. I'm sure you heard the ruckus," said Jack.

"Yeah, we did hear. It's unusual for you guys to fight. I guess the stress is getting to all of us," said his dad.

An hour and a half later, the family loaded up the car for a two-hour drive just over the state border in Wisconsin. Charlie would spend the day at the neighbor's who had a child his age. His dad preferred the scenic roads, and so they headed out on Route 22, and then angled northwest. Jack sat in the back of the car, watching the farms stream past the windows.

His mom insisted that they make a quick stop at St. Raphael the Archangel, a Renaissance structure rebuilt on the prairie. An article in the newspaper had described how the contractor used materials from an old Chicago church. The result transported the visitor to an Italian piazza. Sitting in the middle of nowhere, the architecture took one's breath away. Sunday services were getting out, but the parking lot soon emptied so they had the view to themselves.

"I read it cost the same amount as all new construction," said dad.

"I wonder how many loads it took to haul all that stone from the city?"

"Must have been quite a fleet."

His mom commented that this part of the country was home to some surprising structures. A Norwegian Stave Church, the Bahai Temple, Oak Park's Prairie homes, a Serbian Orthodox Seminary, the Milwaukee Art Museum, Plano's Glass House, Glencoe's Synagogue on the Lake, and

Taliesin in Spring Green always surprised visitors to the Midwest, who only expected the dazzling downtown Chicago architecture.

"You're a regular Chicago booster. You should do tours for the Architecture Foundation."

"Like I've got the time. You know my practice is full," said his mom.

When they reached the town of Lake Geneva the family stopped at a gallery where the art director greeted them. After looking around the exhibit, Jack's mom purchased a small print of a pine forest that reminded her of a summer home from her childhood. The owner rang up the sale, and then looked at Jack's map, pointing out the scenic lake route to the artist's home.

"Prepare yourself. Lutetia is quite a colorful character," said the gallery owner, rolling her eyes.

However, Jack felt some relief that at least this individual was known in the community. As the house was only a mile from the village center, he walked, leaving his parents at a gift shop.

Twenty minutes later, he found the field stone home perched on a hill with a lake view. A magnolia tree, pregnant with buds, was ready to bloom. It seemed early for magnolias. A tinkling wind chime blew in the breeze as Jack made his way across the porch. Hoping someone was home, Jack knocked. After a few moments, a girl about eighteen years old opened the door.

"Yes…um. Hello?"

She looked distracted, and maybe a little sad.

Jack introduced himself, and showed her the cylinder, explaining the coordinates. The girl's aunt joined her in the doorway.

"Aunt Lutetia, it looks like the cylinder you found the other day," the girl said.

"You did?" Jack asked.

The aunt then introduced herself as Lutetia Langdon, and her niece, Esme. They invited him inside. The girl was dressed in an oversized mohair sweater, and a flowing pleated skirt. She led him to the living room, gesturing him to sit near the fire. Jack surveyed the room as he sat in a chair made from bent wood.

A live edge table with ceramic pots sat off to the side. Wooden beams crossed the span of the ceiling, and tribal rugs covered the floors. A rectangle of chartreuse silk with primitive ink stampings hung on a natural brick wall. Everything looked handcrafted in subtle shades of earth tones. Pillows cut from Indian rugs sat propped on a leather mid-century sofa. A copy of *The Boy Who Drew Cats* sat on the table.

He noticed Esme had a far-away look in her eyes. And that she moved like his cousin, a dancer. Although this girl was easy on the eyes, she looked high maintenance. At least she didn't look bossy, like Grace.

Lutetia settled in an oversized chair. Fishing an antique chain out of her bodice, she produced an identical gold cylinder.

"I found this trinket *so* interesting. Last week the piece was resting at the bottom of my koi pond. Can you imagine that?"

She handed it to Jack, placing her hands over his. "It's yours, dear. When the universe speaks, we must listen."

"Look, different numbers are etched here."

He explained that he had been following the coordinates, on a kind of a quest.

"to get some answers and …."

"Oh, I just *LOVE* a quest! You see I define myself as a seeker. Following what I believe is an authentic path." Lutetia sighed.

"SO, so much more interesting than living a conventional life."

Esme, taking this as a cue that this conversation was going to take a while, excused herself. Jack could hear the clink of glassware in an adjoining room. She returned shortly, balancing a tray with a pitcher of sun tea and antique tumblers filled with ice.

Lutetia poured a glass for Jack. Her chandelier earrings and bracelets jangled with her movements. As she gestured, Jack noticed an exotic fragrance. Seeing his reaction, she shared,

"It's a Cartier perfume."

"I *must* give you a sample to take for your mother," said Lutetia as she reached over and opened a drawer that was filled with unusual containers. Choosing a red lacquered vial, she floated out of the room.

"I'll be back in a moment," she called over her shoulder from the hall.

Esme smiled and Jack could see the family resemblance. Aunt and niece presented with the same ethereal quality, as if they breathed a different, more refined air.

"This chair is cool. Bent wood?" Jack said, trying to engage Esme.

"Mm ... Hm ... my aunt only chooses special items. Curated really," she said. "It's all about earth tones, and textures ... and, of course, what touches your soul."

Jack could almost see the drama oozing from this girl.

Lutetia bustled in, carrying a tiny funnel, and a round bottle filled with amber liquid. Carefully, she poured perfume into the vial. Sliding the small container into a velvet pouch, she handed it to Jack.

"Your mother will *love* this scent ... so, *so* special ... just takes you away to Paris, or to the island of Rhodes."

Her gaze rested on the far away horizon through the window.

Jack thanked her. Then he steered the conversation back to his mission.

"So I'm following the coordinates on this gold cylinder. There's a rogue scientist ..."

Lutetia immediately cut him off.

"Oh, that rascal Vincent Marcov!" her face darkened as she grabbed his arm.

"One of the dangers of a seeker's life is that, off a conventional path, it can be difficult figuring out good and evil. Can you believe I used to date that guy?" Lutetia glared.

Jack recoiled. But the woman seemed not to notice. She rattled on, warning him about the importance of staying away from bad people.

"Vincent was so full of himself, vain, and downright mean. The man was incapable of passing a mirror without preening and checking his hair. The relationship was brief. After I discovered the potion in my tea, I poured the drink down the drain. Vincent was furious when I wouldn't drink his special tea, or answer his calls. He was relentless, finally sending a dozen black roses. The hideous bouquet was infested with these tiny black bugs. They moved like something mechanical. And there was a note, condemning me and my darling niece to feeling dissatisfaction with *anything* ordinary. As a result, we remain drawn to all things *special*. Aren't we, my dear?"

"So true. Only art, literature, and music hold any interest for me. Other subjects remain too dry *and boring*," said Esme.

"I hate to tell you, but those bugs were nanobots. You should get checked out by a doctor. Other people I've met had this same thing happen," said Jack.

"That's *very* upsetting. Actually, we *did* go to the doctor, but he assumed we were exaggerating. Being hysterical, hypochondriacal."

Jack could see how the woman might not be taken seriously. Too intense, and way too dramatic.

But Lutetia switched topics, maybe to manage her anxiety about the threat. Because now she was raving about a new opera production at the Lyric, telling the story of Orpheus and his love, Eurydice, trapped in the underworld. Jack thought, woah, who booked this show? A tsunami of emotion crashed into the room. But there was more to come. Lutetia, riding the wave of the opera, admitted that she actually *relished* the inner pain as it "fed her art."

"Can't say as I've ever been to the opera," Jack said, hoping to put the brakes on this runaway drama train.

"Oh, but you *must*. This season offers some *glorious* performances. And the Art Institute, *don't* get me started. We wouldn't miss them for *anything*. I have a pied-a-terre in Chicago so we can enjoy *every single* performance and *all* the exhibits."

"A pied what?" asked Jack.

"It's French slang for an apartment," said Esme. She bit her lip.

Was she *laughing* at him?

Jack thought she was, but maybe Esme only looked uneasy, sensing her aunt's ramblings now were going off the rails. Jack returned to the topic of the rogue scientist.

"Marcov has messed up the lives of a lot of people." he said.

Lutitia paused, considering now.

"I wonder *what* I can tell you about him?"

Then her eyes brightened.

"I know. Vincent absolutely *detests* art. Let me show you an *amazing* piece that he hated . . . he actually broke out in hives."

Escorting Jack out to her studio, they passed by paintings, half-finished canvases, and mosaics. But by far, the most arresting item in the room was a brass chair with cast human arms. Lutetia was pleased with Jack's reaction.

"I know . . . amazing. My son made it as part of a series. It's a marvelous piece of modern sculpture . . . new, yet somehow old. It's titled *Shift & Shadow*. About the soul's journey toward authenticity, according to the sculptor."

Jack could see this sculpture belonged in a museum, and he felt drawn to touch one of the brass arms to see if it was warm. Somehow it embodied the shift he had felt when his fear turned into fury on the ride back from the vet clinic. But the action of the arms also matched the movement he had experienced when he returned to a centered place. Great art was supposed to move you in this deep way, he had heard. Somehow, he sensed this sculpture would remain with him for a long time.

Jack thanked her for taking the time to talk with him. He said it was time to meet up with his parents in town. Lutetia showed him to the front door, and Esme gave him a sweet smile.

They closed the door and counted to ten to make sure Jack was gone. Then Lutetia and Esme turned to each other and high fived.

"Now THAT was fun. Excellent performance, my dear," said the aunt.

"We scared the living daylights out of that *stupid* boy," said Esme.

"Not that stupid. He seemed to grasp the importance of the sculpture. Could be dangerous," said Lutetia.

"We could have done *so* much more," said Esme. "I could barely stop myself from adding some potion to his iced tea," said the girl with a dark gleam in her eyes.

"No, no, dear. Vincent insisted we only *scare* the boy. Apparently, *fear* remains his Achilles Heel. My Vincent needs, or I should say, *requires*, this victim for himself."

The two entered a small enclave under the stairs. A votive candle flickered under the portrait of a leering Cronus given to them by Dr. Vincent. This mythological deity who had devoured his own children, provided the ideal patron for the Marcov cult's mission to destroy the planet for future generations. The aunt and niece pulled black veils over their heads, muttering some incantations. When the planet's climate flipped, this capricious duo knew they would be among the lucky ones.

Jack headed back to the town center. When he saw his parents sitting on a bench, it surprised him how grateful he was to see them, after the intensity of the artists. The story he had heard that morning had rattled him. More nanobots.

Jack couldn't help but compare Lutetia to his mother and father. His parents could be a pain, but they were *so* normal. He'd take grounded any day. Art was great, but to live with it day in and day out. Too much. However, the power in that sculpture would stay with him. Seemed to embody his interior struggle. But also, the possibility of a shift to a better place.

The Abernaults shared a meal sitting on a deck over the lake. While they ate, Jack told his parents about Lutetia and Esme, and their dealings with Dr. Marcov. He added that there seemed something about Lutetia that reminded him of Aunt Catherine. At the mention of his dad's sister, his parents exchanged a knowing look.

On the ride home, Jack filed away the information that Marcov detested art. Apparently, it was like his kryptonite. Jack settled in the back seat of the car, taking in the cool breeze coming through the window.

Two hours later, the Abernaults rolled up their driveway. Grace was sitting on his front steps, her agitation visible.

Jack felt his insides constrict.

Couldn't get even twenty-four hours without her. Grace was intense. Like those artists. But in a different way. They existed in a world of high culture while Grace lived to rule. Different things set them off. But, as for being around them, a little went a long way.

"What's up?" he asked, irritably, still annoyed about the previous night.

Grace ignored his tone.

"I need to show you something."

"I'm tired. Can it wait?"

"No, it can't wait. Look, sorry about last night. I even called Mike to smooth things over. And I sent you a bunch of texts . . . which you ignored."

"Had my phone off," said Jack.

He had turned off the device on purpose. Grace needed a time out after her behavior the night before.

"Look, my bad. But, while you guys were whining, another huge portion of the arctic fell into the sea. Watch this polar bear trying to keep his head above the water. It's horrible."

She handed him her phone with the video. They watched the struggling animal, fighting for his life. The scene turned his stomach.

"That's not all. Today, I got this text."

Jack looked at her phone. The text included a video. Jack started the clip. A view of the arctic appeared. A menacing voice gave the grim forecast. As polar bears struggled, the entire arctic icecap disappeared into the sea. An hourglass appeared and the sand began to fall, faster and faster.

"Won't be long now." Then a maniacal laugh came from the phone's speaker.

"Like we need a reminder," said Jack.

"We've got to find that scientist and destroy his headquarters," she said.

"Woah ... take out his place?" asked Jack, feeling sucker punched by her words.

However, he could see why she was riled up. The struggling polar bear, the hourglass. A count down on the ice cap. Jack already was freaking out. The burned-out remains of the Mason's house. The killing nanobots. The laser satellites.

Woah. Woah. Woah, filled his head. How could he put the brakes on her idea? "Before we even consider taking out his place, we would need a *really* good plan," said Jack.

Just then, Mike walked up. Grace showed him the struggling polar bear and the hourglass video.

"That polar bear is going to *be us* if we don't do something," she said

"Woah." Mike looked grim.

"That's what I said."

Jack imagined Mike's mind, envisioning a hospital bed ... no, a cemetery. Because that's what he saw in his own mind. But Grace continued.

"Look, I know this is scary stuff. But there's no getting around it. We *must* think offensively. Or we're done for."

"We do have to act. But with a plan. And at the right time," said Jack.

He knew he was a fan of a good defense, but he couldn't deny the hourglass posed a threat. They *did* need a plan. *And* a plan B. Jack felt a shiver settle on him, like he was wearing an icy shirt right out of the freezer.

"I could set up a decision tree that might help with some strategies," said Mike.

Leave it to Mike to offer a sensible idea that would slow Grace's careless momentum.

"So, we agree to start looking into a way to take Marcov down?" Grace asked.

"Ok, yes," said Jack.

"You don't sound convinced," said Grace.

"Uh, I already have the quest ... and the book. So, I'm kinda busy. But we *should* have a plan. And we don't even know where the guy lives," said Jack.

Grace was ready to press on, but Mike cut her off.

"I'll start tonight."

Grace looked satisfied that things would move forward now, and Jack felt his heart soften toward her. You had to admire her passion.

Their time in the swimming pool came to mind, and warmth began to build inside him as he watched her walk down the sidewalk . . . truly, a force of nature. Was it always going to be like this? He'd get fed up, and then she'd reel him back in, like a stupid big mouth bass.

That evening, up in his room, Jack laid on his back, staring at the ceiling. Scanning the large blank square always seemed to clear his thoughts. Reset his mind. But then the inner chatter resumed.

Grace, Grace . . . she was killing him. Then, he turned over, and his eyes landed on the cloth bag with the vial Lutetia had given him. He couldn't wait for his mom's birthday. With all the trouble around, he wanted to at least cheer somebody up. He grabbed the pouch and found his mom reading a psychology journal. It seemed she was always learning something to help her patients. Jack handed her the perfume, explaining the artist in Lake Geneva wanted her to have it.

His mom opened the vial and dabbed some drops on her wrists, and sniffing.

"This is incredible. The woman certainly has impeccable taste like your dad's sister. We'll have to get her a bottle for her birthday. What's this called?"

She squinted at the label, translating from the French.

"*Kiss of the Dragon*. Uh, no . . . Catherine would take offense at that name. Maybe this will be my new scent. I love it, although it's a bit heavy for springtime."

Jack knew his Aunt Catherine *was* kind of a dragon.

Grace was a dragon as well. Dragons could be exciting. Thinking of the episode in the pool at Morningside, he needed an excuse to get her back up there . . . alone. There was something about being in the water that evened the energy between them. Maybe cooled her down. Under what pretense might they return to the Lake Forest house? Maybe hosting a school event on the estate would give him some extra time with her while they designed the festival program.

At lunch, the next day, Jack said, "What do you think of an outdoor party at Morningside for a school benefit? The planning could act as a cover while we research taking out Marcov's headquarters. Maybe an international theme? The money could go toward the arts, and science programs."

"Everyone would figure we're busy with the event. But we can have a committee do most of the work," said Grace

"I don't ever want to get on your bad side. That's quite devious," said Mike.

"Only good strategy," she said.

Grace started jotting down ideas. By the time they finished lunch, they had an outline, and list of committees.

First thing, Monday morning Jack texted the student council president about his idea for the festival at Morningside.

But the response was less than encouraging.

"I don't know. That sounds like too much work," came the reply.

Annoyed this guy wasn't jumping at his plan, Jack fired off a second message.

"I can organize it. Thought you might want to be involved."

"You can't have an event unless the student council approves it, and I say *no*. Maybe next year. You need to drop it."

Jack felt his cheeks flush. This guy was a control freak, too stubborn to at least hear him out.

We'll see about that, said Jack to himself. Still fuming, he went to his next class.

Mike immediately sensed something was wrong.

"You look like you want to punch someone."

"I DO want to punch someone."

And he told his friends about the student council guy.

Grace confirmed that, in her experience, the student council always said *no*, because the kids on that council only funded sports.

"They're all jocks, so they never let the arts or sciences have an event. And now I want to punch him *too*," said Grace.

Mike and Jack laughed at this.

"And you might really do it. That guy is already kind of intimidated by you. Remember the incident in seventh grade?"

"The showdown over the last custard pudding in the cafeteria lunch line," Grace recalled.

They all smiled.

"But really, this is ridiculous. What can we do?" asked Jack.

They tossed around ideas, including sending pizzas to his house. It was fun to think of the overbearing guy answering the door, trying to explain to the delivery man how it was impossible that he ordered pizza as he never touched carbs. Laughing, Jack shook his head.

"So, no punching and no pizzas," Grace said, with a mischievous look.

"Well, I am going to talk to the Parent Association," said Jack.

Going over the head of the student council president might work.

A few days later, after his appeal, Jack called to order the first meeting to organize the benefit. The parent group had been all in when they heard about highlighting world cultures. Evanston maintained a national reputation as a welcoming community. Promoting diversity was a great selling point. Jack asked for volunteers to head the committees.

"Who wants to do the decorations?"

A girl named Lucy waved her hand.

"Done," said Jack.

A sophomore offered to take on the chairmanship as she had good organizational skills. Another girl volunteered for advertising. David, a big kid who liked to throw his weight around, said he could handle tickets at the gate. Sandy, the oldest of five, offered to set up a first aid station. A junior wanted to assemble a dance floor as he had experience from his summer job. Two friends, Madeline and Lorraine, volunteered to set up tours of the house. Jack surveyed the group, smiling.

"This was awesome. That took like twenty-five minutes."

This was doable. Delegate the jobs. Research security systems on the side. And, hopefully, more alone time with Grace.

"Let's meet in two weeks to check on progress."

Leaving the building, Jack approached the bike rack. Right away, he noticed his flattened bike tires. The voice of the Student Council's president sneered.

"Hey, having a problem? Seems like you should have thought twice before making an end run around me."

Jack's fists tightened, and his cheeks flushed. Though this guy was bigger, Jack knew he could take him with a few karate moves. Then he remembered Joseph Spencer, and he took a steadying breath.

"Sorry, but I gotta say the arts and science labs could use some money."

Then Jack looked up to the security camera.

"Hope you smiled for the CCTV up there."

The boy's face drained of color as he spotted the shiny surveillance camera attached to the light pole. Jack felt a guilty rush of satisfaction, watching the bully calculate the ding on his school record.

"See you around," and Jack rolled his bike away to find some tire patches.

* * *

Two Weeks Later

The follow-up meeting for the festival did not go as smoothly as the initial one. First, the girl in charge of decorations expected a check for five hundred dollars to reserve a fog machine so the festival would have a *magical feel*. Groaning erupted from all four corners of the room.

"Here we go," said one guy snidely, rolling his eyes.

Jack could feel his discomfort grow as the girl whined

"I only want it to be special. It *has* to be beautiful," she said.

Before Jack could respond, shouting erupted in the back of the room.

David, flipping up his black leather jacket lapels with his thumbs, bellowed that he would not be bossed around!

Glaring at him, the chairman, hands on her hips, scolded that he and his buddies would *not*, under any circumstances, handle security. They could *only* accept tickets. She insisted that the Parent Association would handle the safety and money collection. But, he could, if he wanted a larger role, set up chairs.

With a purple face, David stormed out, slamming the door as he left the cafeteria.

Way too much drama, Jack thought. Guys, it seemed, could be dragons, as well.

Then the girl in charge of advertising complained someone was pulling down the posters that she had displayed all over town. Exasperated, Jack looked over the room.

"Well, is there any good news?"

Fortunately, a number of kids had progress to report.

"The nurse's station is all set. And games for the younger kids are ready in bags."

"Lots of families signed-up to donate dishes. Tours of the Morningside clock collection are all booked."

"I can report the finances are on budget, except for the fog machine issue."

"A family donated the dance floor and canopy."

"*Cattle of the Lands*, that local band, and a Dee Jay are booked to play music."

Jack returned to the fog machine problem. He saw the girl in charge of decorations dabbing her eyes over the rejection of special effects device.

"The fog machine would be cool. But the ground is uneven and so there's a tripping hazard," said Jack.

"Well, then can we have an art contest?" she asked.

"Sure, good idea."

The girl started making notes on getting art supplies. A few minutes later, the meeting adjourned.

Outside on the school's lawn, Jack pulled his bike out of the rack. He was about to ride off when he noticed Grace talking to a guy named Jesse.

Jack saw him lean in and kiss her. Then they walked off toward the park, holding hands. A sharp stab took his breath away. Blindsided. Jealous. Deceived. Hurt. Jack wanted to cry. His eyes stung. How long had this been going on? She had never even mentioned him. He had thought the time in the pool had meant something. Then he realized he had neglected to make any more dates with her. He'd been too preoccupied. But he assumed she understood his feelings.

CHAPTER EIGHT

Morningside Festival

O N A GORGEOUS SATURDAY IN LATE APRIL, the lawn at Morningside filled with festival goers. A warm weather pattern had settled over northern Illinois, bringing up the tulips. Trees blossomed overnight, dressing the branches in festive pastels. Chicago weather was famous for flipping from freezing to summer temperatures in a matter of days. However, this year, the weather was noticeably hotter, more like July than April.

The festival seemed to be going smoothly as folks carried plates piled with food from the buffet. Grace had been correct that the event would offer a good cover for the friends to investigate Vincent Marcov. In the end, though, they also had pitched in with the planning for the fest. Grace had come up with an idea of printing a cookbook of recipes from the community. They already had sold out, and more copies would be available at a local bookstore.

Jack had learned that Jesse worked at the bookstore, and this was how the two had struck up a relationship. Jack feigned disinterest. However, he was *seething*. It took all his strength to steer his thoughts away from what they might be up to. The festival, it turned out, was a welcome distraction, because left on his own he would have moped around the house. He learned from Mike that Jesse was scheduled to work that weekend, so his rival was out of the picture for the day. He didn't think he could have stood it to watch them together.

Jack looked over the main lawn that was strung with paper lanterns rocking in the wind. Over near the patio, the art contest was in full swing, with the chairman hanging art so everyone could view the submissions. The girl who had been such a pain at the meeting, had turned out to be Ok after all. Her lantern decorations were great, and an art project making paper chains kept the kids happy with an activity. A line of children ran with the paper linked streamers, darting through the crowd, like a happy train of miniature jesters.

Jack knew the entrance booth had collected thousands of dollars for the arts and science departments. However, gradually Jack felt a vague sense that he was missing something. Then it hit him. None of the jocks had shown up. He thought about taking some extra precautions, sharing his concerns with the festival chairwoman.

"That student council guy is on a power trip. Lots of chest thumping, My older brother dropped out of sports because his team hassled him so much about his interest in art. His girlfriend quit the booster club in protest," said the chairwoman.

Jack nodded and called the Lake Forest Police and asked for extra security. The dispatcher assured him that several squad cars were on their way.

Jack breathed a sigh of relief. He went to the ticket booth to see if anyone needed a break. Then out of the corner of his eye he saw something moving fast. A half dozen figures jumped over the hedge, and hoisted giant water guns in the air, drenching the people, and the paper lanterns. Dressed all in black, the intruders wore animal masks, yelping as they moved through the festival. Screaming kids and shouting parents ran to seek shelter on the pavilion. Jack hoped his call to the cops had not been too late.

Moments later, with lights blinking, four police cars blocked the drive. Lake Forest officers hopped out, and with the help of the parents, they corralled the hooligans. Soon they were on their way to the station. Only the soaked animal masks on the grass left evidence of a disturbance.

Mike shook his head, predicting the soon-to-be-former student council president, would likely be participating in some extended community service.

"They'll probably try throwing their weight around. Caveman posturing. Parents of bullies often show the same behaviors." said Mike.

"So lame," said Jack.

"I've trained you well," said Grace.

Mike and Jack shared a look. She was preaching to the choir. And *they* were not the ones invested in overbearing behavior. *Grace* was the one overdoing it, channeling bossy behavior much of the time.

The sun's rays soon dried the damp clothes and paper lanterns. Jack grabbed the microphone, "Everyone, have some more food, and the band will take requests for your favorite song."

Jack joined the group on the dance floor where Grace planted herself in front of him. But when the music stopped, he walked off with the excuse of talking to the groundskeeper. Ten minutes later, he returned, pulling the hand of the decoration chairman as his dance partner.

That would serve Grace right. Her turn to feel some jealousy.

On the sidelines, however, Grace was not about to be left out. She grabbed Mike's hand, pulling him on the floor.

Jack felt aggravated. Grace was like a cat. Always landed on her feet.

The music ended, and the band took a break.

"I have to get back to the art booth. That was fun, though," said Jack's dance partner, and he watched her walk off.

Several hours later, the band announced the final song, Soon, a line of red taillights processed down the main drive. The cleanup crew moved in, dragging huge bags filled with garbage to the corner of the pavilion.

Jack, Mike, and Grace, walked slowly up to the house. The group and their parents would spend the rest of the weekend at Morningside.

Beautiful in the late afternoon light, the estate seemed magical, as the unseasonably warm breeze added to the specialness. Exhausted, they collapsed in the living room. Mr. Abernault ordered in a tray of pasticcio, and they all talked about the festival, and the water attack by the jocks. Jack wished he could freeze time, locking out Vincent Marcov, and his rival, Jesse. But Grace, oblivious to his feelings, horsed around with Mike, Charlie, and the puppy, Lad. At eleven o'clock everyone went to bed.

While they slept, Dr. Marcov's satellite took down three more ice cliffs. Air Force jets had scrambled, but the attack had come from above their flight capabilities. With the protective dome still unfinished, the ice cap remained vulnerable.

* * *

Like a golden disc hurled by a giant, the sun ignited the horizon over Lake Michigan flashing on the eastern boundary of the estate. Jack awoke to chirping that reminded him of Max and Izzy's native tongue. Light streamed in between the heavy drapes. He pulled on his jeans and a sweatshirt, descending the staircase to join the others. His friends lazily were eating bowls of cereal at the kitchen counter. The adults were out for a walk to the village center, so the three friends had the house to themselves.

"This festival served as a great cover. I got all kinds of research done on security systems. I just emailed you guys the info," said Mike.

"That's great," said Grace.

"You're the man," said Jack.

Grace and Mike wanted to swim so they made their way to the pool.

"So, Grace, did you bring your *real* bathing suit *this* time," Jack said.

He couldn't resist.

"I did, actually," said Grace.

Then she pulled off her jeans and top, revealing a one-piece black swimsuit.

"What? Did Grace skinny dip in here?" asked a surprised Mike.

"I won't tell," said Jack.

"Tell all you want. I didn't hear any complaints out of you," said Grace.

Jack laughed.

"You're shameless," he said.

"You wish," said Grace.

"What's going on here? Am I missing something?" asked Mike.

"Nope. Only thing going on is Jesse, as far as I know," said Jack.

They dove in the pool. She splashed them both. Then she turned and began to swim laps.

Grace drove him nuts. Wonder what the whole story was with Jesse? Bet her parents didn't like him . . . too old for her. The guy looked like trouble. Book store, my ass. Probably took the job just to get girls. Couldn't she see through that? So stupid.

Mike looked confused.

"What's with her?"

Feeling guilty, Jack knew he needed to clear up the record.

"No, she didn't skinny dip. Just swam in a bikini that looked like underwear. But it's fun to tease her."

Jack grabbed a ball from the side of the pool, tossing it to him.

A moment later his friend dunked him, holding him under the cold water. He knew Mike was letting him know that he thought Jack had acted like a creep.

It was lowdown to infer things that weren't true, and now Jack felt shamed. Although, he reasoned, Grace could have denied the skinny dipping. But that wasn't her style. She wouldn't give away any power . . . wouldn't let anyone think she cared a whit about her reputation.

But over the past few years, the three of them had talked often enough about how rumors were hatched. Jack had to ask himself, how he had stooped so low. Somedays he didn't recognize himself. What was happening to him? Acting like a creep. Then he thought of Jesse. Her betrayal. Grace was the problem. It was *her* fault. Not him. *She* was driving him nuts!

But his concerns seemed dwarfed when compared with the news about the attacks on the ice cap. Politicains were all running around in circles, pointing fingers at each other. Countries blamed each other, political parties claimed the high ground, only to have exposes counter their pseudo facts.

At the high school on Monday, the three friends watched the clock's minute hand slowly lurch forward on the homeroom wall. The teacher's voice droned on. Times like this. Pure torture. So much they had to endure seemed like time fillers until the bell rang. It was maddening. Agonizing.

The earth couldn't wait. The planet was failing, but the adults only talked about meaningless stuff.

"Clean your room. Take out the garbage. Sit up straight."

The three friends felt the urgency of the climate's demise, and Grace felt they had to find Vincent Marcov's base of operations.

Finally, the bell shrilled, and the class headed out. For the next forty-five minutes, the three friends listed ways to take down the scientist. They still didn't have an address, so there was that.

At four o'clock they met again at Evanston's downtown grill. Over root beer floats they considered their next move. Exasperated, Grace said hacking was the best option.

"No, Grace. No. No hacking. Period. You *really* are nuts if you think I'm going to court again. But more importantly, don't you think the FBI already tried hacking?" asked Jack.

"The only solution is physically breaching his security system. And to do that, we need data about all the hardware components," said Mike.

"So forget about hacking," said Jack.

Grace's cheeks flushed, as she hissed.

"You both are wusses."

But on this day. Finally, on this day, Jack saw through the bravado. Her sheer impulsiveness. Maybe the Jesse thing was good, giving him some distance, and more perspective. Helped him see her more clearly. Jealousy put the brakes on his desire to impress her.

"How about this," said Mike.

"I'll keep looking at available information about security systems. Follow the logic. Rule out dead ends." He sat back, pleased with his suggestion.

"Great," said Jack, understanding this could take weeks, maybe months.

Meanwhile he would keep on with his quest which he saw as their best hope. While it was hard to see how meeting these odd people could save anybody, he needed to trust his promise to Spencer's legacy and to the Council's mission. Afterall, there was no way he could ignore his experience on Sophia.

Grace was not happy with the way things were going, so she changed the subject. Apparently, she and her very proper mother, were battling again over her clothing choices.

"So, I opened my drawer and there sits a pink cashmere sweater. Can you believe it?"

Mike and Jack *could* believe it. Grace's mom had waged a losing battle over clothes for the past decade. They knew Grace would have viewed this innocent pink item as a hand grenade nestled among her black T-shirts. But there was no denying, her mother could be relentless, if not subtle. A *steel magnolia*, born and bred in South Carolina. A dragon, dressed in pearls and pastel cashmere.

Grace, as everyone knew, shopped at army surplus for camouflage . . . and, occasionally at vintage shops for black pieces . . . or, anything studded to add that *Don't Mess with Me* vibe.

"The nerve," Jack said, his eyes sparkling.

"Maybe, your mom should have bought you a proper swimsuit, Grace," said Jack, and he tried to high fived Mike.

But Mike just stared at him.

"Really. You want to go there again," said Mike, looking disgusted.

"By the way, Jack filled me in on your swimming attire that did *not* involve skinny dipping," said Mike.

Grace's eyes softened.

"So you decided to man up, Jack."

Shame reddened his cheeks. But aloud he said.

"Well, we couldn't have Jesse hearing about this, now could we? He might get the wrong idea."

Zing. Take that Grace. A flush rose from his collar.

"Jesse actually has been to France so I don't think he would be shocked. Not so parochial as you two yokels," said Grace.

"Oooo . . . *parochial*, big word. Did you learn that from Jesse too?" asked Jack.

"Yeah. He's teaching me *lots* of things," said Grace.

Jack felt a grenade go off inside him.

Mike, uncomfortable with the verbal zings flying across the table, changed the subject. He proceeded to update his friends on his younger sister who had ruined a sweater belonging to the older one.

"You're a regular Cinderella, with two ugly sisters," said Grace.

"So true," Mike said, shaking his head in agreement.

Jack fumed quietly. Grace had won this round. And he could see that Mike and Grace were bonding over a sweater theme this afternoon, and after their recent blow up at Jack's house. It felt like two against one now. If it hadn't been for Jesse, making him the odd man out, it almost would have felt like old times. Maybe it was easier for Mike now that he thought Jack wasn't mooning over Grace anymore because she had moved on to Jesse.

On the way home, Jack got to thinking about how Grace loved to live in the eye of the storm. It seemed she packed a funnel cloud in her bag that she pulled out if things seemed too calm. He could see how the ongoing battle with her mother carried over into her relationships. Then he thought about his friends' home situations. Crazy siblings would have driven him nuts. Grace's mom could be super intrusive. Then he recalled how his own mom had hovered over him until Charlie came along. Now he enjoyed a kind of benign neglect. Of course, his dad kept bringing up the arrest, so he had his own troubles. Then again, Jack knew his friends didn't worry like he did. But, if he thought about it, they did other stuff. Grace could be *out there*, impulsive and explosive. And Mike often seemed oblivious, missing important things going on around him.

When he opened his front door, Jack found his little brother playing in the living room. The baby looked up and flashed a huge toothy smile. It was then Jack saw the item in Charlie's chubby hands. It was an oversized nanobot!

Jack grabbed the thing with a towel, and he ran outside to the curb. Stomping it, towel and all, he kicked it down the sewer drain. The thought occurred to him that Marcov could have filled the thing with tiny nanobots, like a devilish Trojan horse.

He knew he should tell his parents. But *something* stopped him. Overwhelmed by terror, and guilty that he had brought this danger to their door, a kind of paralysis took over.

CHAPTER NINE

Lincoln Park

The following Friday...

THE OLDER MAN OPENED HIS BALCONY doors and took in the cool breeze coming off the Lake. Rustling leaves muffled the sounds of the traffic as he looked out over Lincoln Park. Below him on the street, he could see the Streets and Sanitation trucks rolling slowly, stopping frequently to pick up trash on their route. Joggers loped past the blossoming trees around the lagoon, and moms in their yoga pants pushed strollers on the path. A contented Dr. Bernaski breathed in the fresh air as he loved this view from his condominium, built in the 1920's. It never got old.

Then he turned away and retired to his leather armchair so he could catch the morning news. He paid special attention to the humidity which he saw as Chicago's only flaw. Today, however he learned, the air would be on the dry side. His phone vibrated on the table, and dinged, alerting him to a delivery in the lobby.

He showered and dressed in a starched shirt and silk tie. Then the professor pulled on his seersucker jacket, descending in the brass cage elevator to the lobby. The uniformed doorman handed him a small brown package from behind the marble counter, along with his usual morning greeting.

The professor thanked the young man, noticing the label on the box, scrawled with fancy silver colored ink.

"How festive," he said.

Dropping it in his satchel, he took off on his morning walk to work. The crowd on the sidewalk, was filled with people of all ages hurrying to their jobs. Kids, in less of a rush, slowly meandered toward the local public school down the block.

Twenty minutes later, the security guard at the Newberry Library held open the heavy glass door for the director. Nodding at the young man, Dr. Bernaski pinned on his name tag and made his way up to his office. Then he remembered the box, pulling it out of his bag, he put it on his desk. He cut open the package with a letter opener.

"Hmmmm," he said, looking at the item, his brow furrowing, as he read the note. Then he picked up his phone and pressed a speed dial contact.

After a brief exchange, the voice on the line told him to stick to the plan.

"So just the one extra ingredient? And the harrowing tale? Ok, understood."

* * *

On this same Spring morning, Dr. Marcov put down his phone. Why couldn't these idiots follow his directions? They kept questioning the wisdom of turning over the gold tubes to the kid. Didn't they understand that he *required* this cat and mouse exercise of letting the young man chase his tail all over the place? Marcov certainly preferred to work alone, but he recognized that sometimes he required some help. There was no question in his mind that his plan was flawless. He would prevail over the Council's efforts to stop him, as he had *always* done in the past.

These days he was busy plotting his next environmental disaster. Sitting at his desk with a giant painting of the Titan Cronus hanging on the opposite wall, Marcov stared into the eyes of his patron. He identified with this fiend, this destroyer of future generations who embodied the essence of his mission. Although Marcov hated art, he was drawn to this single image. For an instant, Vincent wondered if Cronus also had been bullied on the playground of mythological Mount Othrys. Afterall, the Titan had twenty-three siblings. Lots of opportunities for intrigue and betrayals there, he thought. Then Marcov focused and got back to work.

His fingers tapped over the tablet's keyboard, as he prioritized a list of ideas that included DNA tampering, tornado inducement, pandemic, and earthquake from fracking. His brow furrowed, drumming his fingers on his desk, considering the logistics. While his goal remained the polar ice cap demolition, he needed these sideshows for his own entertainment.

*   *   *

After school that same day Jack checked the coordinates on Lutetia's cylinder, and he was relieved to see a place he knew, a Chicago landmark library.

Jack boarded the number seven bus, finding a seat near the back. A spring shower began to fall, and the rainwater on the bus windows distorted the buildings and utility poles. He wondered what more he would learn this afternoon about Marcov?

Then the image that he most wanted to push away rose in his mind. The baby holding the nanobot. This haunted him. Although he had tried to stash the memory of Charlie with the dreaded object into a small spot in the attic of his mind, the horror of seeing the baby with the deadly toy popped out like a menacing jack-in-the-box. Sometimes, he pinched his arm, until the pain blocked out the scene. Other times Jack stayed busy. Anyway, he told himself, it was too late to confess now. His parents would be wild if they knew at this point about the nanobot and Charlie. Probably was nothing, he told himself. After all, he reasoned, he hadn't actually *seen* any small black-like bugs. Marcov probably had sent the thing to rattle him.

By the time Jack stepped off the bus, the rain had slowed to a sprinkle. He pulled up the hood on his anorak. A chill hung in the air. Water splashed on his head, dumped from leaves heavy with rain. Water torture came to mind, and the thought that a doctor could have checked out Charlie. If he had spoken up. Jack clenched his fists, insisting his brother would be fine. Or it wouldn't be his fault. His parents should watch more carefully. Hire a nanny if they couldn't pay attention. Shouldn't be *his* problem.

Jack dodged puddles. He arrived at the library building on Walton Street. A security guard asked for his credentials. Jack showed his school ID and the guard waved him inside. Towering over his head, a vaulted ceiling displayed old world maps, impressing a visitor that scholars were at work. Jack's shoes were soaked, and he stomped his feet before trusting the slick terrazzo floors. Then he approached a marble counter and asked directions to the main office.

"Follow me, please," said an elderly man.

Jack noticed the gold pin, identifying him as the library director. The man led him into an office separated from the library stacks by an imposing glass wall. The director gestured to a leather armchair and shuffled around his desk, introducing himself as Professor Bernaski.

"So, tell me, young man, what brought you to these hallowed halls this afternoon?" Jack showed the gold cylinder with the Newberry Library's coordinates, setting it on the desk.

"These numbers give the location coordinates for this library," Jack said.

"Hmmm . . . interesting," said the professor. Then he placed an identical cylinder beside it.

"I've been expecting you."

Jack met his eyes.

"A messenger delivered it to my lobby this morning with a note informing me of a special visitor, a green-eyed teenager."

"Did you get a description of the messenger?" asked Jack.

"No, I assumed it was from my sister. She's always sending me gifts and adding little riddles."

Jack nodded. He told how one cylinder had fallen out of a book's spine, one discovered on a vet clinic floor, another at the bottom of a koi pond, and now this one had been delivered by messenger. Dr. Bernaski told him the Newberry held a special collection. Usually, these artifacts were kept away from the public because they required expert interpretation. Professor Bernaski added he wanted to call in a consultant.

"Sure, if you think it will help," Jack said.

The man picked up the phone and he turned away in his chair, so Jack failed to hear all of the conversation. He did catch the name, *Dr. Vincent Marcov.*

Jack felt his stomach roil at the mention of Marcov, unconsciously letting out a groan.

Dr. Bernaski finished his call, and then told Jack he should return on Wednesday at four o'clock if he wished to proceed with the cylinder.

"Do you know Dr. Vincent Marcov?" Jack asked.

"Not now, we will have time to talk on Wednesday," and it seemed clear that the professor was dismissing him for now.

"It's only that I heard you say his name."

"Wednesday, come back on Wednesday."

"O.K., I'll be back," said Jack.

At a grill on Clarke Street, Jack ordered a sandwich. Soon he sat at the bus stop, eating the grilled cheese. Delays were so frustrating.

Hate having to wait till Wednesday. Patience and *process.* So annoying. The worst. The northbound bus pulled up, with a splash of water, as the brakes screeched. Jack settled in a seat. For the next forty minutes, he watched the neighborhoods pass, this time in reverse order, and now, minus the distorting effect of rain on the window.

Soon the sign for Evanston appeared, as the bus took a bend, passing the old cemetery. Jack noticed a large mausoleum with the family name, SPENCER. He wondered if this was Joseph's family although Morningside seemed a world away from the city. The bus moved on, winding comfortably around Sheridan Road, and into a mass of old trees that marked the Evanston Historic District. Jack relaxed as the sharp glare of the urban neighborhood shifted into restful light, the road canopied by a cathedral of elms. Sprawling homes built more than a century ago with their expansive lawns processed by the window. The month of May was beautiful in Chicago and Jack noticed the temperature let down a few degrees as the bus continued north.

A few days later, Jack returned to the Newberry. At four o'clock, Dr. Elizabeth McGloin from the University of Chicago, walked briskly into the library office. She was dressed like a scholar out of central casting, in a tailored linen suit, with her hair pulled back in a classic chignon. A tribal beaded necklace broke the severity of her outfit. Professor Bernaski introduced Jack and then brought out the two golden cylinders, setting them on the desk.

Dr. McGloin looked at the golden tubes, and said, "These items must possess an interesting provenance."

Seeing confusion on Jack's face, she said, "I mean to say that I believe they have a special origin."

"You could say that." Jack said.

She frowned, seeming to consider his response inarticulate.

"I've been collaborating with the chemistry department for a number of years. My area of expertise lies in ancient artifacts and texts. Some of the old documents and items I've run across contain formulas for, dare I say … potions."

"Really?" Jack asked.

But he was thinking, here we go, more crazy town.

Dr. McGloin continued, her voice now strained in a higher pitch.

"This is cutting edge work, and I admit, *very* controversial. Modern scientists generally reject these old formulas as wishful thinking. However, wisdom remains in the alchemy of ancient scholars who mixed materials in their primitive labs. Most of their efforts, of course, were attempts to create gold out of base metals. But a few of these formulas have proven quite effective as medicines. Others reduce the effects of pollution in the Amazon. And one mixture brings out special qualities in golden objects."

"Wow," Jack said.

But he was thinking, she might have degrees, and might dress the part, but this made no sense. He thought after all the strange occurrences on this quest, nothing would have surprised him. But this information *sounded* bizarre. Alchemy? Potions?

Then he recalled the Council had advised him to maintain an open mind. Sometimes, he knew he had the habit of pushing aside information that challenged his beliefs, or that frightened him. This might be the time to consider new data and learn to manage the inner tension it might produce. He recalled the Council's letter had instructed him to listen with his heart, head, and gut intuition.

Dr. McGloin opened her bag and brought out a vial with an amber colored liquid. Wiping off the desk with a tissue, she set the vial down. Jack recalled the amber perfume from Lutetia, but quickly pushed the memory aside.

"I think this formula may help if we sprinkle the fluid on the two cylinders. Keep in mind, taking a calculated risk is a necessary part of any quest. Betting, and playing the odds appear in many traditions as far back as Plato. Trailblazers always operate at the growth edge in any field of study. In science, we mold the intuition into a hypothesis. So, in effect, we toss a dice, hoping to produce an 80% significant result."

Jack got the scientific method part, just not the potion stuff.

"It's also important to trust others along the journey, and to ask for help. This requires humility, acknowledging that you alone don't possess all the necessary skills. Collaboration is the way to go. If there's one thing I've learned, it's that knowledge and wisdom aren't the same. Wisdom tends to arrive when pride that you have all the answers steps back, so you accept input from others," said McGloin.

"What if the liquid corrodes the metal?" Jack asked.

"It's a risk. But remember, you sought us out," said Bernaski.

Then he brought out a vial filled with clear liquid.

"This ingredient will serve as an antidote if it seems the metal is disintegrating."

Dr. McGloin looked surprised at his suggestion to use an additive, but she nodded as she trusted her colleague.

Jack tried to take in all this information. He jotted down the new coordinate numbers in case they were ruined in the process. Then he took a deep breath, and he looked into the eyes of Dr. Bernaski. Somehow, he was hard to read. Jack couldn't quite get a beat on him. But Dr. McGloin, she was different. Once Jack had tuned in to her story, he sensed her honesty. There seemed a truthfulness about what she was saying. This was a gut feeling, an intuition really. But she seemed trustworthy, independent of her impressive degrees, decades of experience, and crazy sounding theories.

"Ok, *do* it," Jack said.

Dr. McGloin opened the vial, and a powerful smell filled the office. The odor, not bad exactly, maybe pungent described it. She swirled the vial, tipping it, as a brown liquid fell from the lip and coated the cylinders. For a moment, it seemed the metal was disintegrating, sizzling before their eyes.

"Seems too much," said Dr. Bernaski, and he poured the clear liquid to stop the process.

They watched and waited. The surfaces frothed and the liquid evaporated. Then a puff of smoke burst into a tiny golden cloud. When the mist cleared only one cylinder remained. The new longer golden tube was now pierced with holes, the engraved numbers preserved.

Jack noticed Dr. Bernaski showed an odd hint of dismay.

The three stared at the tube, now narrower and longer.

"Is that a flute . . . or a kind of whistle?" asked Jack.

Heat was still coming off the golden surface.

The two professors nodded slowly and began speculating. Bernaski pulled out a mythology book by Joseph Campbell, searching the index for "flute." The story of Pan calling his sheep with a flute, was the first passage he read. Then Dr. McGloin related some of the stories about flutes, horns, and whistles that marshaled the wind to create special sounds. Hebrew scripture described how a horn had brought down the walls of Jericho. Mozart's *Magic Flute* Opera told of the instrument's ability to turn sorrow into joy. Apparently, scores of cultures spun stories about the power of a flute. Even Einstein had written about how everything vibrated at different frequencies, emanating a unique sound.

Dr. McGloin turned to Jack, and asked.

"So are you going to try it?"

"Me?" asked Jack.

"That's why we are all here, dear," she said.

Jack put the golden cylinder to his lips and blew, but the whistle only produced a soft whooshing tone.

However, moments later, startling them, the large window in the office filled with thousands of butterflies, beating their wings on the glass. The three stared at the phenomenon. Clearly, the golden instrument had skills.

"That's incredible. It's like a dog whistle, but for butterflies," said Jack.

The professor produced some cans of ginger ale, and the three clinked their glasses. The scholars shared that too often their findings stayed in academia. It was a cause for celebration when their discoveries made it out into the real world.

Jack then broached the topic of the rogue scientist.

"So, have you actually met Dr. Marcov?" he asked.

"Unfortunately, yes. At a conference years ago, we shared a panel discussing climate in the Amazon. He had us hoodwinked. And he certainly looked the part of a concerned academic," said Bernaski.

"We still have to deal with him because his nanobots disrupt our progress," said Dr. McGloin.

"One never knows when and how he attacks," warned Dr. Bernaski.

Dr. McGloin seemed uncomfortable with this focus on the fiend and returned to the topic of research.

"We know that the solution to climate change needs more than green technologies. How we *see* our fellow humans remains key to sustainability and to our survival as a species," said McGloin.

"My family talks about this all the time around the dinner table. We own all of Ken Wilber's books," Jack said.

But he didn't add that these discussions often were punctuated by flying bowls of noodles when Charlie tired of talk that didn't center on him.

Dr. McGloin and Bernaski shared how the rogue scientist had blocked their grant funding, creating an unproductive competition. Researchers found themselves running around in circles, working against each other, hoarding new data, and ultimately wasting time and money.

At five o'clock, Jack rose to leave, saying he would keep them posted about any new developments. He folded the whistle in a tissue and turned to leave the library.

But Doctor McGloin stopped him.

"Be careful. I've heard Marcov can disappear at will, and leaves a burning smell."

He thought maybe he could smell it now, but brushed this off as the power of suggestion.

That evening Dr Bernaski arrived at the entrance to his condominium building.

The doorman greeted him, telling him there had been another delivery. Then he gave Dr. Bernaski an envelope. On the elevator ride up to his place, he opened the package, and smiled at the large donation to the Newberry signed by Vocram Corporation.

He hoped Dr. McGloin would never find out.

CHAPTER TEN

Meeting

THAT NIGHT, JACK WENT TO BED EARLY because he was not feeling well. The day had been exhausting. It was unsettling to hear about the rogue doctor and his capabilities. And perhaps breathing that potion had brought on an allergic reaction? All he wanted now was to curl up in a ball. His joints ached, and he felt feverish.

A cool patch of cotton pillowcase gave him a moment of relief until it succumbed to the heat from his body. Turning the pillow over, he found another cooler section. But this lasted only for a moment. His misery grew as his forehead burned like a hot griddle. A glass of water sat inches away on the nightstand, but he was too weak to reach for it. At some point, he passed out.

After midnight, he awoke with a start.

Standing beside his bed. A dark shape. A figure. The stooped scepter of a thin man. Sharp features. Birdlike eyes. A sagging cardigan. Leaning over Jack's face, he planted a menacing wet kiss on the youth's forehead.

Jack could not move. Paralyzed, he smelled foul breath with a hint of a lemon drop. Dr. Marcov grinned. His dark beady eyes glowed. A vice-like grip held the boy's jaw, while Jack felt swabbing inside his mouth from an insistent hand. Jack felt the cotton swab withdraw. Choking, he screamed. The smell of sulfur filled the room as the figure evaporated.

The bedroom door opened, and his parents rushed to his side. Feeling his burning head, his dad brought a cool wash cloth, pressing it over his brow. After twenty minutes, Jack's heartrate began to settle, and when the ibuprofen kicked in, he went back to sleep. His mother watched his face relax, but she felt uneasy. Something was very wrong.

In the morning, his temperature was normal. Jack chalked up the nightmare to a spiking fever. But his mother insisted that he stay home from school. Missing a day of school at this point was not going to make a big difference in his grades that were in free fall. So, he ate oatmeal, but soon he felt tired again. It was laundry day, so he went upstairs, pulling the bedding on the floor.

Fear hit him like a bolt of electricity. On the sheets, the remains of a lemon drop. A melting sensation hit the back of his knees. That had been no nightmare . . . but a *visitation! The doctor had been here, in his room, and he had swabbed his DNA!*

Jack felt invaded. He ran to the bathroom, retching up the oatmeal. Turning on the faucet, he tried to wash away his disgust. But the presence of the twisted spirit that had invaded his space, his body, seemed to clutch in his throat. Ringing startled him. Grace's name appeared on his phone's glass display. Jack paused, picking up the call.

"Uh . . . Grace . . . Now's not a good time . . . Can I call you back?"

"I'll see you at first period," she said.

"I'm sick. Not going to school today," his voice cracked.

"What's going on? You sound weird."

He drew in a deep breath, closing his eyes, desperately willing himself back to normal.

"You woke me up," he lied . . . too unsteady to speak about the night visitor.

"Well, good thing I did. You sound kind of freaked out."

"Yeah, umm, Ok, then." he said.

"Well, get some rest. Talk later?"

"Ok, bye."

Jack's dad entered.

"I'm working at home today. Your mother tells me you should get some rest."

Jack looked at his dad. He just couldn't tell him. How the danger had come into their home. *Again.*

But he couldn't stay in that room . . . in that bed.

"Maybe I'll nap on the sofa."

He slept most of the day. Exhausted. Checked out.

In the next room, his dad worked on his laptop.

* * *

The next week, Jack pulled out his books every chance he got. He hoped studying for finals would give him some normalcy, that memorizing would occupy his thoughts. However, memories of Marcov shoved their way into his mind. The stink of his rancid breath. The overlay of stale lemon drop. The vice-like grip on his jaw. The swabbing inside his mouth.

Maybe, worst of all, though. Jack felt he *deserved* this hell for the unforgiveable crime of neglecting to see that his little brother got checked out after his exposure to the oversized nanobot.

* * *

A week passed. A flurry of end of the school year activities kept Jack on the move. There wasn't time for guilty ruminations.

After dinner one evening, Grace called. She insisted that she needed to talk to him, and that he had to come over right away. Jack grabbed his backpack, welcoming a break from studying calculus. When he turned the corner on Normandy Place, he saw Grace on her front lawn, sitting on a blanket. Jack knew her presence outside was a sign she was avoiding her mother.

Now he regretted his decision to ride over here. Getting drawn into her family drama was not something he needed just now. Jesse could play that role. Jack was done playing the patsy who did her bidding. He looked at Grace's pretty face but envisioned the image of a carnivorous blossom, ready to snap, poised to devour him.

"I can't stay long. Promised my dad I'd help him with the garage," Jack said, planning for a quick exit.

She patted the spot next to her.

"I love sitting outside before the mosquitoes take over. Do you realize we only have a few more bug free weeks?"

What was she up to, now? She moved in close one week, then picked a fight, the next. Grace seemed to have two settings, making him jealous or luring him in.

Jack sat down, not next to her, but deliberately across from her.

"So, Grace, what's going on?"

"Thought it would be nice to catch up, without Mike around, *every* second."

"OK, but I thought you two ironed out your problems."

"Oh, we have. But I wanted to ask if you had plans to go to the Spring Formal?"

Jack, who had just taken a swig from his water bottle, sputtered, snorting at that idea. Grace had consistently made a big show out of mocking these traditional events.

Then he saw she *wasn't* kidding. It amazed him how she could turn on a dime. You just never knew what she was cooking up under those blonde curls.

"Ok, what's the *real* story here?" Jack asked.

"Well . . . you see . . . my Mom is trying to fix me up with the son of our former neighbor *And* . . . I was kind of hoping to have an excuse. It's not that this kid is awful, or anything. But I don't want to get involved in a big mess, with everybody, in the end, mad and hurt."

"Since when did you start concerning yourself with how other people feel?"

"Now, that's just harsh. If you don't want to go, I can always ask Mike."

"What about that guy Jesse?" He couldn't resist.

"Oh, that's nothing. We only flirted a little bit."

Grace shoved him playfully, delivering a kiss on his cheek.

Jack flushed. Confused, angry, but wanting her, all at once.

"*Well*, I haven't asked anyone yet. Guess I could help you out," he said, hiding his bewilderment, and pushing down his excitement.

Grace's mom called for her.

They rose, and Jack got on his bike. On the ride home, he felt his heart soar. In spite of all her craziness, he could feel joy filling him like a giant party balloon. The hope he had felt in the pool at Morningside rushed in.

CHAPTER ELEVEN

The Mirror

HAROLD WALKED THE DOG AROUND THE BLOCK, passing the bookstore. His favorite author's new book was showcased in the window. Later, he'd come back with his wallet and without his German Shepard who was pulling him down the sidewalk. The boy was careful to steer the animal around the metal sewer covers planted in the cement. Only last week, he had heard a news report that an electrical shock from one of these round plates had injured a dog. Harold was taking no chances.

He rounded the corner, scanning the front of his house, a contemporary brick structure, with iron grills on the windows. Entering the code, he went inside and released the dog from the leash. The animal made a bee line to the water in his stainless-steel bowl. Then Harold sat down to catch up on the news. He was not about to get caught missing a severe weather notification or any other threat, for that matter.

* * *

The following Saturday, Jack checked the coordinates on the whistle. He knew he should be studying. But the memory of the cotton swab scraping his mouth made it difficult to focus. Every chance he got he washed his mouth out and brushed his teeth. Taking this step seemed to calm him.

Jack did have one bright spot in his life, and that was the school dance. Time with Grace served as a parallel universe that pulled him away from the worries crouching in his mind. Jack also found some relief, keeping a routine. This morning he planned to visit the next spot on his quest, and he would study in the afternoon, that is if he made it back in one piece.

Jack looked at the map on the web. He recognized the house that could have been mistaken for a small office building. Often over the years he had passed this brick block of a structure on the way to the library.

Twenty minutes later, Jack parked his bike behind a fence on Sherman Avenue. He walked up to the contemporary house with the iron grill covering the windows and rang the doorbell. The glass storm door displayed a sticker that read *Viet Nam Veteran*, and a decal from a security company. The door opened a crack, and a boy, looking wary, peered out at him.

"Hello?" The boy said tentatively.

Jack stepped back, introducing himself.

"Hey, I know you from Soccer." Relief flooded the boy's voice.

He removed the chain, opening the door. Jack was surprised that this was a kid from his sport's team. He asked if he could talk to him for a few minutes.

Before the boy could respond, a massive German Shepard bounded into the hall, skidding on the tile floor as the boy called sharply for him to "*Halt!*"

Ordering the dog behind a gate, the boy glared at the animal. The dog lowered his tail, looked somewhat deflated, and switched directions. Jack, satisfied that the dog was in retreat, entered the hall, following the kid to the back of the house. They reached the family room, and Jack recalled the boy's name was Harold. He remembered at a soccer practice the coach once had called him Harry. And Harold had corrected him, saying he was named after his father. For sure, this kid could be serious, and sometimes talked more like an adult. However, Jack also knew he played well, and always helped pick up equipment after the practices.

Jack showed him the coordinates of Harold's house on the whistle. The boy studied it carefully, and Jack recognized fear in the boy's eyes. Harold's breathing accelerated and Jack feared the kid might have an asthma attack, Harold pulled out an inhaler, took a deep draft, and his shoulders relaxed. Jack, as well, let out a sigh.

"My dad won't be happy when he hears what brought you to our house. We try to keep a low profile. You see, we moved to Evanston to get away . . . from

"Let me guess…Vincent Marcov."As if the villain could hear, Harold responded in a whisper.

"How did you know?" His eyes widened.

"Can you tell me what happened? It seems I've been recruited to learn more about his ways."

"Well, I guess it would be Ok. Because I know you from school, and all."

He took another deep breath, like he was ready to jump off a cliff.

"My dad worked at this lab. Dr. Marcov was on the staff and he sabotaged their projects until he was discovered. We left town to get away. My dad was a worker bee type, responsible and dedicated to following through with research. Vincent Marcov *terrified* him."

Jack knew that he and Harold were alike, wanting to avoid trouble. At school, they were not the show ponies, but the behind-the-scenes kind of kids. Tey valued responsibility and.

Jack sensed that there was something Harold wasn't telling him.

"Did Dr. Marcov use any nanobots?" asked Jack.

Color drained from Harold's face.

"They killed my little sister." Suddenly tears streamed down his face.

"She was only five years old."

A bolt of sheer terror hit Jack.

"I'm so sorry," he said, trying to control the feeling of being torpedoed.

The bots had killed a child. The memory now of the mechanical device in Charlie's hands melted his insides. He pushed down tears, sitting with Harold for a while. But his panic was mounting. Jack needed to flee, to run away as fast as he could from this house. He had to get out of there.

"When all this is over, we should hang out." Jack tried to control his voice.

Harold seemed to recognize that Jack was like him. Worried. Sensing danger. Scared.

"Yes. We need to be careful. Where we go. Who we see," said Harold.

Jack, however, knew *he* hadn't been careful when it came to protecting his brother. For sure Harold would hate him if he knew the truth. After all, he was disgusted with himself.

* * *

Meanwhile, in a secret laboratory deep within his compound, Dr. Vincent Marcov grinned. He had finished programming the satellite for another polar ice attack. Now it was time to work on Jack's DNA. He had divided the sample from the cotton swab, one Petrie dish for CRISPR so he eventually could edit his own genes, and one sample for Jack's virus.

Marcov glared at the two photos pinned on his wall, one of Joseph Spencer and one of Jack Abernault. There would be a delicious symmetry, eliminating both with a virus. Dr. Marcov snickered at the red X slashed over Morningside's previous owner.

One down and one to go.

* * *

That evening Jack shared Harold's story with his parents, leaving out the part about the boy's little sister. As he talked, he could see worry growing on his mother's face.

Jack thought about telling his mother now about Charlie. She would never forgive him, of course. The baby should have been checked out, right when it happened. Now, it likely was too late. Tortured by his guilt, Jack struggled to keep it together. Somehow, he *still* could not tell her the truth. Because his mouth just wouldn't form the words. Jammed between his heart and his throat, his confession stuck.

His mother asked him about his nervousness, and if he was sleeping.

"I'm wondering if we should talk to Dr. Segal about some medication, at least until this trouble settles down. I don't know how you are coping as well as you are."

Jack couldn't deny that he felt split in two parts. When his guilt attacked, he escaped into fantasies about Grace, operating out of a different self, one that could more readily suppress his worry.

"Let me think about it. I'm looking forward to the dance this weekend," said Jack.

The next morning the Tribune headlines announced the iron dome over the ice cap was complete. Finally, things were looking up.

* * *

Friday night, Jack sat in a brand-new electric Volvo wagon as his dad pulled up in front of Grace's house. The Abernaults finally had replaced the dusty brown minivan, and his mom now drove a new Prius that she loved.

Jack made his way up Grace's front walk, pushing down his excitement about the upcoming evening. He reached up to ring the doorbell however Grace opened the door and pulled the bouquet of flowers from his hands. She spun around and pushed the posies at her mother.

"Go put these in some water," she said.

But Grace's dad stepped in

"Not so fast, Missy. We need a photo."

"OK, but make it quick," said Grace.

Jack was accustomed to this girl's need to control the playbook, but he took her hand and posed for the parents.

"One more near the evergreens," said her dad.

The couple moved into position. Jack smiled, Grace, not so much.

"Thanks," he said, waving to the parents as Grace pulled him toward the car. Once they settled in the back seat Jack. he asked her.

"What's the big rush?"

"They're making *such* a big deal out of this to annoy me."

Then her tone brightened.

"Hi, Mr. Abernault, sorry to keep you waiting."

"Good evening, Grace."

Then he waved up at her parents who stood arm in arm beaming that their daughter would be attending her first dance. Conforming for once.

"Look what my mother made me do," Grace said, extending her hands.

The fingertips, more like talons, glistened with deep red nail polish.

Jack cringed, acting repulsed.

"Yikes, that looks like blood."

Grace shoved him.

"This was the compromise shade. I wanted black nail polish, and *she* wanted pink. She was paying, so the manicurist pulled out this color called *Vampire Vixon.*"

Mr. Abernault sputtered, then recovered his role as disinterested chauffeur.

"OK . . . You do know you're *never* going to live this one down," Jack said with delight.

He felt his heart relaxing in his chest. He had worried this car ride might be awkward with his dad at the steering wheel. But, Grace, being Grace made it so easy. Then he took in her dress. It was black, of course, but cut away at the shoulders.

"By the way, you look great," he said with admiration.

"You look OK yourself," she said, meeting his eyes. "New tie?"

"Oh, this is all new, I assure you. My mom hauled me over to Old Orchard last week."

Jack brushed some petals off his sport jacket's sleeve.

"Thanks, by the way, for the bouquet. I imagine my mother is busy pressing a few of the blossoms in her scrapbook as we speak."

Jack took her hand. It felt warm, and a little damp. His heart raced with happy, anxious feelings.

The car rolled up to the high school, and they thanked Mr. Abernault who told them to text when they were ready to leave.

'Ok, *Vampire Vixon*, Are you ready for this?" Jack's eyes twinkled.

"Keep that up, and you *will* get a big bite on the neck," she said.

"Oh, I'm counting on it," and he pulled her up the walk.

The gym looked awesome, transformed into a French village by the decoration committee.

"Our next song, *Coucher du Soleil,* is dedicated to our exchange student from Provence, Clemence Duteil, the deejay crooned, attempting a French accent that sounded more like a cartoon Pepe Le Pew.

Jack led Grace to the dance floor and pulled her in close. They moved, rocking gently to the music. She gazed into his eyes as the plinking guitar chords filled his heart.

The next song, by Ariane Grande, shifted the mood in the gym as hypnotic drumbeats blasted from the speakers.

Jack watched Grace move, her arms gyrating in the air. Thinking the modern dance classes certainly had paid off, he moved in closer. Grace smiled, and turned, moving in toward him.

He felt a reset button click on their relationship. He had almost lost her to Jesse. A jab hit his heart. Need to get back up to the Lake Forest house. Back to the swimming pool. Soon.

His thoughts were interrupted by the deejay.

"We're gonna take a break now, so get yourself some food. See you in fifteen."

Jack and Grace moved over to one of the food stations that was serving French fries with a variety of sauces.

"These are amazing. Try the peri-peri dip," Grace said, popping one into Jack's mouth.

The flavors exploded, Jack groaned.

"More, please."

But Grace, of course, could not resist.

"Get your own," she said playfully.

He felt his heat rise, and he put his arm around her waist.

"Hey, buddy," said Mike who suddenly appeared with his date.

"Hey, Mike . . ." Jack said, trying to conceal his annoyance at the interruption.

"Hi, Ellie," said Grace.

"That dress is great."

"Oh, thanks, that's a great dress, as well."

"Jack, we need to meet tomorrow. I found some interesting stuff to show you about you know what."

"Sure," Jack said, feeling disappointment as the evening was morphing fast into the school lunch table. And for tonight, at least, he wanted to block thoughts of Vincent Marcov.

Grace and Ellie turned to make their way to the rest room. Mike started in on the coding talk, but Jack barely listened as he was watching Grace's hips slide through the crowd.

Soon the deejay resumed, they all returned to the dance floor, and the evening passed. The closeness they had exchanged earlier seemed lost, deflected by their friends and the loud music.

At eleven thirty, the lights blinked to signal the event was winding down. Jack pulled out his phone to text his dad, but Grace caught his arm.

"Not so fast, buddy," she said.

She took his hand, dragging him willingly into the hall. Around a corner, he pulled her in.

They made out next to the lockers, until footsteps approached.

Over Jack's shoulders, Grace saw her math teacher, hands on hips.

"Achem," the teacher interrupted.

Jack tucked in his shirt, feeling sheepish.

"Well, *well* . . . *Grac*e," the teacher's tone indicating that she was not surprised.

"Time to move along, dear," the woman insisted.

"Sure thing," Jack said, his face reddening, as he ducked behind the teacher.

But, Grace, unwilling to cede any ground, responded coolly.

"Ahhhh . . . Ms. Pugano. *So* nice to see you this evening. What a *fetching* ensemble," she said, refusing to be intimidated by the faculty chaperone.

Ms. Pugano actually let out a laugh at Grace's chutzpah.

Pulling out his phone, Jack texted his dad, and nudged Grace toward the exit.

Twenty minutes later, Jack walked Grace up to her door. And hoping his dad wasn't watching, he kissed her. Later that night, after it was all over, Jack collapsed on his bed, contented.

CHAPTER TWELVE

Party Girl

THE MUSIC FILLED THE HALL, AS DAISY swung her arms above her head, bouncing her hips to the beat of the rhythm. She called to her Zumba class, clapping her hands, as they followed along dressed in their candy-colored yoga pants. Forty-five minutes later she toweled off her forehead and sent her ladies off to do their errands. Grabbing a bottle of water, she drank it down. The seventeen year old loved this part of her summer student internship at the Evanston Park District. While her parents kept reminding her that a college degree in recreational management entailed more than dancing and games, Daisy wanted to enjoy her time in high school. She popped a candy in her mouth, and then she prepared for the next session.

* * *

The month of June finally had arrived. Jack wanted to put the school year behind him. Final exams had been rough, with his grades slipping to new lows. There was talk of dropping him down an academic level, but he couldn't seem to care. He had juggled a mountain of trouble, from Charlie and the nanobot, to the Council's challenge. Jack felt he was stumbling out of spring, like a soldier on his hands and knees in the mud, escaping the battlefield. The one good thing had been Grace.

This morning, Jack slept in. He awoke at ten o'clock, feeling rested for the first time in weeks. After a bowl of cereal, he checked the whistle again. He was surprised to find a destination nearby, the local fieldhouse on Noyes Street. Hopping on his bike, he rode three blocks, cruising under the elevated station. Jack had spent many hours at the fieldhouse over the years, signed up for sport camps and crafts before he gained veto power. While he protested when his parents pushed him, usually he ended up enjoying himself.

Jack leaned his bike in the rack, and walked past the tall nineteenth century windows, the frames heavy with too many layers of paint. The old Noyes Street School, built back in 1892 by architect Daniel Burnham, now served the community with theater and the arts. His grandmother, Mimi, recalled a Halloween Haunted House set up here in 1955. And sixty-five years later, reported she still could feel the sensation of the cold noodles, passed off as worms. Jack appreciated these family connections . . . anchoring his roots to Evanston's history. Charlie would begin classes in a few years, following the tradition. Jack entered the building, the golden oak floors waxed so heavily, his rubber soles squeaked as he walked. He turned into the office where he saw a girl absentmindedly bouncing a ball on her knee. She looked up, flashing him a big smile. Sparkling rhinestone letters on her sunflower yellow shirt claimed that *Girls Just Want to Have Fun*! A giant air conditioner thrummed, blowing red ribbons that seemed to signal a celebration as well.

"He," said Jack.

"If you need to register for a game, arts or crafts? Sign-up sheet is on the counter," she said.

"No, thanks . . . I think I need to talk to you."

"Sure," she said brightly, motioning him over to a round table in the corner. Jack introduced himself, and the girl said her name was Daisy.

Thinking she looked familiar, Jack could not place her at first. Then it dawned on him that he stood in the presence of high school royalty as Daisy reigned as captain of the pom pon squad.

Football, Big Ten or high school games, was the highlight of autumn weekends in Evanston. Daisy had ridden atop the Homecoming float that rode down Central Street. He recalled this girl throwing smiles like she was tossing gold coins to the crowd.

Jack looked at her kindergarten colored outfit that matched the girl's upbeat attitude.

Pulling out the golden whistle, Jack set it on the table.

"Wow that's cool," said Daisy.

But Jack began telling her about Vincent Marcov.

Daisy's face went ashen.

"No. No. No. Not HIM Again," she said.

"What happened?" asked Jack.

"My dad worked in a lab down at the Circle Campus, and one day he forgot to enter a file from Dr. Marcov. But it turned out my dad's delay saved the project, because apparently, the guy's real intention was to mess up the data with a flood of errors. Marcov was furious when he was blamed, so he reprogrammed some nanobots to tinker with our brains."

"That's awful. What happened then?" asked Jack.

"Soon my dad and I noticed a whirring sound in our heads that brought on *terrible* headaches. It felt like an automatic hammer was pounding rivets behind my eyes. Luckily, the pain has stopped. But now, I have trouble settling down to work. And I struggle with food, wanting to eat sweets all the time. Our dental bills are through the roof. And, if that's not bad enough, I started playing a videogame that I can't stop. If something is good, I only want more."

"I've heard other people tell stories about how Vincent Marcov used nanobots . . . . the whirring, the headaches, and the behavior changes. It sounds bad."

Then Daisy picked up the gold whistle and, like magic, they noticed a new series of digits appear on the surface. Her eyes widened as she held up the golden whistle to the light.

"Wow, that's some awesome technology, Is it heat sensitive?"

"Not that I know of. But there *are* smart phones, so maybe it could be considered smart whistle," said Jack.

"The engraved numbers provide latitude and longitude coordinates for locations. You're my seventh visit."

He got up to leave, pocketing the whistle.

"You and your dad are lucky. Some people have died from the brain altering devices," Jack said.

He was surprised he had been so blunt about the deadly bots. But it seemed this girl with her sunny disposition would not be too disturbed.

And he was right. She took the information and flipped it to a positive response.

"I guess we were lucky," Daisy said.

As soon as Jack left the building, Daisy began texting. In a moment, she got a response.

Nice work scaring that stupid kid.

Jack rode home. As he cruised back under the L tracks, it occurred to him that Daisy lived in a bubble of fun even though sometimes she wanted to be more serious.

After he got home, he went for a run, and then spent the afternoon at the beach with Mike and Grace. Playing volleyball on the sand and eating sandwiches on towels, brought to mind other summers at this beach. Jack squinted as he looked up at the old lighthouse looming above him. The landmark, he knew, had a rich history. During the Civil War, the Union army buried the Austrian crystal light in the sand to protect it from the Confederacy. Now Jack thought of his own battlefield. Somehow, the lighthouse's survival in 1865 gave him hope.

Heat filled his pores, and the sound of gulls squabbling over scraps of lunch blocked the dark chatter that had camped out in his mind for so long. The warmth from the sun's rays, and the sounds of the shore anchored him in the moment. Roasting on the sand, he breathed in the waxy scent of his sun block. From behind his sunglasses, he took in the contours of Grace's tanned body and imagined their next time alone.

When he got home, he texted his friends to see if they wanted to come over for Chinese food. At five thirty, with the group around the dining room table, his mother walked in from the pantry holding an armful of serving bowls, and cloth napkins, planning a proper meal. However, the white cartons of food were already making their way around the table strewn with paper plates.

Jack's dad saw his wife's disappointment.

"Hey, fewer dishes to wash. Come sit down."

"OK, then," she said.

"My mom does the *same* thing. Proper this and proper that," Grace said.

"I think parents want to be sure that you learn some manners," said Jack's mom.

"You guys mean well, I know," the girl said.

"Well, thanks, Grace. I'm happy you approve."

"Sure," said Grace, but grimaced, acknowledging her sassiness.

"No worries, dear," said Ms. Abernault settling the topic. She understood that one did not engage with teeangers, who in many ways operated like oppositional two year olds.

"This food is great! Where's it from?" asked Mike.

"Pine Lodge," said Jack.

Even Charlie liked the rice, but soon bored, he started throwing food off his tray.

Mike quipped that his sisters were a pain, but at least they didn't hurl food around.

Grace, teasing the baby, tossed some crunchy noodles back at him.

However, Charlie, not knowing what to make of this unexpected assault, burst into tears. Grace quickly apologized, and Jack's mom plucked Charlie out of the highchair to soothe him.

"Sometimes I go too far," said Grace, stroking her blond curls.

"Charlie's pretty tough. He's O.K," said Jack.

Charlie glowered at Grace, his arms wrapped around his mother's neck. Grace pulled out a balloon, blew it up, and tossed it up in the air. Dazzled, Charlie immediately stopped crying and smiled, reaching to bat the balloon.

"See, he's a trouper." said his dad proudly.

The group finished dinner and settled in the family room.

Jack volunteered to take out the garbage, and Grace hopped up.

"I'll help you," said Grace.

"Of *course* you will." Mike couldn't resist.

Jack threw a bean bag at him, and then left the room with Grace.

Out in back, the two hauled the garbage bags into the bins, and then proceeded to kiss.

Realizing they couldn't be out there too long, Jack pulled back.

"We need to go in," said Jack.

"I know," she said, and then kissed him again.

Smoothing her hair, Jack led her back into the house.

Entering the family room, they saw Charlie who lit up at the sight of Grace.

"Uh oh," said his mom. "Now he's going to want to play."

Grabbing his rabbit, she picked up Charlie, heading for the stairs. The little guy strongly protested, wanting Grace and her balloon.

"OK ... how about Grace reads Charlie a story to settle him down."

Grace hopped up.

"That's only fair as I riled him up before bedtime."

Jack taunted her.

"Yup, you need to fix this. We're gonna have some dessert while you get a taste of bedtime routine gone south," said Jack.

"Hah, *Hah*. This is gonna be fun." said Grace happily, as they disappeared upstairs.

The rest of them finished the apple crisp. An hour later, they could still hear Grace's voice reading book after book, after book. Charlie knew a good deal when he saw it.

* * *

The next morning, Jack's phone dinged. When he saw the display with University of Chicago, his insides froze. He picked up the call.

"Jack, good, I'm glad to speak directly. This is Dr. McGloin."

"Oh, hi. What's going on?"

"I got a troubling text this morning."

"Oh no," said Jack.

"I'm afraid so. I'm going to forward it to you. It includes a video that's quite disturbing, to say in the least."

"Let me guess. Arctic ice cap, polar bears, and an hourglass?"

"Yes. Did you get one, as well?"she asked.

"My friend Grace got one, and it included a countdown ticking on the ice cap."

"Well, I'm sure you're aware that this summer's weather has been significantly warmer than usual. It's so concerning that the Doomsday Clock on our campus has been set forward as our planet moves closer to collapse. This threat from Marcov suggests we are running out of time before a catastrophe. We seem to be at a point of no return. And Dr. Bernaski isn't returning my calls. I don't know what to think."

Her words hit him like an oncoming train. Jack felt himself float out of his body. Could Dr. Barnaski be working for Vincent Marcov? He remembered how sick he had been after his visit to the library."

"Jack, are you there?"

"Uh, yes. It's hard to know who to trust. Dr. Bernaski seemed helpful," said Jack.

"It's *very* disturbing. I found out that the Newberry received an anonymous donation of ten million dollars just after our visit. That's a huge temptation for a non-profit organization. But I never thought Bernaski would stoop so low."

"Jack, I don't understand your connection to all this. But you did have the golden cylinder. If there's anything you can do, now would be the time. I'm sorry to put this burden on you. But here we are."

Before Jack could respond, the phone went dead. He hit redial, but an automated message said the line was out of order. Jack heard another click. Quickly, he dialed her number, but there was only ringing. Cell service in the city had been spotty due to the heat wave. He hoped it wasn't something more sinister.

CHAPTER THIRTEEN

Tattoo Girl

THE BLENDER'S MOTOR GROWLED, pulverizing the kale and spinach protein drink. Tanya Stokes pushed the stop button, and then drank directly out of the appliance pitcher. She smirked as she recalled her mother's horrified look when she witnessed this habit of hers.

"Tanya Louise! *Really*. Pour that into a proper glass."

And Tanya would respond, with no response . . . only a long, steady glare. And that would be the end of it, with her mom shaking her head in total disbelief.

But, in recent years, her mother had given up on the etiquette tips. Tanya had always felt closer to her dad and brothers, anyhow, as they were more straightforward. She couldn't abide her mother's longing for the good old days, when young ladies didn't were slacks all the time. It didn't help that her mother had grown up in South Carolina, where etiquette was considered high art.

Tanya splashed water on her face and headed off to the L stop at Wilson Avenue. Finding a seat in the back of the car, she watched the blank faced commuters file into the gritty train. Most people found the noise level uncomfortable. However, Tanya loved the ear splitting, screeching sounds as the train lurched around bends, threatening brick apartment buildings built way too close to the tracks. The shrieking noise of metal on metal seemed to resonate with the steeliness that ran through her body.

A crackly voice from the train's speaker announced the Wells stop, and she hopped off, descending the steps to the street. Flipping up her hood, she smirked, thinking of her mother's objection that she spent so much time down here. But the gym had been in her father's family for three generations. She knew her mother worried for her safety, but nobody messed with Tanya. She felt totally at ease walking in this area, as it felt tough, like her.

Tanya entered the gym, and carelessly threw her hoodie behind the counter where it slipped to the floor . . . and where she left it. She flipped on the florescent ceiling fixtures, filling the space with a flush of harsh light. Soon the regulars would be showing up expecting a fresh tank on the water cooler. She hoisted the refill, turning it until she heard the click. Pulling out a jump rope, she began her work out routine, raising her heart rate for the grueling session on the punching bag.

* * *

Meanwhile, fifteen miles north in Evanston, Jack checked the coordinates on the whistle. When he entered the numbers, the location pin dropped on a gym in a seedy section near downtown. Training for the Golden Gloves Boxing Tournament happened there, according to an article that popped up with a web search. Jack taped the whistle on the underside of his bottom dresser drawer. After the suspicious actions of Bernaski, Jack felt he needed to take extra precautions.

He left for the Noyes Street station and took the elevated train down to Wells Street. The map led him to a rundown block, with vacant store fronts and grimy windows. Old newspapers blew down the sidewalk. A homeless man slouched under a blanket, looking dazed and toothless. This didn't look promising. Wonder if he'd meet some behemoth bouncer type guy. Sweat popped on his temple and brow. The day was heating up to be a sizzler. A cloud of ashes blew up from the gutter catching him off guard. The grime tasted like cinders and cheap cigarettes. He spit into a Kleenex.

Jack reached the gym, pulling open the door. A blast of frosty air hit his face, sending goosebumps up his arms. Immediately, a girl blocked his way. "Hey, today is a closed session," she said.

Startled that this shorter kid made him feel off balance, Jack stepped back.

But he'd come all this way. He'd see this through.

"I'm not here to box. Do you have a minute?" asked Jack.

"Don't make me punch you," she said.

When Jack looked surprised, she smiled.

"Only kidding," but then delivered a substantial jab in his side.

"AAGHH" . . . let out Jack. A sting burned his ribs.

"Tanya . . . Tanya Stokes," introducing herself.

Then she told him that her dad owned the gym.

"Can you talk? Just five minutes?" asked Jack.

"Sure, I guess," said Tanya. She stepped aside to let him in the door.

Tattoos of snakes covered her arms, and the oniony smell of sweat wafted off her shirt. Behind her, boxers pummeled punching bags, and for an instant Jack imagined they were hammering away at beef carcasses with their bare fists.

The once white walls oozed a grittiness that he could almost taste. Smells and sounds of the gym assaulted his senses, leaving him with a queasy feeling. His side still stung from Tanya's jab.

"I'm training for a boxing match," said Tanya. "So I can't talk long."

Jack told her that coordinates with her gym's location brought him to the gym.

"Can you show me?" asked Tanya.

"Uh, no. Left the map at home," he said.

Then he asked the girl if he could have a towel as he was freezing.

"Yeah, the thermostat is broken. Hope the repair guy can make it today.

The boxers don't mind, but you have to keep moving."

She handed him two big towels and he wrapped them over his shoulders. She also kicked a rubber wedge under the heavy door to let in some warmer air.

A blast of Chicago summer pushed back the icy gym air. Jack shivered from the shock of the heat after the chill from the out-of-control air conditioner.

Jack asked if the name Vincent Marcov meant anything.

Tanya slammed her fists on the counter.

"That weasel . . !"

"I've heard some bad stuff," said Jack.

Tanya's eyes brimmed with fury.

"Marcov heard about our place and sent some guys over to train as his security detail. Right away, it was clear that these bums refused to follow the rules. So, my dad canceled their gym memberships and banned his goons from our place. Marcov was furious when he heard about it."

Tanya took a swig of water from her bottle.

"The day after all the fuss, a pizza was delivered, and when we opened the box, these tiny bug-like things ran up our noses. Right away, my dad and I had splitting headaches that must have lasted a week. We went to the doctor, but nothing came up on the scans. I think they chalked up our symptoms to boxer brain syndrome. But we *knew* Marcov had done this. After the infested pizza, I noticed I felt more aggressive . . . more revved up. Since then, I've had a bunch of run ins with the cops."

"I've met a number of people who had the same thing happen. It always goes, first Marcov, next nanobots, then headaches or worse."

"I don't get headaches anymore, but I'm still screwed up."

"Sometimes, the effects seem to wear off, but others have died," said Jack.

It was clear this news bothered the tough girl. Was she tearing up?

Tanya said it was time for her next boxing session. Jack left the gym. His ribs still smarting, he headed back to the elevated station.

Back in the gym, Tanya Stokes felt an ice-cold grip on her neck. She turned and found Vincent Marcov leering at her.

"So did you insert the nanobot?" he asked in a raspy voice.

"All done. Jabbed it in when I punched his side. He didn't know what hit him."

"Knew I could depend on you, my young pugilist," Marcov said.

"Timing couldn't be better. He was due for a second dose."

"Too bad he didn't bring the whistle," said Tanya.

"Not to worry. Prefer cash or a check?"

"Cash . . . always cash," she said.

As Jack rode home on the L train, he thought about how Tanya Stokes could end up in big trouble if she didn't get that temper under control. His side still burned where Tanya had punched him. When he got home, he lifted his shirt and looked in the mirror. A patch of deep red swelling showed on his ribs, so he taped on a cold pack to ease the pain. Then he checked the whistle. New numbers glistened on the surface that Jack committed to memory. Then he returned the gold item to its hiding place.

That evening, Grace called. The anger in her voice felt like lightning bolts in his ear. She was frustrated because of a serious setback with the web searches on the Marcov project. Jack held the phone away from his ear, not needing the speaker feature. Insisting that he come over, she would not accept his excuse that he had a headache. Finally, he agreed, thinking the fresh air might help.

Apparently, she and Mike had spent the whole day cataloguing security systems on the market. They were making progress, even narrowing down the designs that might be best suited to protect a lab. But, then the computer had crashed, and they had lost all the information. An electrical power surge, followed by rolling outages, had occurred over Northern Illinois due to the heat wave. Just then the lights went dark in the Abernault house. Jack looked out the window and saw no streetlights and dark windows in all the neighboring houses.

Still on the phone, Jack walked out his front door, assuring Grace that they would figure it out. He ended the call and rode his bike through the darkened streets. Headlights from a few passing cars illuminated the road. Suddenly, it occurred to Jack that Grace reminded him of Tanya Stokes . . . like sisters from another mother. The blast-furnace-like anger was the common denominator.

Fifteen minutes later, he arrived on her porch and knocked. After a moment, Grace's mom opened the door.

"Your friend is in the kitchen."

Her voice had an unusual tone that Jack noted as he made his way down the hall.

The kitchen was lit with candles, the heat, stifling. Around the table, sat her dad . . . and Grace's uncle, the police detective. The room felt like a pressure cooker. Grace's eyes glared; her arms crossed over her chest.

Jack met her gaze, and he felt a bolt of fear. Like how he felt the day of his arrest. What was going down?

"Hi," Jack said tentatively.

"You can save the pleasantries. Sit," said Grace's dad sternly.

Ouch. Anxiety, like a swarm of bees, enveloped him.

Apparently, Grace's dad had overheard her phone call about the security system searches, and her uncle just happened to be over. This was bad. Very bad. Mike arrived, and when he read the room, it seemed clear he felt ambushed.

"I can come back later. Looks like you're in the middle of something."

Mike started to back away.

However, Grace's dad, glared at him.

"Sit yourself down here Mike," as he forcefully pulled out a chair, insisting the boy, *park his backside* next to Jack.

It was the arrest all over again. Jack, back in the federal van, with a law enforcement badge glistening from the detective's belt. The nightmare, the day the rift formed within his family. The day any trust his dad had in him had left the premises.

Now the adults around this table accused them of hacking . . . . again. Grace had been caught red handed. The kitchen felt intense, like a pressure cooker. Skin glistened with sweat. Jack's shirt felt like a wet canvas tent had collapsed on him and the pain in his head intensified. His temples pulsed, feeling like two demons were taking turns with red hot pokers.

"You know you were all extremely lucky to get off last fall with some community service. And Mike, your dad would be pretty upset that you're tempting fate again. You were told, in no uncertain terms, to avoid any form of hacking. How much clearer can we make it?"

Why had Grace been so careless to make that phone call about security systems where she might be overheard? The adults were expecting a response.

Jack felt something like a capsule open in his head, and suddenly found words tumbling out of his mouth.

"Oh no, this is just a misunderstanding, Detective. Grace was only helping me with my robotics project that I'm entering in the state competition this fall. There's no hacking involved. See, I'm looking into a way to disable the other entries with a coding sequence. It's not against the rules or anything . . . and there's absolutely no hacking involved. None."

The fact that the lie slipped so smoothly from his lips, shocked Jack. Sweat rolled down his face. He hoped they chalked it up to the lack of air conditioning.

Relief flooded the faces of Grace's parents,

The adults really had no clue about coding and robotics. To them, Jack's explanation sounded plausible. After all, Jack was the careful one, the one who followed the rules. Now the parents wondered if they indeed had jumped the gun, making assumptions, and premature accusations.

"*See!*" Grace, said, shifting from defense to offense, her comfort zone.

"I *told* you this was nothing. Why do you *always* think the worst?"

Mike sat there frozen in his chair, attempting maybe to be invisible, and possibly imagining how he could beam up to someplace safe . . . or at least, someplace cool. Then Grace's mom intervened, breaking the tension in the room.

"Well we were concerned that you might get in trouble again. You all have such bright futures. It would be a shame to jeopardize that."

Jack knew that this motherly tone in her voice drove Grace nuts. At these times, her mother's southern accent seemed exaggerated.

"I've got to get back to work, but I don't want to hear about anything like this again. Are we clear?" said the detective.

The teenagers nodded.

Just then the appliances groaned. Lights flickered on. The TV began talking, and most welcome of all, a blast of cool air flowed from the vents.

Sighing relief, Jack stole a look at the face of Grace's uncle.

Jack could tell the detective wasn't buying it. Grace's uncle was not as gullible as the parents, as he had seen too much on the job. The look on his face showed that he knew his niece was a spitfire, a genuine bad ass, and that Jack just had served up a steaming plate of BS.

A half hour later, the friends sat on swings at the park, congratulating Jack on his quick explanation. An evening breeze blew off the Lake and the moon appeared over the water, as clouds slid aside like curtains in a theater production.

After his initial relief at sidestepping the parents, Jack worried. He felt guilty that lying had been so easy. Now, Grace's family was in the mix, and he suspected the detective knew the truth. It bothered him that he was edging closer to breaking the law again. However, a little bit of him, still, was pleased that he had rescued Grace from that kitchen.

Grace, however, did not appear to fully appreciate his actions. Rather, she seemed undeterred by parental threats. The showdown around the table occupied only a minor annoyance, a tiny blip in her day. Moving beyond the kitchen showdown, she insisted that they had to keep going to find the scientist's place, and then work around the security system. Jack tried to take her hand, but she pulled it away, in no mood for closeness. She still had a pile of anger to unload and now she seemed to direct it toward fueling the mission.

Her cavalier attitude toward the family confrontation amazed Jack. She seemed to chalk up the clash in the kitchen as only the latest run in with the parents. Mike, on the other hand, dialed down his feelings. It was clear he was pushing the unpleasantness away, smoothing over any ripples of upset that remained. He would not worry *his* dad might hear about this.

Jack marveled how Mike and Grace clearly did not have his scruples. He always, *always* felt guilty. His headache was getting worse.

Jack's phone dinged with a text. He touched the play icon, and the dreaded hourglass video began to play, showing a noose tightening on the planet. The three of them watched as the clip highlighted the baking hot, dry weather, fires in California and coastal flooding.

Jack felt a vice like pressure bear down on his temples. The news of the world was weighing him down. The powers in Washington D.C. sat twiddling their thumbs, acting like the proverbial frog swimming contentedly in the warm pot as the temperature climbed to the boiling point. The kids rode their bikes back to their homes heavy hearted.

That night the moon hid its face, and a darkness slithered into Jack's restless sleep. Trapped in a mammoth hourglass, he pounded frantically on the surface. And, this time, he was not alone. The frightened eyes of his little brother looked up at him, sand falling on their heads, burying them alive. The last thing Jack saw was Charlie's curls disappearing under the deluge of sand.

CHAPTER FOURTEEN

Namaste

WINNIFRED WEAVER PULLED UP HER EYE mask, hoping it was not time to get up yet. Now she regretted staying up way too late, binging on House Hunters International. Exotic travel remained a dream of hers, and someday she hoped to see the world. These days, however, it took real effort just to make it downstairs to the communal kitchen.

She groaned as she remembered it was her turn to prepare the oatmeal for the house residents. Why couldn't they just have toast? Why the big deal about a hot breakfast? If she had her choice, she'd skip the morning meal, and snack on cashews if she got hungry. Her frustration grew . . . but only momentarily. Because as always, she lowered her irritation by turning her attention to something pleasant. Maybe that afternoon, she would catch the next three episodes of House Hunters. She pictured herself, draped over the long sectional, enjoying a chai tea latte, covered in a fluffy blanket. Within minutes Winnifred dozed off . . . sending up a series of soft snores, as she drifted away.

* * *

That morning Jack awoke early, and he pulled out the bottom drawer and took the whistle from the underside. Checking the coordinates to be sure he had memorized correctly, he entered them on a map search. The pin dropped on an ashram up in the hills near Galena and the Mississippi River. Jack returned the whistle to its place and slid the drawer back in the bureau. Then he heard anguished voices coming from his parent's bedroom. This was unusual. This couldn't be good.

Jack went down to the kitchen and a half hour later, his parents followed. They seemed calm, but when he approached them about a spur of the moment trip, they looked at him with annoyance.

"We can't just pick up and go. You could have asked us about this last week, but you didn't plan, did you? So, *no*. We can't go. Everything is not all about you," said his mother.

Jack backed away, reeling from the attack.

"I'm sorry. It's OK," said Jack.

He retreated to his room, feeling like a bad dog. Then he heard more raised voices discussing Charlie's recent physical exam. Fear shot through him. What if his brother was *not* Ok?

The image of the nanobot in Charlie's hands landed with a thud. Of course, the baby had been infected, infested. Contaminated with filthy little, brain altering nanobots.

Jack had to get away. Maybe Charlie could have been treated. Keeping this from his parents was unforgivable. He was a terrible person. An awful brother. Deceitful and selfish. A coward.

He had to get out of the house. What would his parents do if they knew the truth? He would go to Galena. At least he could follow through with the quest. Do one thing right. He started walking to the bus station. Checking, he found, there was a 9:47 bus.

Jack arrived in time, jumping aboard. Walking down the aisle, he settled in a seat next to the window. He texted his parents. A minute later, they responded, clearly not happy that he had taken off.

Thoughts of Charlie and his parent's heartache brought tears, but he brushed them away with the back of his hand. He swallowed hard.

Then Jack had a most uncharacteristic thought.

Everybody lied, didn't they?

He doubted telling his parent's the truth would have made a difference. He shouldn't feel bad. It wasn't *his* fault. A tiny voice deep inside his mind protested, but this new, stronger voice silenced the doubts.

Jack stared out the window. An endless string of storefronts with bargain signs made him want to turn away. Sometimes, the city looked like an infinite strip mall.

An air hammer started up. The arms of an orange vested construction worker vibrated as he brutalized the cement. The drill's ear-splitting noise reverberated in his skull. Hell must be filled with air hammers.

Why wasn't the bus moving?

Car horns and blasting noise added to his misery, and he had left the house without his sunglasses. His headache flamed.

After creeping along for what seemed forever, the bus finally sped up. They passed the turn off for the airport, and blessedly, the traffic flowed. Another fifteen minutes and the streets cleared of the metropolitan mess. Jack drew in a breath.

The sun now had free rein in the cloudless sky, beating down, cooking the vehicle's metal roof. A flat landscape offered their bus as a sacrificial object for the sun's delight. Jack moved across the aisle seeking a cooler spot. Damp air cranked out from the air conditioner. Jack's stomach began to turn. He put a piece of gum in his mouth, hoping the spearmint would help.

After several hours, Illinois prairies gave way to bluffs near the Mississippi River.

Jack's bus rumbled into Galena, turning into the depot. He stepped down on to the hot pavement. Burning diesel filled the air, and he moved away to escape the fumes. A shaft of sun drenched his face. It was even hotter here. Looking up the hill, he saw a row of three-story brick buildings built over a hundred years ago. Jack ordered a car service, and ten minutes later, an old jalopy pulled up with a peeling Grateful Dead decal on the bumper and the Lyft placard in the window. He got in, directing the driver to the ashram.

The car seat gave off a tangle of smells that worked their way up from the patched vinyl. Jack bounced around in the back, because the vehicle seemed to lack shock absorbers, offering a veritable rodeo ride. When they arrived at the destination, the driver asked if Jack wanted him to wait. But he shook his head and got out at a wooden gate.

He saw the homestead sitting on a hill, with several pine trees standing next to an old barn. Young people tossed a frisbee in front of a big house with a wrap-around porch. They directed him to the entrance, and he headed toward the house. He was feeling unsteady from the ride across Illinois.

As he got closer, the smell of curry wafted from the porch. This heavy scent did not help Jack's queasiness. Wishing he had stopped for a sandwich before coming out here, he took in some deep breaths, trying to bring up his energy.

He reached the door and saw a brass plate with the official Illinois seal. After Jack knocked, a teenage girl greeted him with *Namaste*. She showed him into a living room with tie dyed hangings, most likely done by the residents. In the corner, a fan turned and wobbled on its stand, humming out a blast of tepid air.

"I'm Winnifred Weaver, the hostess at our ashram . . . Well, this week, anyway," she said.

"Our next meditation class is going to be at two this afternoon. You're welcome to join us then."

"I took the bus from Chicago because I'm following some directions," said Jack.

"I'm not here for meditation."

Then he explained the golden whistle and showed her a paper with the numbers, and the coordinates that had led him here.

"Have you ever heard of Dr. Vincent Marcov?" he asked.

Winnifred's eyes widened and then she swooned to the floor. Jack called for help, and a boy rushed in with a bottle of water.

"Do you need a doctor?" Jack asked as the girl opened her eyes.

The girl shook her head, assuring him she would be ok. After more water and an apple slice, the color returned to her cheeks.

"Sorry. Didn't mean to upset you," Jack said.

"We can talk another time, maybe on the phone?" But Winnifred insisted that he stay.

"It was a shock, hearing that name again."

Her voice shaking, Winnifred began to tell how Dr. Marcov caused a disaster that left her an orphan. As she talked, Jack could feel acid churning in his stomach. He had fled his house this morning to get away from the sadness. But Marcov's threat reached across the miles, filling him now with dread.

"Our ashram here was founded when that environmental disaster killed our parents. It was in all the newspapers."

"I remember my parents talked about this. Everyone was shocked because the town was so far west of Chicago, away from factories and industry," said Jack.

Winnifred began to cry again. She took another sip of water and began telling the sad story.

"I was ten years old when we moved to a new house. At first, we were happy to have the space, a big backyard, with a pretty stream. But soon the neighbors up and down the street in my subdivision began to get sick with strange cancers. Everybody had breathing problems. My dad got a weird lump on his leg, and my mother needed an inhaler to get through the day. Funeral hearses became a common sight. It wasn't long before the Environmental Protection Agency found a cluster of cancers. Soon my neighborhood was crawling with scientists in hazardous material suits".

"*That* must have been frightening," said Jack.

"They discovered a laboratory a mile from us with safety violations. But the toxic chemical valve was never fixed. This company lab poisoned the air and water. Finally, the place was shut down, but not before my parents died."

"I'm so sorry," Jack said.

"In the end, the state social workers brought us survivors to Galena. Everyone was kind, and under the circumstances, we felt fortunate. The police found that the Vocram Company who owned the lab was a shell company. Vocram is Marcov spelled backward."

"No wonder you fainted when I said his name," Jack said.

"Marcov disappeared before he was sentenced. The cops looked everywhere, but he seemed to have vanished. Then a package arrived here that was filled with these mechanical bugs. By the time we saw the note from him, it was too late. We were all suffering from terrible headaches. So, while it's peaceful here, we can't seem to get any projects completed. We just put them off."

It occurred to Jack that the intensity of his own headaches recently had increased. And he thought about his growing tendency to lie. He was turning into a regular Pinocchio.

Jack noticed that as Winnifred talked, she spoke without inflection, rolling out the facts in a monotone voice, almost on automatic pilot.

"So terrible with so many dead," Jack said.

He explained other people had told him a similar story. The nanobots, then the headaches, sometimes a whirring sound, and the personality changes. All after an incident with Vincent Marcov.

Winnifred took a sip of iced tea, but then, her face suddenly brightened. Reaching in her pocket, she pulled out a handful of sparkling crystals. Winnifred explained that she thought these colorful rocks might help defeat Marcov. Jack didn't know quite how to respond. After all, he believed in science, certainly not in the power of crystals, seeing these glassy stones as an abdication of personal power. However, they gave comfort to some people . . . and, no one could deny, they were beautiful. So, Jack thanked her, accepting a small bag of colored stones. Then he left the ashram, telling Winnifred that he would let her know if there were any developments. Jack called for a Lyft, and a driver arrived in a newer model Chevy. Once the car reached the highway, and after he checked there were no cars following, Jack tossed the crystals out the window. His paranoia was growing, and he worried they might be toxic, might house nanobots. The driver looked at him in the rear-view mirror and frowned.

Jack leaned back in the seat trying to calm himself. He was freaking out. Hearing again about the killing nanobots. Maybe he should see a doctor. Get checked out. The headaches were bad and getting more frequent. But then, why did *he* deserve medical help when his brother's health had been neglected? Did Charlie have headaches? The toddler didn't have the words to tell them.

Jack dreaded learning the truth about the baby's medical tests. On the bus ride back to Chicago, Jack felt a tsunami of chaos heading his way. The skyline appeared on the horizon, a dark menacing cloud hung over the city.

Jack opened the front door at nine pm and found his agitated parents standing in the living room.

"I know, I'm sorry I left like that," Jack said. Too tired to get into it with his parents, sometimes it was easier to apologize up front.

But his parents didn't seem to register what he was saying. They looked broken. He could tell his mom had been crying.

"We need to tell you something," said his dad.

Jack's heart constricted.

"What's happened?"

"Charlie's lab work came back. He has damage . . . from a nanobot."

There it was. Jack closed his eyes. A steel door slammed in his heart.

"Charlie hadn't been sleeping well. And there was the falling issue, so we had him checked out," said his dad.

"No, not Charlie," Jack said, dropping into the sofa.

"I should have refused the inheritance. Not gotten us involved."

"You couldn't have known," his mom said. "None of us could have known."

"Can the nanobot be removed?" asked Jack.

"The device passed out of his body after it weakened his muscle tone," said his mom.

"But, at this point, we need you to stop this quest. It's too dangerous. Let law enforcement deal with Vincent Marcov. He's a psychopath. It's ludicrous for you to be involved."

"Charlie has to come first," Jack said, immediately recognizing his hypocrisy.

"I'm glad you understand," his mom said.

"What can be done for him?" Jack asked, trying to move forward, away from his complicity.

"All we can do is get him some physical therapy. Time will tell. There's no research on this type of brain damage," said his dad.

Brain damage. The feared words. Charlie had brain damage. At the time he had told himself that stomping on the thing had been enough. But he couldn't deny that he had suspected the toy was filled with *real* nanobots. But he had been too caught up with Grace and with Morningside . . . and most of all, with himself. Jack had wanted to impress a girl with his inheritance, with his importance. And now he kind of hated her.

Up in his room later, he felt only emptiness. His quest was over. Charlie was damaged. He took the whistle from its hiding place, noticing the numbers had not changed. He wondered what this could mean. It was as if the whistle had overheard and now sat silenced with the shame of it all.

* * *

For the next few days, Jack walked around in a fog. When Grace called, he didn't pick up.

Jack tried to ignore the news and avoided his friends. A week went by.

Then they all left town on family vacations. Mike to the Ozarks, and Grace to Minnesota. The Abernault family spent July and August in Charlevoix, Michigan with his grandparents. His parents took leaves of absences from work. They needed to spend more time with Charlie, hoping the change of scenery might help with his rehabilitation.

Mike had called, of course, and they had talked about the attacks on the ice cap. The hourglass texts had stopped. But this silence seemed ominous. Jack told Mike about Charlie's condition, and so his friend understood why Jack was stepping back. He said he needed space. Mike said he would try to bring Grace around, try to get her to understand, but she was fuming at Jack's rebuff.

* * *

September came, and the Abernaults returned to Evanston, and resumed their routine. Jack felt rested. Walks with his grandmother relaxed him. Rather than dole out advice, she kept an ongoing needlepoint project that posted her thoughts in silk threads. Adding to it every now and then, the latest version of the linen fabric read; *Notice beauty and mystery, Use your gifts, Create little projects of hope. Be grateful, Learn something every day. Help someone out, Listen more.*

On the ride up to Michigan each year, the family tried to predict what kernels of wisdom grandma wished to impart to her daughter and grand-children. They always got it wrong. She surprised them this year because it seemed the septuagenarian had taken up breathwork and meditation. They had not seen that coming.

Charlie, tanned from all the time at the beach, had loved digging in the sand with his grandma. He seemed more content, although there was a clumsiness when he moved. Every time Jack saw the child topple over, he felt a piece of his heart shrivel.

Jack dreaded going back to school. Mike had called and told him he had heard a disturbing rumor. Apparently, there was a story circulating that Jack was involved in a conspiracy theory involving spaceships.

Somebody had talked, or somebody had overheard. Mike had countered the gossip by putting it out there that whoever started the crazy story only was envious of Jack's inheritance.

Mike was a true friend.

That first week back walking through the halls at school, however, Jack imagined kids staring and whispering. Grace acted icy when they met. To make matters worse, he had seen her holding hands with a senior on the debate team. Jack felt terrible. All he could do was to throw himself into his schoolwork. He needed to get his grades back up. It was sophomore year. Time to knuckle down.

And Jack had settled on a new trick . . . cheating. He told himself it would be stupid not to help himself out. Lots of kids did it. It was all part of the game. A faint voice inside him protested, but Jack cranked up the volume on the heavy metal music pulsing through his earbuds.

At the end of that first week of school, Jack breathed a little easier. He had made it through, keeping his head down. Making lists and checking off tasks seemed to help manage his anxiety. He worked with Charlie on the physical therapy exercises, and he kept up his running routine. He sensed his parents worried about his isolation. But at least, Mike dropped in for a short visit on Saturday night, before he headed out to a party.

In mid-September, Jack received an unexpected text from his school counselor. Apparently, some visitors from Chicago's corporate community planned to visit the science lab at the school. The principal asked him to serve as their tour guide.

Jack showed up at the main office after his last period, and his counselor introduced him to three prominent CEO's. Tanned and manicured, they wore expensive suits and shoes, and looked like mannequins who had broken out of a Michigan Avenue window display.

"Well, Jack, it's nice to meet you. We read about the robot you're assembling for the state competition. We're always interested in meeting up and coming engineers."

"Thanks, I'm happy to show you around," Jack said, feeling a flush of pride.

For the next forty-five minutes, he showed the visitors around the computer lab, explaining the interface with his robot.

"Very impressive. Jack, we would like to offer you a special apprenticeship. Now you would need to talk it over with your parents and get back to us."

"That's amazing, thank you. Is it focused on robots?"

"Yes, and other cutting-edge technology. It would involve spending a week at a conference center in Minnesota."

At this point the principal intervened.

"You would get extra credit, of course, boosting your math, and science grades. It's really a wonderful opportunity. I've called your dad to let him know the details."

"Wow sounds great," Jack said.

They continued to discuss the mission of their Fortune 500 group, describing the robotics used in their industry. They walked outside where an amazing automobile was parked in the school lot. The principal held the door open and gestured for Jack to get in the car. The vehicle was equipped with features not yet on the market.

Jack was dazzled by the automobile. He got in the passenger side.

The black Maserati resembled a patent leather shark. When the car pulled up in front of his house, several neighbors out for a walk, stopped to see who was in the flashy coupe. Evanston residents were accustomed to seeing understated family cars. The people here spent their money on tuition, displaying college decals on the bumpers of older model cars.

That night Jack brought up the topic of the apprenticeship with his parents. Given their son's willingness to stop the Council's quest, they thought this distraction might be good. This experience on his resume would get Jack's academic record back on track after his poor showing the second semester of freshman year. Focusing on robots, and spending a week away sounded promising.

"Well, it's up to you. Maybe a good opportunity," said his dad.

"Getting extra credit seems reason enough," said Jack.

Later Jack checked the apprenticeship website and found the sponsor actually was a big oil company. The CEO's had withheld that bit of information.

However, this apprenticeship would give him time away from Grace, and the rumors.

Jack always could pretend he didn't know about the oil company sponsor if someone found out.

This betrayal of his values went against *everything* he professed about renewable energy. Six months ago, the oil company connection alone would have been a deal breaker.

*   *   *

Several weeks later, his mother hovered as he packed his suitcase for the conference.

"You know it's going to be cold. Be sure to pack sweaters, and warm socks. They have a winter that lasts from September to May," said his mom.

Jack packed for two seasons, as it was still in the high seventies in Chicago.

"Wonder, if the melting ice cap has changed Minnesota weather?" his mom asked.

"The polar vortex sometimes dips so low that Illinois is colder than the North Pole," Jack said.

"The satellite attacks on the artic shelf definitely are making all this worse," she said.

"I feel guilty that I've abandoned my promise to the Council."

"I know. But really, you were tricked, being shuffled off, kidnapped really, in that glass cube. Talk about intimidating," she said.

"And your dad still hasn't found a way to deal with this. Everything is *classified this*, and national *security that*. The Council needs to find someone older. Someone with top scientific credentials in the military. Our family has suffered enough. Charlie was sacrificed," and she started to cry.

Jack wrapped his arms around his mother. He held her, feeling the heaving of her sobbing body.

"It'll be all right, mom," he said. But he didn't believe it.

* * *

The next morning, Jack boarded the train headed for Minneapolis. He sat next to the window looking through the thick plated glass. His family stood waving on the platform. Charlie's broken body in his dad's arms, was the last thing he saw as the train slid out of the station.

After twenty minutes rocking gently through the city's steel and brick, Jack let his mind wander. Trees with yellowing leaves streaked past. Miles of grey rooftops, and finally the station in west Lake Forest marked the end of the suburbs. Soon farms appeared and a spattering of cows ignored the train's passing.

Jack closed his eyes, sighing. He was glad to get away. Even from his family, and it had been hard seeing Grace with that guy. He dreaded the hallways at school, fearing a sighting of the couple every time he turned a corner. Still, he hoped she was impressed that he had been picked for this apprenticeship. For sure, Mike would have told her he was one of only five high school kids chosen from the Midwest. When Jack described the week long opportunity to Mike, he left out the fossil fuel part. And Mike would have been disgusted if he had known about his cheating. Jack felt his deceitfulness, coiled in his throat. Lying had become his thing, and sometimes that meant he just withheld all the facts.

Several hours later, Jack's train pulled into the Minneapolis Metropolitan Station. Cold air hit his face as he climbed down on to the station platform. It seemed more like late fall, a contrast to Indian summer lingering in Illinois. Jack put on his wool coat and scanned the crowd at the terminal. As expected, a young man in a uniform held a sign with *Abernault*. A scheduled car was part of the plan, as the apprenticeship was to be held at a conference center near the Boundary Waters.

Jack settled in the vehicle and texted his parents that he had arrived in the city. The driver handed him a box lunch and told him they had a three-hour drive. Sitting in the limousine, he thought about the CEO's and imagined how he would feel wearing custom suits, and expensive watches.

Some kids at his school came from families who took exotic vacations, or who had memberships at country clubs. Their parents generally worked in finance or the corporate world. Now, with the Morningside inheritance, he had that kind of money. Jack considered how it would feel driving a ridiculously expensive car. What would it be like picking up Grace for a date in a Lamborghini? This fantasy took off in his head like a silver tipped Lear jet climbing into the clouds.

This thought, however, was followed quickly by a stab in his heart as he knew Grace had moved on. Although, he couldn't deny that he had pushed her away. Maybe he felt that he didn't deserve love. After all, he was a liar and a cheat. Abandoned his brother to the effects of the nanobots. Thrown him to the wolves. Despicable. Unlovable.

Empty, his life was a wreck. The girl, the mission, all gone. He looked out the car window, noticing the weather turning bitter cold, mirroring the way he felt inside. The sky shifted as the sun slid ominously behind a dark panel of clouds, the kind one sees in the dead of winter. Snow flurries began to swirl, and the wind picked up. Sinister pines leaned into the highway, threatening to swallow the vehicle, dragging it off the road and into the dark forest. Drowsy from the travel and the darkening scene, Jack's eyes closed, and he fell into a deep sleep.

* * *

Jack awoke, shivering in pitch blackness. His socks and coat missing, he was on his back. He struggled to his feet, staggering a few steps until he felt a wall of dirt. He seemed to be standing in a deep pit. A raw fear rushed through him. What was going on? He screamed for help. Darkness swallowed his voice.

Had he been kidnapped? Had the car veered off the road into a ditch? Or was this some kind of insane initiation? Nothing made sense. Bitter cold gripped his body. Howling wind rushed overhead.

Jack's mind faltered, his body shivered. Had Marcov taken him? Had he been drugged? He could not see his hand in front of his eyes. It seemed he stood in the pit of the world, abandoned. Freezing to death. Would his parents miss him? Would his last text keep them from worrying?

His throat felt lined with razors, as he tried to swallow. It hurt too much to scream. His mind began to play tricks on him. What was crawling on his legs? Could they be nanobots? Frantically he tried to brush off whatever was attacking him. Then the creeping sensation on his skin ceased, frozen maybe, too cold to register.

Jack knew he had to do something. He had read a book once about a prisoner in solitary confinement who kept his sanity by organizing his thoughts. Jack focused on memories of his family.

Willing himself to recall his earliest recollection in life, Jack conjured up the scene of a fire in the house across the street. He must have been age three. The memory now played out like a movie. Blaring sirens had awakened him from a nap. He recalled how scared he had been, watching the long red trucks pull up to the curb. Flames from the house where his friend lived burst from an upstairs window. He heard plaintive cries for help. Then, it seemed out of nowhere, these wonderful big figures in shiny black coats carried his friend Nathan out of the burning house.

Clinging to his mother, Jack remembered seeing the mask and tubes pulled over the little boy's face. Several hours later, the fire was out, and thankfully, everyone survived. Nathan had come home the following week from the hospital. The Abernaults had brought over a casserole for the family. Jack could still feel the sense of his friend's bruised hand in his.

This significant event marked a turning point in Jack's development. It had created a lasting impression of what a hero could do. After that fire, little Jack announced he planned to be a firefighter when he grew up. The trauma of that incident also left him with the understanding that the world could be an exceedingly dangerous place.

Now, in this dark hole, Jack drew in a breath, recalling Nathan's rescue. The actions of those firefighters, imprinted in his young mind, burned a lasting impression of courage, and loyalty. Every year after, during Evanston's Fourth of July Parade, his heart skipped a beat when the venerable hook and ladder truck slowly rolled past. Jack understood these were the *special ones* who rushed into trouble, protecting others from harm.

As the years passed, however, he discovered science and math, and let go of the notion of becoming a firefighter. What had stayed with him were the core values of loyalty and service. Honoring tradition, following a path under the direction of teachers and mentors, felt right to Jack. Even the rules of math, and now engineering, fit his need for structure. They also seemed a path for making a contribution of some kind. This feeling of responsibility created a rudder that, up to this point, had guided him. All that was true, up until recently, when he had begun to lie and to cheat. Become a master of rationalizing his actions. Abandoned his brother.

Darkness had followed him into their home, and it had landed on the most vulnerable . . . Charlie. He'd been a rotten big brother. Deserved to be in this pit. Betrayed his values. Put Charlie at risk. Gave in to the temptations from the CEO's. Even his commitment to green energy had collapsed like a house of cards in favor of a desire for glory. A bit of his soul had cracked off. He didn't recognize himself anymore. Had he been a victim of nanobots? There were the headaches. But no whirring sounds. However, there had been the white noise. Had he been infected? He kept putting off the doctor appointment. Afraid to know the truth.

Some of those people he'd met on the quest couldn't be trusted. Definitely, not the Masons. Not Trip Grainger. Not Bernaski. Maybe they'd all made stuff up? But why? To scare him? To warn him off the quest? Who *could* he trust? Not even himself, he thought bitterly. Jack thought of Mike, peaceful and gentle, always ready to soothe over any trouble. And Grace, outspoken and bossy, seemed even now, to reach across the miles. Despite the fact they were no longer together, he sensed her presence.

Most of his life he had depended on these two friends. It had only been in the past year that Jack had been more apt to keep his own council, fearing Grace's judgement. He wondered what they were doing right now. He tried to imagine their faces, but he was fading fast. Lightheadedness overtook him. His head cradled in the dirt, he passed out.

It must have been hours later, he stirred. A glimmer of awareness flickered in his mind. He had to decide. Give in to the cold and the signals his body was sending. Or take charge of his situation. The face of Joseph Spencer now appeared . . . Was it real? Maybe in his mind, he decided.

Jack marshalled his will and began to sit straight-backed, with legs crossed. Willing himself to focus, a technique he had learned at the karate dojo, he sat. First, he told himself, get in touch with a felt sense in the body. Second, he must find an image that fits the bodily tightness, and lastly, come up with a word to match the image, and physical sense. Working this sequence, he moved his awareness from sense, to picture, and to word, over, and over, and over again. And it was working. At each stage, he felt a release, along with a deeper breath. The tightness in his chest shifted a bit.

Jack saw the *wheel of fortune* in his mind, turning around, up and down, pausing a moment in the best place and then spinning down into the worst. Moving his feelings from the highs and lows on the circumference of this circle, he moved his attention to the center, to the hub of stillness. He breathed in the moment. From this place of centeredness, he would prevail. Will himself into this experience for whatever came. Jack now switched into a meditation pose. Moved into a place beyond his attachments. Under his fear. Even beyond his hope for rescue. As he did this, he acknowledged his attraction to worldly honors, drawn in by the CEO's. He confessed veering off his true path, lying and the cheating.

He drew in a deep breath.

Then softly, Jack's chest released.

He was free.

At that moment, a flood gate of lights blasted into the hole.

Jack awoke, finding himself miraculously still in the car heading north to the conference. His head was pounding, and his throat raw. Had it all been a terrible nightmare? Or had he been drugged? Convinced that he had hallucinated the terrible ordeal, he fell back into the car seat, his forehead burning up.

By the time he arrived at the conference center near the Boundary Waters, he was running a high fever. The worried director, called a doctor, who insisted they arrange to have a corporate jet fly Jack back to Chicago. He didn't know who he could trust because he felt all alone. He had no choice but to board the plane on the private airstrip.

Hours later, in his room at home, Jack sat on the edge of his bed. As he pulled off his socks, a shot of fear ran through him. Inside out, they were covered in dried mud!

CHAPTER FIFTEEN

The Anamchara Text

RECOVERING FROM A SEVERE BOUT OF STREP took Jack weeks to regain his strength. He languished in bed for days, watching TV and napping. The best part was Grace came to visit. Jack almost cried when his mom had called up the stairs, asking if he was up for a visit from her. He sat up, plumping his pillow behind his back. Grace poked her head in the door.

"Hey ... sleepy boy. How you doing?"

"Grace, hey, come on in. Doing better. The medicine wears me out. All I do is sleep"

She brought him a peace offering, a black knit cap.

"My mom knitted it for you. But I picked the color."

"Thanks, it's great. I'm hoping to be back at school next week, at least for half days."

"We all miss you. *I* miss you," said Grace.

"It's going to be hard catching up on work."

"Don't think about that. You need to rest up. That's the most important thing."

"I've never felt this wiped out in my life," said Jack.

"You do look pale," said Grace.

She hadn't stayed long, but the effect on Jack was like a shot of interferon. The previous day, Mike told him that Grace and the debate team guy had broken up. This news sent hope flooding into him.

The glow lasted for the rest of the afternoon, however as evening approached, Jack's mood darkened. Now that he had started to recover physically, memory of the pit haunted him. When he tried to push the experience off as a feverous hallucination, the dried mud on the socks offered contradicting evidence.

But what exactly had happened?

Confused and conflicted, Jack felt a roiling in his chest, like a *fight club* had taken up residence where his heart should have been. From the four corners of this boxing ring the contenders glared. In corner #1, his need for self-preservation, in corner #2, the promise to the Council, in corner # 3, his family's safety, and in the last corner, the earth's survival. These warring forces felt like vicious dogs tearing him apart. Then the antibiotics thankfully kicked in, and sleep took over.

In the morning, after some breakfast, he felt stronger. But then his thoughts turned to Grace and what she must think of him abandoning the quest. He figured she knew about Charlie's diagnosis, and how his parents had asked him to stop. It was all too dangerous for the family.

Jack pulled out the items from Sophia. As he stared at them, it seemed that even the gold whistle, was content to sit dormant. No new numbers had appeared on the engraved surface. He hid it, taped under a bookshelf for safe keeping.

The following week, Jack returned to school. His morning classes tired him more than he had anticipated. If he could make it through lunch and English, his dad was picking him up for early dismissal. This shortened day worked for the first week back. The following week Jack felt stronger, and he resumed his full day of classes. Mike and Grace had been careful to let him recover. But now that he was better, Grace couldn't resist, bringing up the topic of taking out Marcov's headquarters. Going over the same ground, she laid out her argument. But Jack stood firm despite his low energy, and Mike backed him up.

"What part of *no* don't you get?" Jack stared Grace down.

"No, *you* don't get it. The best defense is an escalated offense. *Art of War*, Sun Tzu."

"Sun Who?" asked Mike.

"Don't pretend you don't know who I'm talking about. Look, I get it that Charlie, and your family, have taken a terrible hit. But, if you think that backing down will stop Marcov, you really are bat crap crazy. Power is the only language he speaks. Time to double down, not back away. That monster will only ratchet up the attacks," Grace said.

"Have you seen Charlie wobble as he tries to walk?" asked Jack, his eyes glaring.

Hearing his friend's voice crack, Mike said.

"We love Charlie, too, you know. We're here for you."

"Some of us, more than others," said Grace, taking a shot at Mike's reticence.

"Enough. Stop," said Jack.

But Grace did not stop.

"Look, Jack, the best way to shield Charlie is not to ignore the reality. That encourages bullies. If we can figure out which security system Marcov installed, we can do this. Don't we always say people give up too easily? If we stick to the course, we can protect your family . . . and maybe save the polar bears. The ice shelf attacks happen every few days. Somehow Marcov's satellite lasers are evading the Iron Dome. The planet is slipping toward a point of no return. He doesn't even bother to send threatening texts anymore. He thinks he's won."

Tired of going over this ground again, Mike said.

"Here's a thought. Grace and I keep looking for chinks in likely security systems. Meanwhile, Jack can learn what's written in that Anamchara Text. You didn't promise your parents you wouldn't look at it. Right?"

Mike was correct. While he had promised to stop the quest, nothing had been said specifically about the text. And anyway, what harm could come from reading a book?

"OK, I see what you're saying. That could work," said Jack.

Then he thought of Charlie.

He did not want to tear up in front of Grace so he escaped to the washroom. Splashing water on his face, he gripped the cold ceramic basin. He looked in the mirror. Clearly, he saw exhaustion, but he also saw resilience. Maybe things would work out? Spencer's words came to him, *Do the next right thing*.

He took a few minutes to practice some Navy Seal deep breathing: inhale for four counts, hold breath for four counts, release air for four counts, lungs empty for four counts, and then repeat. After four sets of this sequence, he felt centered. He checked the mirror, and he saw a new steadiness. The bell rang and he went off to class.

After his last period, Jack skipped a math club meeting and went home. He entered the house and found his mom, sitting at her desk. She gestured for him to keep it down as Charlie was sleeping. In the kitchen, he stood in the opened refrigerator, looking for sandwich makings.

Plate in hand, he took his food, moving carefully up the stairs, passing Charlie's door. Sitting on his bed, he ate his sandwich, brushing the crumbs off his spread. Then he opened his drawer and pulled out the Anamchara Text.

Weird how the book weighed next to nothing. Better lock the door. His mother would freak out. Finding him with this book open. But he had to do this. He'd promised the Council. Breathe.

Jack opened the book. Pages of degraded writing stared back at him, challenging him to break their code. Reading the lines was slow going. He took a few notes. Written in English, the fancy calligraphy, and awkward phrasing, made his eyes feel like they were plodding through mud. Some of the letters looked Arabic, graceful like a waterfowl leaning over the edge of a pond. Missing text. How was he ever supposed to figure out the meaning?

With so much inaccessible. He rolled over on his back, exhausted, feeling defeated already.

He stared at the ceiling. His eyes scanned the blank surface, taking in the emptiness. He blinked, and drew in a breath.

The words from the Council's letter spoke.

Listen with your heart, with your head, and with your gut.

He repeated the words, *with my heart, with my head, and with my gut.*

Jack sat up and flipped the book's pages to the diagram with the star encircled symbol. With fresh eyes, his mind began to put something together, like a puzzle dancing into place. It dawned on him that he had made *nine* visits, and there were *nine* points around this circle. Turning to his notes, words now popped off the page, *anger, pride, deceit, envy, avarice, fear, gluttony, lust,* and *sloth* . . . nine points, nine visits, nine flaws.

This couldn't be a coincidence.

Resting back on his pillow, he thought about the people he had met on his visits. How had he felt in their presence? Margaret Mason bristling with *anger*, had made him feel attacked. Her nagging had registered in his gut, making him want to lash out.

Jack's mind sensed a key turning inside a lock, opening the secret of the coded diagram.

Lindy Simons, made him recoil with her self-denial. His reaction had been to pull away from the neediness, making him shield his heart. Her impulse to one up everyone came from *pride*.

Trip Grainger used relationships like pawns in a game. The Graingers operated in a transactional way. They gave to get, and to win. Their shady business deals were based on *deceit*. And they expected others to lie like they did. Jack couldn't deny that his own cheating and lying was like the Graingers.

Jack sat up. His mind was building a scaffold of understanding.

Lutetia set herself apart, rejecting anything *ordinary*. Her *by-pass* into art required constant comparisons, the stuff of *envy*. She was dramatic, but somehow lacked authenticity.

Dr. Bernaski hoarded data, a description of avarice. The volume of ideas flying in that library that day had given Jack a headache. The professors seemed a perfect example of an *Ivory Tower*, stockpiling information.

However, Dr. McGloin's work restoring the Amazon showed something better. The truth about these personality styles seemed more *dynamic than static*.

Harold remained on alert for threats. Jack could relate, as he also anticipated worst case scenarios . . . a wheel of worry spinning in his head. But he also knew he could move away from the fear. With the breathing. He could recalibrate.

Then there was Daisy and her appetite for *More*. On a *gluttonous* path, she focused on plans for fun and novel entertainment.

Tanya Simons, on the other hand, *lusted* for power, punching her way through life. Anger fueled her, and Jack's gut had felt the threat, but also the impulse to strike back.

Winnifred admitted she could be lazy. Her monotone voice did not match the facts in her terrible history, suggesting she pushed down tremendous anger. The effects of trauma seemed ready to explode, or to come out in sneaky ways . . . like being late, or incompetent . . . or living in the midst of a mess. *Sloth*, atop a pile of rage.

But there still was a problem. Where on the circle, in which position, did each of the nine people fit?

Well, there remained two problems really, because he also didn't know what the connecting lines meant in the enneagon diagram.

Just then, Charlie began to howl. Jack jumped off his bed. A moment later, he lifted the baby out of the crib. The damp curls and warm little body smelled of sweet baby sweat. With Charlie's arms circling his neck, he carried the little guy down to the kitchen. Jack sat him in the highchair and maneuvered the tray in place till he heard the click. Then he poured a bowl of cracker octagons, adding some cheese cubes to the tray. Charlie kicked his legs, pointing to his cup.

"You want milk. I'm moving as fast as I can, Bub."

Grabbing the milk, he filled Charlie's favorite blue cup.

His mother called down the hall.

"I have to run some errands. Can you watch Charlie? I'll be back in a few hours."

"Sure. No problem." said Jack.

His mother picked up her car keys and he heard the door close.

Watching his brother chomp on the snack, Jack's mind began to wander. The diagram of the heart, head, and gut body centers from the Anamchara Text seemed to appear now on the edge of the round table. He considered how each of the nine made him feel and react.

The *body map* snapped together. Tanya Stokes, Winnifred Weaver, and Margaret Mason operated out of the gut center from *anger*. Tanya exploded with anger, Winnifred dialed down her frustration, while Margret Mason released her rage with a steady barrage of criticism. Jack recalled how talking to these three people had made him notice his own anger, in his gut.

He poured more milk for Charlie. While he waited for the next refill, Jack considered the anxiety he'd experienced in the presence of Lindy Simons, Trip Grainger, and Lutetia Langdon. Overly concerned with relationships, he'd felt an urge to guard his heart. Lindy managed her *anxiety* by serving people. Trip Grainger needed to impress others. And Lutetia ramped up her specialness, as a means of channeling her anxiety.

Jack shook more crackers on the tray for his brother.

Dr. Bernaski, Harold, and Daisy stirred up his own fear, setting off his natural tendency to worry. The professor managed *fear* by gathering information, and Harold by scanning for trouble. Daisy avoided fear by escaping into fun and by planning for the future.

But the question of who fit where on the diagram remained.

Charlie now was fussing.

"Buh-ee. BUH-_EE!" he demanded.

Jack loped up the stairs to find the bunny.

He looked in the usual places, crib, floor, toy box . . . but no bunny. He checked his room. Sometimes, Charlie wandered in there.

The treasured rabbit sat slumped next to his bed. Jack scooped it up. Then something caught his eye. The gold whistle was perched on top of the nightstand, next to the lamp. He knew he had left it taped under the bookcase. Jack picked it up and saw a new engraving etched on the surface of the gold:

Mason 1:00 pm.

What *could* that mean?

Then a sudden flash of understanding. He could barely control his fingers as he texted his friends.

A half hour later, Mike and Grace sat around the Abernault's kitchen table, while Jack explained his theory about the text.

"The problem is. We don't know who fits where," said Mike.

"We do now," said Jack, setting the golden whistle on the table. They stared at the new engraving.

"This hint puts Margaret Mason in the one o'clock position on the circumference of the circle. Now we have the orientation. I'll add the other people in the order I met them," said Jack.

"Let's see if that makes sense. Grab some index cards. We can map this out."

Jack got a text from his mom asking if he could babysit for another few hours. His parents wanted to go out for dinner.

"We have some extra time now," said Jack.

Jack returned a thumbs up emoji. He certainly didn't want his parents seeing what they were up to. They'd be mad.

The teenagers added names, numbers, and attributes around the edge of the table, in the order of the visits.

"This orientation works for the nine types, and the three centers (head, heart, and gut). But each type has *two* lines connecting them to other types.

What does *that* mean?"

Picking up the Anamchara Text, Jack flipped through the pages, scanning for diagrams.

"The lines maybe could be **vectors;** you know directional arrows. That would explain a path to soften the main flaw of that point," said Jack.

"You mean a way to *balance* a personality?" asked Grace.

"Except, each point is connected with *two* lines," said Mike.

"Maybe these points on the circle were more like *comfort zones* for different types of people. And one could move from a preferred base of operation to *improve* or *regress.*"

"Let's try it out," said Grace.

Jack grabbed some string, red and green, from the drawer.

Looking at the book's diagram, they cut and taped, adding the segments to the points as they considered the meaning.

"Tanya Stokes #8 is connected to Lindy at #2, and to Dr. Bernaski, at #5.

If she became more like the professor, she used her power to hoard. *That* can't be good.

However, if she took on Lindy's kindness, she used her power to protect other people. Right?"

Jack looked up. He added red string and green string to mark the two paths, one positive, and one negative.

"Try another combination."

"Winnifred at #9, moved on this connecting line toward Harold, at #6, her laziness merged into his routines. That would make her even *more* tuned out. On the other hand, if she moved to Trip Grainger's point at #3, she became energized and effective."

"That totally makes sense."

Keep going," Grace said.

"If Margaret Mason, #1 moved to Lutetia's point, #4, she collapsed into a miserable victim, whining that everything wasn't perfect. But, if she adopted Daisy's point at #7, she lightened up, gained some perspective. Had some fun."

"Let me do the next one. If Lindy Simons, #2 took on attributes of Tanya's point #8, she manipulated people. But, if she developed Lutetia's creativity at #4, she'd be more independent, and enjoy being alone."

"My turn. If Trip #3 moved to Winnifred's point# 9, he merged with his deceit, but if he moved to Harold's position, he used his talents for the good of the group," said Grace.

They continued, discussing the paths, adding Lutetia, Bernaski, Harrold, and Daisy.

Lutetia at #4 needed to move to point #1. Rising above a fog of feelings, she would focus, make lists, and prioritize her tasks. Moving to 2 would only make her seem precious, and less authentic.

If Bernaski, at point 5 moved to point 8, he sent knowledge into the world. However, if Bernski moved to 7, he used humor as a way to avoid taking a stand.

Grace added one green string for the positive direction, and a red string for the negative path.

Harold and Jack, at point 6, improved with the peacefulness of point nine. Their fear became courage. However, if they moved to 3, adopting a false courage, they turned into vigilantes. The type 6 needed to develop an authentic inner authority, and to not swallow a party line from an outer source.

Daisy at point 7 needed to take on the prudence of type 5, reigning in the appetites. On the negative side, a seven type, at point one, released anger by needling other people.

Jack made a list of the nine types, the gifts, and pitfalls . . . or more accurately, the nine *points on a path.*

1. The Perfectionist . . . Righteousness . . . correctness overdone becomes anger
2. The Giver . . . Love/kindness . . . overdone becomes pride
3. The Performer . . . Effective/ successful . . . overdone becomes deceit

4. The Artist . . . Individuality/creativity . . . overdone becomes envy

5. The Observer . . . Competence/ knowledge . . . overdone becomes avarice

6. The Loyal Skeptic . . . Security/loyalty . . . overdone becomes fear

7. The Epicure . . . Satisfaction/appetites . . . overdone becomes gluttony

8. The Boss . . . Power . . . overdone becomes lust

9. The Mediator . . . Peace . . . overdone becomes sloth

"So, progress is moving . Regressing is moving *with* the arrow's direction," said Jack.

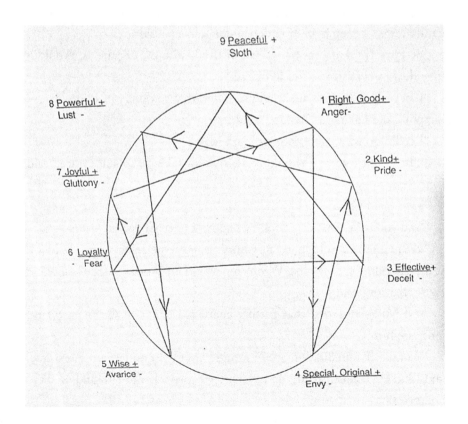

Although the paper was crumpled, this was coming together. A path through the diagram's web, and the mysterious phrases in the text. No longer an enigmatic star design. The code was broken. Jack felt tears well up, but he choked them back. Mike and Grace, he could tell, were also moved by the treasure of these insights.

"So, these types are points on a path, as a type could *never* contain your total identity," said Mike.

"Yeah, but this map shows a good first step. In order to find your authentic self, you need to know your starting point, and see how you over-value a sliver of reality." said Jack.

"And it deals with the blind spot, the stuff we hide from ourselves," said Mike.

Again, Jack and Grace stared at him. Apparently, underneath his calm nature rested a deep pool of understanding, like an old soul.

"So guys, think if I took on some of Lindy Simon's sweetness. Would it tone down my feistiness?" asked Grace.

"Uh, yeah. Although, we wouldn't know what to do if you started wearing pink, and baking us cookies," said Jack.

"I could do with some cookies," said Mike.

"Uh . . . but I guess I shouldn't use this for taking shots at Grace," said Jack.

"*Yeah*," said Grace.

"And you bake your *own* cookies, buddy." Grace smiled at Mike.

"We're *supposed* to look within ourselves, not type *other* people. If I look at myself, calming down like Winnifred would interrupt my focus on worst case scenarios," said Jack.

And Mike conceded that getting energized like Trip Grainger would motivate him.

"Wonder if a meditation group would help us get under our chief flaw," said Jack. He recalled Mimi up in Charlevoix with her breath and meditation practice.

"That's a *great* idea," said Grace.

"Ok, here's a thought. Imagine the nine points as types of boats. The number one type acts as a border patrol craft, the number two serves as a hospital ship, and the three type is an impressive yacht. The four type skims through life as an elegant sailboat. The five type acts as a research vessel. The six type works as a tugboat, the seven type, a fun cruise ship, and the eight type is a battleship. The nine type is a pontoon boat, floating on the lake." said Mike.

"Yeah, that's a nice way to look at the surface image of the types. But those nine boats show only the strengths. We should look at the nine, tap-root flaws, or to use your boat metaphor, the nine different rudders that drive the direction of each craft. These negatives hide under the gift, altering the course or sinking the boats."

"But we need to check this out with an expert. We can't ask Jack's mom, the psychologist. Not yet, anyway. Could we call your grandfather, Mike?" Grace asked.

Mike agreed and set up a call with his grandfather to get his opinion about this personality map they had laid out around the edge of the table. Grandpa Joseph was a respected Jungian analyst, and Mike trusted him. The septuagenarian listened thoughtfully while the three teens explained the layout on the table. Suddenly, his face brightened.

"I want to look at something. This reminds me of an unpublished paper. I'll call you back," said Mike's grandfather.

The three heated up a frozen pizza while they waited.

About forty minutes later, the Facetime screen lit up and jangled. A smiling Grandpa Joseph appeared.

"I found it. This paper, *The Tangled Wing*, described how people got tripped up in different ways. The author was the director of a school in Paris in the 1920's. All sorts of people attended the classes from avant garde writers to a Russian ballerina. I recall I was quite taken by the ideas in these writings. However, at my university the professors remained closed to different approaches. They shut down without looking into the complexity and usefulness of the system. However, new research in neuroscience suggests even mice exhibit 60 discreet behaviors that appear hard-wired, offering data that personalities are ingrained. And mice are genetically similiar to humans. The next step seems to research if the sixty behaviors cluster into nine types, or at least into three body centers. That would point to a biological basis for personality. But even if these types are physical, surely they also are impacted by environment.

But here's the important thing. Early on, in the long road to *individuation*, a youngster adopts a personal world view that colors how they proceed in life. It's as if, around the age of seven, a child stands in front of nine doors, and walks through one. Now behind that door is three more doors, and so on and so on. The enneagram in the Abamchara Text sounds like these writings.

The nine paths show varying identity formations impacted by nature and nurture. Individuals struggle to become more themselves, more authentic. And we are all unique. But it's easy to get lost without a map of some kind.

We are told to "be good," but often that requires different paths for people with different impulses. It helps to be aware of your particuliar path so you can make adjustments. Over the years, I've watched how a patient's potential becomes upended by specific pitfalls. While some of my colleagues reject the idea of personality types, I feel it's just not helpful to deny these trends.

The ancient Greeks described the Apollonian Way, becoming better, versus the Dionysian Way, falling into excess. The goal is to modulate, to stay in the moment, and to respond appropriately. I do think often these rigid patterns soften as people age. The world and life experiences tend to sand down the false facades. But this map you have shown me offers a young person a perspective into their path and shows them a way forward. Maybe save them lots of pain and wasted time. But it's important that you remember that no one type is better or worse than another type. It's all about softening the flaws because the world needs all nine types.

Mike was taking notes. Grace looked thoughtful. Jack was excited.

The map made sense to someone they trusted, someone with credentials and experience . . . a *discernment.*

At ten o'clock, Grace and Mike went home, and Jack went to bed.

However, three hours later Jack was still tossing and turning. His excitement about breaking the book's code, and the encouraging words of Mike's grandpa, had been replaced now by a painful self-evaluation. He knew he had to make some changes. The task felt overwhelming. Then he reminded himself that change was a long process. This was likely an early step in the first leg in the hero's journey. And he knew he *had* made progress since his confession in the dark pit.

But he noticed that when he let fear run wild in his head, it morphed into anxiety, making his breathing shallow and fast. This fueled a tendency to lie. However, when he breathed deeply moving his breath into his lower gut, it calmed him, and he resisted the impulse to deceive himself and others.

The Council had told him to spread the wisdom in the Anamchara Text. He was the messenger. He'd never be perfect. But he could do the next right thing. Jack took a deep breath, releasing a mountain of anxiety.

He knew a sizable percentage of the population would need to take these lessons to heart. If the climate was going to have a fighting chance, the people would have to evolve . . . and fast. How was that supposed to happen? Seemed impossible. The digital clock glowed three am before Jack finally fell asleep.

The alarm clock's buzzer sounded the next morning, beating out Charlie as the designated rooster. A dull haze camped between his temples, and Jack's insides refused to rally. He sat on the edge of his bed trying to muster some energy. Finally, he managed to make it down the stairs where he found his dad in the kitchen.

"Rough night?" asked dad.

"Couldn't get to sleep," said Jack.

"Sounds intense," said dad.

"It was. Did you enjoy your dinner out with mom?" asked Jack.

"Yeah, sure did. Did Charlie go to sleep OK?" asked his dad.

"Yup. He slept like a log once he had all his stuffies in his crib," said Jack.

"That bunny of his sure has a lot of friends come bedtime," said dad.

"Hah . . . Well, I did read him, *Don't Let the Pigeon Stay Up Late* . . . maybe he picked up some new stalling tips," said Jack.

"Grace and Mike came over for a while?" asked dad.

"Yeah," said Jack. Then he rested his head on the counter between his arms.

"You look really wiped out," said dad.

"I am," said Jack.

His dad poured him a cup of coffee.

Coffee was a rare thing for Jack. But the bitter hot liquid hitting his stomach seemed to help.

"Let me make you some eggs," his dad said.

"Thanks. My body feels like I'm speeding a hundred miles an hour, and then slamming on the brakes. Like jet lagged."

"Go take a shower while I fix breakfast."

A few minutes later, with hot water blasting his frame, his skin reddened. Surrendering to the rush of the spray, he began to feel better, hoping the soap's lather would wash away the fatigue. He toweled off and dressed quickly.

The fresh cotton next to his skin, scrambled eggs, and more coffee seemed to glue him back together. He felt kind of new born.

"Thanks, dad," said Jack.

"No problem," said his dad.

Jack met Grace and Mike before first period. They talked about the night before and Jack admitted some things were bothering him.

"Have to make some changes. Hard to admit this stuff," said Jack.

"Yeah. I can relate," said Grace. "I barely slept."

"Me too," said Mike. "The description of Winnifred made me feel like a butterfly pinned to a board."

"Ok, but remember this type is only a sliver of our true self, even if it nails the parts that could use some fixing," said Jack.

"It's about overdoing a good thing. Relying on one habitual response. Not being in the moment, using a stale set of behaviors. But it also shows us where are gift lies." Jack sighed.

"True," said Mike.

"And it showed me a trap in my personality, like a stealth rudder that steers me off in the wrong direction."

"The blind spot," said Grace.

Then Jack brought up the problem of how to get the word out about the personality map. Although he feared his parents would find out that he had continued with the Council's mission, he had to go forward. He reasoned that technically, the Anamchara Text wasn't the quest, however he knew they'd feel betrayed.

But Jack knew the stakes high. The danger his parents feared *already* had attacked them. There was no way back. He *had* to act. He took a deep breath and turned to his friends.

"Let's teach this *people map* to everyone we know. If they find it helpful, they'll pass it on. Hopefully, enough people will react the way we have. We can say we learned it from an old book that was found in the university library stacks."

"Ding!" Grace's phone notified her of a tweet.

The lightbulb emoji registered simultaneously in their heads. The answer of how to get the word out was obvious.

Social media

Their fingers got busy. Tweeting, texting.

It wasn't long before the enneagram was the hot topic at school. Everyone wanted to learn more about their talents and how people saw the world from a different perspective. First, they learned about the *gift* at each point, then about the needed shift. It seemed *Being good* had nine different paths.

Grace started a blog, and Mike managed an Instagram account. They asked the school social worker to start a meditation group. After the first session they appreciated how this kind of awareness allowed them to *sit in the moment*. When the social worker finished the guided meditation, the participants looked around the circle, seeing acceptance in the eyes of the others. Jack noticed his heart felt more open. Grace's eyes glistened with tears.

All this was very Kumbaya. However, when Jack's parents found out that he had deciphered the Anamchara Text, his mother did not talk to him for a full week. His dad let him know that he didn't buy the argument that the book was different from the quest.

Jack felt their anger, but he knew that part of growing up was taking the heat from your parents when you knew you were right.

And of course, the proverbial cat was now very much out of the bag.

While the Abernault's home brimmed with tension, kids in the town started changing. Some of the teachers commented that their classes seemed easier to manage. Bullying reports were down. Kids at the dinner table talked about how they could make other people happy, even their siblings. Grace noticed how her classmates appreciated differences in other kids, learning they each had a gift.

The social workers suddenly found kids lining up outside their offices with questions. At the faculty meeting, the question arose, *What in the world was going on?* When the adults questioned the kids, they told their parents and teachers about the personality lessons.

Facebook pages of Evanston parents lit up with stories about how their kids were suddenly cleaning their rooms, helping out with younger siblings . . . even volunteering on Saturday morning. Other kids started a *go fund me* page for removing plastic from the ocean. Homework was turned in on time. The list went on and on. Kids still talked back sometimes, and came home late, but these things happened less frequently. In the halls of the high school, there was a change in the air that you could feel. It felt lighter, friendlier.

One afternoon, a neighbor stopped Jack's mom in the grocery store and thanked her for her son's work. This woman related how her daughter had sworn off drugs as a result of learning more about herself. Jack's mom came home and told her husband about the encounter and how the woman had tears of gratitude in her eyes. Their son seemed to be having a real impact on people. One parent commented that her kid seemed more tuned in to her inner life. Previously, this teen had been preoccupied with images on social media that created unrealistic expectations.

One of the families with a kid who had made a U turn in his behavior had an aunt in Montecito, California. A well-known talk show host happened to live on the same cul de sac. Over cocktails on a neighbor's patio, the television celebrity heard about the unusual phenomenon taking place with the teenagers in Evanston, Illinois.

The following month Grace and Mike sat with the Abernaults watching the television broadcast when Jack and Dr. McGloin were interviewed about the lessons in the Anamchara Text. Jack's parents eventually had come around after a few weeks of uncomfortable tension in the home. Charlie sat on his mom's lap while his parents sat amazed as they saw their son on the television screen.

"Thank you for joining us. Today we are going to be talking to a young man, Jack Abernault, and Dr. Elizabeth McGloin from the University of Chicago."

The host gave a brief description of the enneagram and the significance of the teaching.

"So, I understand this material came from an ancient text. Is that correct?"

"Yes, we translated this Anamchara Text that was sitting in the college archives," said Dr. McGloin.

"And Jack, you helped figure out the personality puzzle by chance? You met this scholar while you were researching a school assignment?"

"Yeah, I happened to be in the building. I overheard Dr. McGloin discussing the diagram with the librarian. On their table I saw a familiar design. I recognized it matched the one in my paper about Pythagoras."

Then, the interviewer said, "Even I remember Pythagoras from my high school math class. So I understand you believe these insights could help solve climate issues? How can that be? That seems quite a leap?"

Dr. McGloin explained.

"Well, I've been researching the reasons why green technologies haven't caught on. It turns out that the problem lies within people. The enneagram, in the Anamchara Text, shows nine gifts, each with its own blind spot. Everyone has one of these. The teaching tells how to recognize the pattern and then to make a shift in a specific way. With this new clarity, people can change their priorities. Green choices become a viable option. Policies follow the evolved leadership of individuals. The result is that we can turn back the tide on climate. Of course, we must act fast."

"What a wonderful coincidence that you two met. And I understand that the National Institutes of Health along with the Department of Energy are funding the personality type podcasts as we speak."

"Yes, it's a collaboration," said Dr. McGloin.

"So, Jack, I hope you got an A on that project."

"Yes, ma'me, I did." Jack smiled into the camera, knowing Grace and Mike would be howling.

"Oh, my gosh. He's *such* a good liar," said Grace, throwing a potato chip at the TV.

"Well, he couldn't very well talk about aliens and a flying glass cube, now could he?" said Mike.

CHAPTER SIXTEEN

All Vehicles, Big and Small

THE NEXT WEEK, JACK AND HIS FRIENDS presented the personality map from the Anamchara Text at the high school. There had been so much interest after the television broadcast, that the faculty felt it was time to offer a workshop. The morning was going well. During the questions, one girl who sounded irritated asked if the enneagram was stereotyping, putting people in boxes. Jack responded.

"You see, the thing is, you're already in a box. We all are. This model offers a way to get out of the box."

"Interesting. I'll have to think about it," the girl conceded, and sat down.

Suddenly, the auditorium went dark. A loud buzzing filled the room. Kids called out in distress. Jack reached for his phone, flipping on his flashlight feature.

"O.K. everybody, stay calm. Turn on your phone flashlights, and we'll see what's going on."

Jack passed the wings of the stage, and then walked out in the hall that was also dark. He heard running. He spun around to see a figure in the dim corridor moving fast. Jack thought the person somehow looked familiar, but he couldn't quite place him. Mike joined in the chase, but they lost the guy when he took an unexpected turn, disappearing between the gym and the cafeteria. Finally, they went back to find someone to turn on the lights.

A minute later they passed another exit, and Jack saw a copper-colored sports car peel out of the parking lot. The car triggered something that he couldn't seem to put together.

The building custodian rounded the corner.

"Someone called the office about the light issue," the man said.

The loud buzzing continued.

Mike and Jack followed him into the storeroom, seeing rows of metal boxes with levers and wires for each bank of lights.

Flipping the switches, the custodian smiled.

"Someone must be playing a prank on you all today."

Suddenly, Jack felt a jolt. A sudden understanding. A body alarm in his gut. Without a word, he reached up and set off the fire alarm.

"What the hell! What are you doing?" The custodian said.

"We *have* to evacuate the school," Jack said.

Running back into the auditorium, Jack passed students streaming for the exits. The buzzing had stopped.

Minutes later, they heard the thin stream of sirens growing to a loud wail until six fire trucks pulled up in front of the building. The heavy brakes screeched to a halt.

Jack waved down one of the firefighters.

"Don't go in their without hazmat suits," Jack warned.

"You have to stand back."

"You don't understand. I think someone released nanobots," said Jack.

"Nano what?" The firefighter asked.

"Nanobots. Mechanical bug like things," said Jack.

"Are you the one who pulled the fire alarm?" asked the firefighter.

"Yes, to get the kids away from the nanobots," said Jack.

The urgency in the man's expression shifted then, as something seemed to dawn on him. Signaling the EMT, he said quietly into his body microphone.

"I think we may have a 10-96."

Seeing the exchange between the firefighter and Jack, the principal walked over and spoke with the firefighter.

Jack overheard his name.

"He's been under a great deal of pressure, and his grades have dropped," said the principal.

"Look, he's walking away," the chief said.

Jack was approaching a group of kids, standing at the curb.

"Anybody have a bad headache?" asked Jack.

Several sophomores who had been sitting in the front row raised their hands.

Now the EMTs were coming for him . . . with a stretcher.

Jack's eyes widened, his panic growing.

Protesting he resisted the EMT's who were urging him to sit on the stretcher.

"These kids say they have headaches. They've been *attacked* with nanobots," said Jack.

"Sit down here a minute and tell me about them," said the EMT. In his soothing voice, he was clearly trying to settle Jack down.

A second EMT covered Jack's shoulders with a foil blanket.

Did they think he was in shock? Maybe having a psychotic episode? Or a drug overdose?

Jack was frantic and he was blurting out words.

"A nanobot is a tiny mechanical delivery system. It puts drugs in the body. Tinkers with the brain. You need to tell the hospital right away," Jack said urgently.

He sounded crazy.

"And I *don't* need a blanket," he said, pushing it off his shoulders. His body, however, was trembling.

By then, students were complaining they didn't feel well. The first responders could not ignore the symptoms, so they pulled on their protective suits. Several more ambulances pulled up and the teenagers with headaches were ushered to the side.

The principal insisted all the classes get checked out by a doctor.

After an hour in the auditorium, the firefighters, returned, hauling sensors that had detected no foreign substances.

"Nothin in there. They're all imagining their symptoms. Power of suggestion," said a firefighter.

Jack struggled. He felt the EMT's steady him and pull tight the straps over his chest.

"*Something's* in there," he said, begging them to look again.

Quickly, they rolled his gurney toward the ambulance, set on his hospitalization.

Mike saw his friend's frantic plea.

He phoned his dad for help.

Mr. Farrell listened to his son. Immediately he contacted the police chief, demanding they take Jack's warning seriously or there would be legal repercussions. Well known in the community, this attorney was not to be ignored.

The fire chief's cell rang. It was the hospital. The doctor told him that nanobots had indeed appeared on the first of the brain scans.

"The kid is right. They found nanobots," called out the fire chief to the police captain.

"And I *still* don't know what a nanobot is! Just how am I supposed to find them?" asked the fire chief.

Jack was now in the back of an ambulance, and he called out the back hatch.

"Nanobots have a metallic component. The construction site at the corner over there has an industrial magnet. Use that to sweep the school."

The firefighters huddled. After a moment, four of them rushed off to the construction site.

Two hours later, the fire fighters exited the school, carrying special containers. Shaking their heads in disbelief, they had captured over a thousand nanobots.

Four black SUV's screeched to the curb. A dozen FBI agents walked at a fast clip toward the police chief. The FBI guy who seemed to be in charge wore a jacket with *Bernstein* on the back. After flipping his badge, he took custody of the containers with the high-tech devices.

Jack now sat on the curb, wiped out.

What a close call. Could have been wrong. They'd been ready to put him away . . . in the loony bin. But that guy running away. The buzzing. The copper car. Triggered something in his gut.

Hope those kids were Ok. Should get checked out too. Better tell Grace and Mike.

His teeth chattered, and he was still shivering.

Attacks were coming from all directions . . . at Charlie, at the school, and at the polar ice cap.

Pulling the foil blanket back over his shoulders, Jack rocked. Then he was taken to the hospital and underwent the long overdue brain scan.

What had begun as a day of lessons from the Anamchara Text had descended into the largest terror attack in Illinois history. However, that was *not* the story reported to the public.

The local television news that night led with a story about an electrical mishap at the high school. According to the news anchor, chemicals from the cooling system left some students hospitalized. Agent Bernstein had seen to it there was no mention of nanobots. Scores of nondisclosure paperwork had been signed that day. The FBI would see to it that the facts were suppressed. Because if the truth got out, there would be panic.

Surgeons, under the direction of the CDC, implanted miniscule screens to filter any nanobots from the blood streams of the teenagers.

Jack feared what the doctors might find on his brain scan

* * *

That evening, a furious Vincent Marcov paced in his compound. His attack on the school had been thwarted. And he hadn't received the publicity he had anticipated. Assuming it was only a matter of time until the climate collapsed, he figured nanobots released at Jack's school would offer him an entertaining sideshow.

He had watched Jack's interview on television, and it drove him wild that lessons were taking place right under his nose.

The fools were taking counter measures!

That could not stand.

The situation *had* to be remedied. Marcov figured he was home free with his mission to destroy the earth's climate. But now, with the Anamchara Text's dangerous teachings spreading like wildfire, he couldn't have the population growing in self- awareness. He was too close to completing the murderous virus, knocking out the polar ice cap, and escaping to Sophia.

So, he had contacted a dependable operative, arranging for the nanobot deployment at the high school. There remained plenty of complicit folks, greedy for more of the proverbial "pie," and who remained eager to add another shiny car to the driveway.

Then, that insufferable kid alerted the cops, and the hospital scans discovered the nanobots. He needed to switch tactics. Before the day was out, the scientist accepted delivery of a giant 3D printer. He read the assembly instructions, and after several hours scrutinizing the illustrations, he added the last component. He fired up the massive copy machine, fed the data, and watched as the contraption built a vehicle out of liquid titanium paste. The printer head hummed, moving side to side as the scientist glowered. Two hours later, the first satellite bumped off the platform. Excited with the quality of the workmanship on the craft, he reloaded the tank on the machine.

Vincent Marcov knew it was time to go big. He needed a base of operations, a compound out in the wilderness where he could build and house his satellites. Before the day was out, he had paid bit coin for a ten-thousand-acre tract of land in the Canadian wilds that included a large hangar. His new fleet of satellites would be manufactured there, and then deployed, bringing him one step closer to obliterating the entire polar ice cap.

CHAPTER SEVENTEEN

Debriefing

THE FOLLOWING AFTERNOON, TWO FBI agents appeared at the Abernault's door. Soon it became apparent that Jack remained a prime suspect in the school attack. Hadn't he been the one who reported the barely visible nanobots, setting off the emergency? The agents wanted to know how this was possible.

"So, we understand your son has been ill. That he's been under a lot of stress. We also know he received a lot of attention after his television interview."

Mr. Abernault's face went purple.

"Are you kidding? My son *saved* the kids yesterday. And now you come here and imply he had something to do with that attack?"

"Well, it's just that sometimes, kids want to play the hero. Maybe need the attention," said the agent.

"Let me explain," Jack said.

"Nope. Don't say *one* word. We need a lawyer here," said Mr. Abernault.

The doorbell rang. Jack's mom returned in a moment. Behind her, filling the door, stood the FBI agent in charge the previous day.

Jack's mom introduced him as Agent Bernstein.

The large man addressed the other officers.

"I'll take over here. Agent Walker, Agent Reilly. You're needed in the office right now."

After the two agents left, Bernstein turned to the family.

"Sorry about that. Lots going on today. I assure you that Jack is *not* a suspect. Anything but."

The Abernaults looked relieved. Jack slumped on the sofa. Letting out a deep sigh he closed his eyes.

"Can I get you some coffee?" asked his mom.

"That would be great. Thanks."

Bernstein turned to Jack.

"How are you feeling today? I understand the doctor checked you out and there's evidence of a previous nanobot," said Bernstein.

"WHAT?" said the Abernaults all at once.

"This is the first we're hearing about this," said Jack's dad.

So, he *had* been infected. The devices *had* kept him from telling his parents about Charlie and the nanobot. And *had* caused his cheating in school?

But then he thought. *No*, if he was honest with himself, and although deception had been easier, deep inside, he knew that there had remained a choice to choose truth each time he had lied, each time he had cheated, and each time he had withheld information.

"I'm sorry to drop that information on you like that. Results of your scan were just finalized by the radiologist," said Bernstein.

"Apparently, the nanobots have cleared your system. The damage was minor."

"And *you* know all this, before *we* find out? What about HIPPA?" asked Jack's dad.

But Jack cut him off.

"Actually, that explains some things," Jack said.

His parents looked uneasy, wondering what Jack had been hiding.

"Tell me everything. Start from the beginning. Ok if I record this?"

Jack nodded, looking at his dad, who shrugged his shoulders. Clearly, he was processing the privacy breech of Jack's medical record.

But Jack knew he had to trust someone, so he told how the lights had gone out, and how a loud buzzing had filled the auditorium. And that he had seen the guy running, and then driving off in a copper-colored sports car. He explained the guy looked familiar.

"I suddenly had this overwhelming feeling that nanobots had been released. There'd been a loud buzzing sound," said Jack.

Ms. Abernault returned with the coffee, and Bernstein took a sip.

"Nice, Thanks."

"I happen to have some background on nanobot attacks," said the agent.

"So, we don't need a lawyer here?" asked Mr. Abernault.

"No, but what I'm going to share is classified. For reasons that will become apparent, your family is cleared to hear this information. However, you'll need to check with me if someone else needs to know. National security overrides everything, even HIPPA regulations."

And with that, he pulled out some confidentiality papers for the three of them to sign.

Relieved that Jack wasn't in trouble, Mr. Abernault carefully read the documents. Then they all added their signatures. Jack had signed similar papers the previous day at the hospital, feeling he existed now in a world of secrecy.

Bernstein gathered up the papers, sliding them into a folder. Then, the agent began to talk.

"Ok. Where to start? Several months before you met Joseph Spencer, he hired a private investigator who pulled Jack's DNA from a paper cup he threw out at a soccer practice. You see, it seems when your mother submitted her DNA to that genealogy database, Spencer was alerted that a match for him might be found in your family. The private detective's work and the DNA confirmed what he suspected."

"Apparently, Jack, you shared a rare string of chromosomes with him, a certain maternal haplogroup, K2B1a. This blood line remains unusual, even within your extended family. While the gene has popped up on all the continents, the sequence seems connected to green eyes and to possessing a talent for problem solving. The migration route of this gene cluster was studied by the National Geographic. This line traveled from Africa to Southeast Asia. There's a bloom of the haplogroup in the center of China, then east along the Silk Road, back into the Rhine Valley. From there, it disperses, down into Italy, and north to Finland. Seven percent of Ireland's population contains this sequence. But you and Spencer have some additional mutations."

"Whaaaat!" said Jack. "Spencer orchestrated your meeting at the family reunion, even ordering your favorite apple pie to lure you over to the buffet. You see, he did his homework," said Bernstein.

Jack's ears burned. This felt like a betrayal, like he was a pawn in some bizarre genome conspiracy? Manipulated and lied to, his insides churned.

"Using DNA off a paper cup? Is that even legal?" asked his dad.

"Well, you see, by this time, Spencer was desperate. He had been receiving threats, and he feared he might not have long to live. Wanting to prepare for the worst, he needed to find a relative with his special string of chromosomes to pass on his legacy."

This information was sinking in, while Jack's mind was scrolling through the memory of the reunion afternoon. Now that he thought about it, Spencer had seemed to steer the conversation, even eliciting Jack's passion for solving mechanical problems. He also remembered, the elderly man said something about how, even as a boy, he had been more serious than other kids his age, thinking about his future, and considering his role.

But there was more to this than simple deception. A rush of sadness and disappointment, then fear, but also anger, rushed in. Spencer had feared for his life, intent on passing on vital information to someone he hoped could carry on his work. Jack felt knotted up inside, his feelings snarled and snapped. The connection to Spencer was a tainted blessing. The man had put him and his family in great danger.

On the other hand, the inheritance connected Jack to a larger scheme. But it bothered him that he hadn't chosen.

He had *been* chosen.

Bernstein added that the federal government had worked with Joseph Spencer's company for decades on reducing carbon emissions. And on a regular basis, they had encountered Vincent Marcov's sabotage.

Jack recalled that Harold, Winnifred, and Dr. McGloin all referred to Marcov's criminal record, so it was no wonder that the FBI had kept the fiend in their sights.

Bernstein continued, sharing that Marcov's felonies had spanned decades, escalating over the years to include deadly environmental catastrophes. The European Union and Interpol had issued international warrants for the scientist. To date, Vincent Marcov had stacked up hundreds of convictions for climate crimes. Unfortunately, the agent admitted, Marcov always evaded capture, remaining one step ahead of law enforcement. Different agencies had staged all kinds of traps, but their tactics had never been successful.

"Either he vanishes into thin air, or he repels swat teams with a microwave defense system."

Then Bernstein shifted in his chair.

"There's *one* more thing. This may be hard to hear, but I think you and your parents should be aware of this background," said the agent, looking down at his coffee cup.

The Abernaults looked uncomfortable.

"Last Fall, the video game hacking accusation and your arrest . . ." said Bernstein.

"Wait. What?" said Jack.

"Spencer was behind all of it. Your keyboard was overtaken by his technician. He needed to see how you would hold up under pressure," said Bernstein.

Anger and tears welled up in Jack. All those months of worry and guilt. And he had been *set up* for hacking on that computer.

"That is vicious," said his mom.

"Against the law," said his dad.

"There seemed no other way. Spencer knew he was running out of time. He had to be sure about you, Jack," said the agent.

"Do you have any idea the stress that case put on me and my family?" said Jack.

"In the end, Spencer paid a *huge* fine to make the case go away. Of course, all of this was classified. The community service you and your friends had to complete was just a cover," said Bernstein.

All this time, Jack had blamed Grace for distracting him. Now he recalled, tapping the keyboard into the classified part of the website *was* suspicious. For an instant, the code seemed to shiver, to flip. Now he knew he *had* been right. Grace was innocent and so was he. Spencer was turning out to be *not* such a nice guy after all. Manipulating other people into his web of intrigue? Then Jack figured that someone like Spencer who ran with the *big dogs* probably had a comfort level with bending the rules. A rush of anger came over him.

Jack felt unglued, needing to unburden himself from all the secrets he had been keeping. He wouldn't be like Spencer, drawing unsuspecting folks into his battles.

So, Jack told the agent everything . . . all about Max and Izzy, and the Council, and Sophia.

The agent sat back, sighing.

"I was aware of the space/time portal, but thanks for filling in some gaps. We need to be on the same page. The Sophian children must be part of the Ghost Fleet," said Bernstein.

"The *what?*" asked Mr. Abernault.

"The Ghost Fleet refers to alien visits from an advanced civilization. This information remains highly classified as you can imagine the panic that would result if this news got out."

But before they could respond, Charlie began to howl. Jack's mom left to get him.

Moments later they heard her screaming.

"He's gone!"

Jack felt his heart shatter as they all rushed up the stairs.

Sobbing and hysterical, his mother sat slumped on the floor, holding the stuffed bunny.

"Please, no," begged Jack.

At that instant, Jack felt a seismic shift register in his body. It was as if a pilot light within him ignited in a flash. Any vestiges of doubt about defeating Marcov evaporated. He *had* to save his brother. Agent Bernstein was on his phone.

"APB for Vincent Marcov's black SUV. Check all the CCTV in Evanston. Get the helicopter here. NOW."

"He took Charlie to Sophia, I'm sure of it," said Jack. Bernstein thought this sounded plausible. Then he asked if Jack had a way to summon the glass cube. Because if he did, now was the time.

Just then Grace walked in the hall.

"Door was open. Hi everyone."

Immediately, she sensed something was very wrong, her eyes fixing on the FBI letters on the agent's jacket.

"Grace, Charlie's gone," Jack said.

"Oh no. When?"

"Just now. We heard him cry out," Jack said.

Then a thought occurred to Jack. Maybe going to Morningside might help because the porthole to Sophia rested above the estate. As soon as the words were out of his mouth, the agent agreed. A half hour later, they were running out the door, boarding the helicopter that had landed in the middle of Orrington Avenue. It was decided the parents would stay home.

On the flight to Lake Forest, Jack racked his brain about a way to reach Max and Izzy, berating himself that he had never thought to ask them for a way to communicate. The agent looked grim. He knew the statistics in cases of abduction. The clock was ticking.

They all thought of the helpless baby.

Fifteen minutes later, they hovered above the estate. The blades whirled, sending the leaves flying across the lawn. The pilot lowered the helicopter, landing near the pond. The three quickly disembarked and ran over the stone path. Jack entered the code in the new keypad, and he pushed the door open. They moved quickly down the halls, turning into the stone passage. They followed Jack until they reached the hidden door marked by the stenciled eye within the triangle, behind the tall ship mural. They stepped through the door where Jack had first encountered the two little brothers.

Once inside, they were not sure what to look for, hoping something in the room might help. Grace saw an old-fashioned telephone, but when she lifted the receiver, she found the wires disconnected. Jack picked up a small, oval mirror, thinking a reflection might signal a message if it were positioned in a certain way. But Agent Bernstein shook his head and dismissed it as "too small to signal through heavy clouds and atmosphere."

Feeling a sense of desperation, Jack's eyes settled on a dusty old phonograph sitting in the corner. He noticed it was hooked up to some kind of a high-tech speaker system. Oddly, a decal showed a satellite capability. He grabbed a vinyl recording of Bach's Fugue in D Minor, placing it on the turntable. Carefully, he set the needle on the outer groove. Loud crackling began. After a moment, powerful organ music blasted out of the machine. The three grabbed cushions off the furniture, covering their ears. They grimaced as the music built to a crescendo, shattering the windows with the force. Jack thought he actually could *see* the bursting sound, like in a graphic novel. But, amazingly, before the musical piece ended, Max and Izzy were peeking through the window, wearing giant headphones.

"Holy Cow, turn that off!" yelled Max.

"Nobody in the next three galaxies can get any sleep with that racket," said Izzy.

Jack pulled the plug and, never so glad to see anyone, hugged the boys, and then told them about Charlie's abduction.

Upon seeing the silver and moss green haired children, Grace dropped her bag,

"Oh my gosh, they're adorable. And they talk like little birds, chirping and all."

Izzy beamed with the complement, but Max, bristling, stared her down. Then the two little boys ushered the FBI agent, Grace, and Jack to the glass time cube, which was still hissing from the recent voyage.

"Let's plan while we ride." said Jack.

The group climbed in the cube and moments later they were airborne. The roof and the gardens of Morningside along with the shores of Lake Michigan receded below them. Grace and the agent watched in amazement as they rocketed up, up, up.

"We feared this might happen. Vincent Marcov has been known to flee to Sophia after a crime. Let me check our planet's surveillance." Max said, opening a small tablet.

He tapped in a time frame, creating an electrical fence.

"Sure enough." Max said.

"Here it is! He flew through the portal and landed near a warehouse he owns under an alias."

"What now? What can we do?" Jack looked around.

Max admitted that although law enforcement on Sophia was advanced, Vincent Marcov also had evaded them. Then he looked thoughtfully at Grace and decided to turn the tables on this impudent girl who had diminished him as *adorable*.

"You know . . . Marcov has a soft spot for young ladies in distress. Odd, when you think of his history, but it's a chink in his armor. He's a complicated guy. You, my dear, might be able to breach his security," said Max.

Grace's nostrils flared at being referred to as *dear* and as *a lady in distress* by a cocky little boy with green hair. But then she thought of Charlie.

Max looked her over again. Disapprovingly, he shook his head.

"No, no . . . those Doc Martins and the camouflage jumpsuit aren't going to work."

"OK, whatever . . . Do a makeover," she said.

Hearing that, Max brightened, producing a leather valise stashed under the seats. He dug around, tossing suits and ties on the floor. Then he produced a wavy strawberry blond wig, a pink chiffon dress, and high heels. Noticing their surprise, he said, "Yeah, I know, but sometimes agents from Sophia need disguises for a caper. This one is my older sister's favorite dress," said Max. Jack quickly slid out of Grace's reach, as he saw her eyes pop in fury.

"Well, I do have a Chanel suit and pearls, if you want to go for subtle," said Max.

"Look Grace, I'm going to give you a special spray, so you'll be safe," said Bernstein.

Grace thought a moment.

"It's for Charlie, after all."

"You *sure?*" asked Jack.

"I am, and I can do the country club, girl next door routine. Whatever it takes," she said.

Disappearing behind a makeshift curtain, moments later, Grace appeared transformed from GI Jane to a version of a girl about to attend her first tea dance, circe 1950. Bright pink lipstick, fake eyelashes, and a splash of perfume completed the disguise. The get up made her look twenty-two.

Grace was gorgeous, Jack thought. Resigned to her mission, she sighed.

"The things we do for our friends," gesturing flirtatiously with her hands.

With deep pink press on nails, she knew her mother, at least, would have been proud.

"Wow. You're a looker." Max weighed in.

Grace settled a steely gaze on this cheeky kid.

But, unfazed, Max met her eyes.

"Grace you're a trooper. Now here's the plan. Marcov's security capabilities include air testing so he will be alerted to your presence by the perfume. You claim you have car trouble, your phone is not working, and you really need to call for help. Vincent Marcov has been known to help young ladies in the past. Something oddly chivalrous."

"Here's a spritzer," said the agent.

"Looks like perfume, but really a sleeping agent, so keep it away from your face when you spray it. Get as close to his nose as you can. He won't know what hit him." Bernstein said.

Then the cube landed on a soft patch of grass. The group climbed out of the cube and Jack recognized the familiar scent of Sophia's blossoms. Grace looked around, amazed at the sights.

"This is beyond *anything* I could have imagined," she said.

"Wish this visit was under better circumstances," said Jack.

"That's the capital building."

He pointed to a large titanium shape with gleaming sails that seemed to float in the middle of a pond. In front of this structure, a fountain sprayed bubbles that shimmered like 3D halos. Acres of ornamental grasses turned the landscape into rolling ocean-like waves.

Max ushered them into a small hover van, navigating the vehicle out of the park. After a few minutes moving a few feet above the ground, Max pulled back on a shift. They could feel the wheels contract and the van lifted eighty feet in the air. Caught by surprise, the earth visitors fell back.

"You could have warned us," Grace said irritably as she smoothed her crinoline skirts.

"Maybe use those seat belts," Max said.

Then he expertly steered over the treetops. Soon the warehouse roof came into view, and Max lowered the van behind a hedge of tall bushes. Jack's heart froze, recognizing the danger facing Grace. She was putting herself at terrible risk. But when he looked over at her, she radiated courage and purpose. She wasn't scared. She was determined.

Grace jumped out and raced over to the warehouse entrance, surprisingly adept at maneuvering in the high heels. She pushed the bell. In a few moments, a voice crackled, asking her to state her business. The overhead camera swiveled, and Grace smiled sweetly, explaining her predicament. The voice hesitated, but the door lock clicked, opening. Grace stepped inside the warehouse and found herself in a dark hallway. Ahead a light glowed at the end of the passageway and she began to move toward it. When she rounded the corner Grace came face to face with the infamous Vincent Marcov.

Shocked, she thought he looked more like the neighborhood pharmacist, than an intergalactic criminal. Dressed in a cardigan, and a stained bow tie, the thin man appeared harmless. Grace controlled her surprise, assuming the role of a flustered young woman in distress who was just so, SO grateful that he was at home as she was desperate to call for a tow truck.

"Of course, young lady. I'll make the call."

He turned to pick up his phone.

Quick as a chipmunk, she pulled out the spritzer and sprayed him directly in the face. Immediately, he slumped on the sofa. Grace sent the signal, and the first agent inside, taped a warrant on the entrance. Soon the place swarmed with cops looking for Charlie.

Searching everywhere, they found the baby in a make-shift crib on the second floor. They tried to rouse him, but he seemed drugged, his pulse weak. The baby groaned as the paramedics lifted his little body on to a gurney. Quickly, he was rolled out to a medical helicopter.

Meanwhile the officers rushed to arrest Marcov, but he vanished right before their eyes. Only the tell-tail burning smell filled the room. Marcov was gone.

"No way!" said the cops. Agent Bernstein saw the frustration on the faces of the law enforcement officers. Even on Sophia, it seemed, Dr. Marcov had the advantage. So, it was no small miracle that young Grace had so totally fooled the fiend that evening.

At the hospital, the doctors assured Jack they would do everything they could for Charlie. The next twenty-four hours would be key in the baby's prognosis. Max reminded them that Sophia had advanced treatments. Charlie was in good hands.

A tear escaped, rolling down Jack's cheek. Grace put her arm around his shoulders, pulling him in close.

"This is all my fault," said Jack.

"I should've said *no* to the Council. Charlie might die, or never recover. That innocent baby. What have I done?" He rocked in agony.

Grace tried to comfort him.

"Look we don't know anything yet. The doctor said twenty-four hours. And this is no ordinary hospital. Can you imagine how good the medical advances are? We have to pray."

Agent Bernstein joined them. He complemented Grace on her performance at the warehouse, adding that if she ever wanted a job at the FBI, to give him a call.

Exhausted, Grace looked down at the frothy pink dress. A set of lashes fell in her lap. She felt ridiculous.

Jack buried his head in his hands, curling up to contain his grief. "I'll be right back," she said, and grabbed the bag with her boots and jumpsuit so she could change.

Then she leaned over and kissed him on the lips.

Jack returned the kiss, but then slumped back, when Charlie's face came to mind.

Grace entered the washroom, and minutes later, returned, looking like herself, face scrubbed, dressed in camo, and clad in her signature big boots.

Without a moment's thought, she unceremoniously stuffed the pink chiffon layers, and the wig into a nearby garbage can.

Max, however, remained more than a little peeved that the disguise sat in the trash. And so quickly he darted inside to retrieve the couture. Glowering, Max complained under his breath. It was hard enough for agents to deliver all those gold cylinders without being detected. And he worried what his sister would say if her favorite dress was missing from the collection.

It was decided that Jack and Grace would stay by Charlie's bedside for the next twenty-four hours. All they could do now was wait. Jack watched through the glass in the hospital corridor, observing the doctors scanning Charlie repeatedly with a high-tech wand. With each pass of the device, the nurse adjusted the medicine in the tubes connected to his brother. Another nurse assured him that the toddler was sedated.

Time ticked slowly. Jack and Grace waited in the lounge, and finally dozed off. After many hours a nurse gently shook them awake. They heard voices down the hall, louder, and then more muffled as doctors in white coats turned into Charlie's hospital room. Grace and Jack watched through the glass, as they saw the nurse pull the tubes from Charlie. The toddler began to stir. The nurse beckoned them to enter the hospital room.

Another aide brought a silver pyramid shaped balloon and Charlie's eyes widened as he reached for the string.

Then he started to scream for his mama.

More doctors filed in, and Charlie cried louder. Stepping to the side of the bed, the nurse, put a blue pad on the child's arm. In moments, the toddler quieted down, his eyelids lowering.

"The scan shows some damage. There may be some limping, but overall, your brother is going to recover."

"That's wonderful. Thank you. When can we take him home? My parents must be out of their minds," Jack asked with relief flooding his voice, choking out the words.

"After Charlie has lunch, you can get on your way."

"So soon? Is it safe for him to travel?" Jack asked.

"Yes, we will make sure he's properly hydrated. But he's good to go. You got him here in time, or the outcome might have been different. It appears Marcov was about to experiment with CRISPER. It seems he wanted to graft the green-eyed gene for himself if Charlie, in fact, carries that DNA sequence. His lab notes indicate that he wanted to boost his capabilities as a scientist. And they also found more nanobot devices in the warehouse."

"I don't know how we can ever thank you. We were so worried," said Jack.

Grace took hold of him, kissing him on the lips.

The hospital staff smiled, and they filed out of the room, leaving the two entwined teens.

After a lunch of something resembling carrot mush, the nurses wrapped Charlie in a quilted robe, and slid his feet into little silver slippers. Jack carried Charlie as Max led them to the cube and entered the auto pilot destination. They waved to the hospital staff as the vehicle lifted off, carrying the five of them. Fortunately, Charlie slept all the way home. The cube glided through the portal, and then landed on Evanston's beach, behind some shrubs so as not to attract any attention.

Cold winds blew off the Lake, so the place was deserted. The Abernaults were waiting. A blast of air hit Charlie's cheeks, and he awoke for a few moments, smiling when he saw his mom. Then he drifted off again from the mild sedative still coursing through his body.

They dropped Grace at her home while Jack felt tears of gratitude well up, stinging his eyes. Charlie had survived. A hard lump stuck in his throat.

His mother turned around to face him.

"We're so grateful that you saved our baby."

Jack swallowed hard. If only they knew the *whole* story. Yeah, sure this time he had stepped up. But what about the first time. Could he ever forgive himself? Although maybe his will *had* been weakened by the nanobots. He certainly *had* felt overwhelmed.

As Jack sat in the back of the car, he thought about the rogue scientist. It seemed like it wouldn't be long now before things would come to a head with Marcov. When it came to the planet's survival, Jack felt he'd always be playing catch up. He was no match for the scientist. Maybe he'd have a stroke of luck here and there. A hint of intuition. Help from Max and Izzy. But, Marcov led an army of minions, nanobots and satellites. He could even disappear on demand. It seemed hopeless.

CHAPTER EIGHTEEN

Vincent Marcov

S QUAWKING CROWS AWOKE VINCENT MARCOV the next day. He rolled off the sofa on to the warehouse floor, bumping his head on a crate. Disoriented, a bitter after taste in his mouth brought back the memory of the encounter with the cunning girl in pink who had duped him. *HIM!* The effects of the sleeping potion were wearing off, but all he could think about was revenge.

Vincent knew he had narrowly escaped this time.

The ability to disappear depended on an ancient meditation he had mastered after a visit to a Himalayan monastery. Only two monks knew this method, and, after learning the technique, Marcov had shoved them off a cliff.

An instant before Grace's spritzer's drug overwhelmed him, Vincent had focused just long enough to disappear.

But it had been a close call.

After a pot of coffee, he boarded his space vehicle, and slipped back through the space/time portal, landing near Evanston. It was time to strike back.

Marcov descended the steps in his compound that evening. The rogue scientist always felt he did his best work at night. Gearing up for a retaliatory strike, his thoughts turned to grievances from long ago. Faces of mean children, sneering on a playground, tormenting him. Then the sting of betrayal by his only brother. The brother he had loved. Who had deserted him. Leaving him alone within a ring of bullies. Something inside the little boy had cracked that day as if a piece of him had floated away on an ice flow. The betrayal broke him, crushed him, sending him on a path of revenge. He was left with a festering wound in place of a soul. He was an old man now. But he hadn't forgotten. They would pay. He would destroy the playgrounds, the children's faces, all the children's children, the entire planet.

Marcov grabbed a set of blueprints, spreading them over his desk. He scanned them, his glasses balanced on the tip of his nose. Resorting to paper plans, he feared the FBI might gain access to any designs left on his computer.

It had only been days since the television networks covered the disaster at the high school. Reporters jumping out of the news vans to cover his escapades always gave him a buzz. But then it had all changed.

His nanobots had been discovered, his plans upended. There hadn't even been mention of the devices. And then the girl with the strawberry blonde curls had gone and fooled him. Marcov felt bamboozled. He had tried to help her. Then she had turned around and returned his favor by drugging him. The deceit stuck in his craw.

Now he eyed his lab's refrigerator. Where the glass vials waited. Filled with an almost ready dose. Marcov loved the symmetry of taking out both Joseph Spencer and Jack Abernault with a virus. Anticipation of the kill only added to his pleasure. Marcov could wait, bide his time. After all, he relished the stalking, toying really, with his prey. He could take out Jack at any time, but he fashioned himself a kind of a theater director, producing a performance. His cast of actors. The Masons, Lindy Simons, Lutetia, Tanya Stokes and others, had been instructed to terrify Jack with stories of treachery and nanobots. Vincent Marcov loved his role as puppet master, knowing just how to turn the screws. Carefully, he had targeted his attacks at Jack's most obvious vulnerability . . . the boy's unfailing tendency to worry.

Marcov needed that death for Jack would come with suffering, but not before months of terror. So, no need to rush. At this point, the virus concoction only needed some minor tweaking. Marcov's drama would time the youth's murder after the destruction of the icecap, so the kid would witness the planet's destruction. The green-eyed bloodline would be finished on earth. Then he would graft the remaining *K2b1a* gene into his bride. Because, on Sophia he would begin a new dynasty.

So, with that in mind, Marcov prepared for a night of wonders. He poured himself a hot chocolate, and commanded Alexa to play *The Dance Macabre in G Minor.*

Tonight, the rogue scientist worked on a plan to pollute Chicago's water system. His target was that strawberry blond minx who would drink the tainted water. He had traced her cell phone ping to the Northshore suburbs of Chicago, and he smiled at the image in his mind of her writhing in pain. Still, he felt dumping toxins in the Lake remained too pedestrian.

Nothing short of a spectacle would do.

"Maybe produce tall waterspouts off the shore. Add in some special effects, colorful lighting, some nasty toxins, and . . . Cirque du Lac accomplished. Lovely, but deadly, water columns dancing terror into Chicago," he said, bowing to the portrait of Cronus. Then swaying to the dark chords, he envisioned his environmental destruction. The reviews would be epic.

* * *

The next day, Agent Bernstein answered a call from the Evanston Police Department.

"Great," he said into his cell phone.

"We finally got a break.

The law enforcement drones, the ones that look like gulls, flying along the lake, had shot some interesting video through an open window.

Moments later Vincent Marcov's blueprint popped up as an attachment in Bernstein's email. Within the hour, he gathered experts from his new group of consultants. His team now included people from different backgrounds, with fresh perspectives so they could paint a fuller picture of a crisis. Bernstein instructed them to find a way to stop Marcov's plan.

"Good, you're all here. OK, People. How can we stop a barge equipped with a massive industrial fan from creating waterspouts over the Lake? Keep in mind, toxic chemicals may be in play that would overwhelm the city's water intake filters."

Agent Garcia, a handsome guy with a fresh haircut, spoke first.

"We could enforce a no-craft zone, and regulate his ability to operate the barge."

Bernstein added this idea to the overhead screen. Garcia had come to the task force from the legal department and approached a problem from a rules and regulations framework.

"I don't feel we can justify that action until we're absolutely convinced there are toxins. Too many people would be inconvenienced."

Bernstein noted this empathetic approach, reflected this agent's previous job in human resources.

Agent Ratcliffe made a show of taking off his sport jacket and hanging it on the back of his chair. Then he spoke.

"If the attack comes at night, strobe lights mounted on boats would mess up Marcov's navigation capability."

He looked around to see if he had impressed anyone. Satisfied, he struck a thoughtful pose.

"Interesting. Great, when you guys think outside of the box," said Bernsteion.

Ratcliffe, with a marketing background, knew all about systems, and, also, how to disrupt them.

Agent Cucinelli's talent, on the other hand, was imagining fresh ways of looking at a problem.

"Thinking of special effects, a giant projector could create an image of the skyline out on the lake. . . confuse Marcov . . . sort of a high-tech Potemkin Village."

Peering over her reading glasses, Agent Meyer disagreed.

"Focus on the toxins. Find a chemical formula to reduce the effect of an attack."

Agent Williams, a veteran, added his two cents.

"We need military back up as the threat qualifies as a pending National Disaster."

Dressed in a navy suit, with a pin striped tie, he quickly ran a threat algorithm on his tablet. Somehow, he always seemed to look worried.

As his agents talked, Agent Bernstein scribbled the suggestions on the screen.

"Come on people, I haven't heard from everyone."

The room was quiet.

Then John Yang, an agent on loan from forgery, broke the silence.

"Why not invite him to a surprise party with an attached copy of his blueprint."

Laughter filled the room, clearing the heaviness in the air. Yang, wearing his signature tropical patterned shirt, had been recruited from a Vegas, high stakes gambling table. He had jumped at the chance to join the FBI, always up for something new.

"Torpedo the barge out of the water."

Heads turned to Agent Adebayo, dressed in a dashiki. A man of action, he had come from West Point. He had brains and brawn, and likely would serve someday as military brass.

"OOOOO-Kaay...that's one idea," said Bernstein.

Then he turned to Agent El Safid.

"We haven't heard from you yet. Whatcha thinkin?"

"Stop deliveries to his compound. We know he requires lab supplies. Sometimes, when you slow the process, it gives the criminal more time to slip up."

"Hmmmm, Interesting," said Bernstein.

Then he ran the list of strategies through a computer that calculated the pros and cons of each idea. In a few minutes the computer dinged, generating a best solution. Stopping the deliveries came out first place. Last on the list was *torpedo barge*. However, Agent Bernstein pointed to that last option.

"It may come to that. Thanks everyone. Great work. Now get to work on blocking those shipments."

The next morning Vincent Marcov paced in his office and watched for the delivery truck. He was expecting a crate of glass filaments, but when he checked the delivery status a message from customs listed his shipment as *detained due to national security*. Furious, he threw the laptop against the wall, blasting it to smithereens. He required the lab supplies for his toxin, and now his spectacle on the Lake would need to be scrapped. His retaliation aimed at the strawberry blond girl . . . foiled for now.

* * *

Up, beyond the clouds, and through the space/time portal, the Council on Sophia gathered. News had reached their ears about Charlie's abduction, and they knew Marcov was engineering a virus meant to kill Jack. They also were aware of Jack's nanobot infection, that had left him vulnerable to cheating, lying, and the CEO's apprenticeship offer. The fancy suited businessmen, Marcov's agents, had drugged Jack and left him in the pit to weaken the kid's resolve. Later they planned to recruit Jack into their web of destruction.

However, Marcov hadn't anticipated that Jack's time in the dark hole would serve as a soul-searching experience. Once the boy confessed his betrayal to his principles, Izzy and his older brother had rescued him. Max dressed as a limousine driver, had worn special boots so his feet reached the gas and brake pedals. He replaced the original chauffeur and had driven Jack to the conference center. Izzy had dealt with the first driver, shuffling him into the glass cube and dumping him at a 24-hour fast-food restaurant in the Wisconsin Dells. It was likely he would have some *splaining to* do.

The Council now debated about how they might support Jack. The chairman noted that interfering with Jack's mission could pose a problem because a hero's journey required overcoming adversity. Even when the Anamchara Text was damaged during the transport to the earth, they had not intervened. And their trust in Jack had paid off. Because, rather than give up, he had followed their instructions *to listen with his head, with his heart, and with his gut intuition.* So, in spite of the obstacles, the clever boy had made sense of the book. And he had recruited his friends to help him along the way.

But the stakes were growing. The earth was running out of time. The planet's deteriorating climate, and the threat of mass migrations to Sophia worried them all. They didn't know how they could help. And there was always the danger of unintended consequences. So, the Council decided, rather than fumble with a clumsy intervention, they would wait. For now, Jack was on his own.

In the corner of the chamber, Izzy sat on his little chair, listening with growing concern. While he didn't yet have voting rights, he knew he needed a plan, even if it meant banishment from the Council's apprenticeship. After all, that kid Jack was in serious trouble.

* * *

Back in Evanston that night, Jack went to bed early. Worry was wearing him down. He was exhausted. The attack on Charlie, nanobots at school, and the dying environment had pushed him to the limit. While there had been a big uptick in the adoption of green policies as a result of the enneagram, the earth was running out of time. The progress seemed all too late.

At five am, ear splitting cries woke him up. Jack heard his mom dash into Charlie's bedroom. But the screaming only got louder. He leaped out of bed and rushed across the hall. A horrible struggle was happening. His terrified mother, Max and Izzy, all trying to help the hysterical baby. Over the child's body, a menacing blanket of maroon mist was bearing down, smothering him. His mother wailed in anguish. Max and Izzy, climbed frantically on the sides of the crib, pulling, and pushing, trying to free the baby from the sticky monster. When they seemed to make some progress, the menacing mist reached up like a claw, grabbing Izzy around the neck, strangling him, and slamming him to the floor.

Jack and Max tried to free him, pulling the maroon tentacles off the boy. But the mist glowed orange, burning their hands, and blistering their skin. Izzy's eyes rolled back. He didn't seem to be breathing.

Jack's dad ran in, turned on the lamp, and opened the window. Repelled by the light, the malevolent mist slithered away into the night air. Jack lifted Charlie into his mom's arms, while his dad performed CPR on Izzy. Max called 911.

Maniacal laughter reverberated from the tree outside the window. The thing with gleaming fangs coiled in the branches like a giant serpent. Jack's dad shined a bright light and the thing evaporated. The ambulance arrived, however a burning smell lingered on the second floor. The EMTs pulled an oxygen mask over Izzy's face and he was rolled out on a gurney. Jack and Max were treated for burns.

Max took off in the glass cube but returned several hours later with a medical kit and instructions for the doctors caring for Izzy. Agent Bernstein oversaw the radical medical treatment. The hospital staff had never seen anything like the special infusion prepared by the Sophian physicians. Soon Izzy's condition was upgraded. The attending doctors insisted that the formula undergo analysis. Bernstein agreed but required everyone sign confidentiality documents. If news got out about alien treatments, there would be panic in the streets.

By 8 am, Jack sat on his porch, exhausted. Izzy and Charlie had almost died. Then the morning news reported another attack on the polar icecap despite the iron dome and efforts by the military to block the assault. The only bright spot seemed that the lessons from the Anamchara Text were spreading even faster.

Jack closed his eyes, trying to settle his mind. The lines from ancient scripture came to mind, warning about a spiritual war, and about *battling powers and principalities* ... negative constellations; *anger, pride, deceit, envy, avarice, fear, gluttony, lust,* and *sloth.* And, just yesterday, his dad had reminded them that Dante, back in 1300, had written about these same shadowy complexes.

Jack heard footsteps approaching, and he looked up surprised to see Harold coming up his walk.

"Hey," Jack said.

"Hi ... I'm glad you're home. Are you still trying to find Vincent Marcov?"

"Let's walk?" said Jack.

He didn't want his parents overhearing this conversation. The boys moved down Orrington, and then turned toward the Lake.

"I overheard my dad on the phone talking about Marcov. He was discussing a microwave defense system. I was surprised. No idea who he was talking to."

"Woah, that's weird," said Jack.

"After he got off the phone, I looked at the notepad and his writing left an impression. I tore it off, and like in the movies, I rubbed the side of a pencil over the page. Here's the message," and he handed the paper to Jack.

Jack looked at the note, *building permit #MW1966, 2100 Ridge.*

"Oh, wow, that address is Evanston City Hall."

"I can't go in there alone, but if there's two of us, we *maybe* could get the address and blueprint plans for Marcov's house, given what I overheard," said Harold.

Jack knew the danger. But, at this point, with all the threats around them, doing nothing seemed even more risky.

"OK. But we need more help. I have two friends," Jack said.

"Like could they create a distraction, or something?" asked Harold.

"Yeah, something like that. Let's see if they can meet us at the park?"

Jack texted his friends and half an hour later, they found Jack and Harold sitting on the bleachers.

"I brought doughnuts. Breakfast in the park," said Mike.

"First period starts in forty-five minutes. So talk fast. What's going on?" Jack and Grace looked at Mike with the same shock.

"Since when did you turn into the energizer bunny?" Grace asked.

"Well, I'm trying to be more of a "Trip Grainger . . . the good part. You know . . . on time . . . motivated," Mike said.

"Well, Ok, then," said Grace.

"This is Harold. He has a great idea," said Jack.

Then he noticed Grace's clothes. There was powdered sugar all over her leather jacket. But even more arresting was that, underneath the dark shiny lapels, he saw a pink sweater. Grace quickly zipped up, and Jack resisted making a comment on this unusual clothing choice, or on the evidence that she clearly had raided the bakery box.

Jack described the plan to breach the city hall office, and how they needed to create a distraction. Then he and Harold could slip into the office and photograph the building permit for Marcov's headquarters.

"I like it," said Grace.

The next day the high school had scheduled no morning classes because of teacher conferences. At eleven o'clock, the four teens waited at the bottom of the west side steps of Evanston City Hall. Mike entered the building first, carrying a bag with soda, and three pizza boxes. He wore the red hat and sweatshirt from a local Italian eatery. Grace waited in a wide brimmed felt hat, and long woolen dress coat, borrowed from her mom's closet. She could pass for a young matron. After Mike disappeared in the door, she started up the steps. Harold and Jack followed. They all headed for the third floor. When Mike saw the sign he turned into the Building and Zoning Office. Four office assistants sat behind desks, focused on their computer screens.

"Hi, Mr. Roberts sent me. He was so pleased with the fast inspections last week. He's treating you all to lunch for passing his permit so quickly," said Mike.

The office assistants looked up, and happily moved to the counter, to check out the pizza.

"This is great. So nice." The staff picked up paper plates, lining up for slices.

Then Grace rushed in, bumping into Mike who had set the open soda bottle on the counter. Grace screamed as the soda covered her coat.

"You clumsy ass," she said to Mike.

"This is a Balenciaga!"

The office workers scrambled for paper towels to help her, as Jack and Harold slipped in around the counter.

"*Please* don't report me, I'll get fired for sure. I'm so sorry," wailed Mike.

But Grace continued.

"You *should* be fired. You've ruined my day. I'm supposed to lunch with the hospital benefit committee. I can't go looking like an incontinent crazy person."

Meanwhile, Harold and Jack riffled through the file cabinets lined up inside the interior office. With the threat of discovery, and the clock ticking, Jack opened file drawer after file drawer, his fingers flying through the tabs, trying to locate the permit.

Then, he saw matching numbers.

Grabbing the document, he photographed the building layout. He had just shut the drawer when he heard the inner office door open.

"What are you doing in here?" a voice snapped.

The boys turned to see a large woman blocking the doorway.

Jack swallowed.

"I'm so sorry. I know we should have asked first. This is going to sound weird, but my grandmother graduated from Marywood High School back in the 1960's. Her memory is spotty, but sometimes she remembers stuff from long ago. She wanted to see if there were initials still carved in the windowsill. I'm pretty sure this used to be her homeroom based on her description."

"It would mean a great deal if I could take a photo to her. Her memories are few, and things she does recall are special."

The office manager stopped, her eyes softening. The city hall had been a girl's academy back in the day, before it was converted by the City of Evanston.

"You say the 1960's? My aunt went to Marywood, as well. Let's check the windowsill".

They examined the wood, and under layers of varnish, the faint letters, M.A. were barely visible.

No one was more surprised than Jack, and he snapped the photo.

Thanking the woman profusely, Jack and Harold backed out of the office.

They passed Grace and Mike, as the mopping up continued. Worried they were running out of time, Mike had flipped open one of the pizza boxes. Gooey cheese was everywhere.

"Oh, please don't call my boss. I'll pay your cleaning bill," said Mike.

But Grace was having none of it.

"Oh, my beautiful coat!"

A half an hour later, the four kids entered the halls of the high school, still laughing at the morning caper.

"At least those office workers still got two free pizzas out of our little performance," said Mike.

"What are the chances that windowsill actually would be carved with initials?" said Jack.

"Impossible to calculate," said Harold.

"Oh, I don't know. Teen age girls," said Grace.

Mike and Jack turned and stared at her.

"Wow, that was very Lindy Simons of you."

They could tell Grace was on the verge of making a snotty retort, but then stopped herself.

"I *have* a soft side," she said defensively.

"So that would explain the pink sweater yesterday?" asked Jack.

"I like to keep you guys on your toes." Grace's eyes twinkled.

"By the way, how's the coat doing?" Mike asked.

"Hope that three-hour cleaner lives up to their claim, or my butt is on the line," said Grace.

However, Jack and Mike thought it was unlikely that she ever felt intimidated. Afterall, she had taken down Marcov dressed in high heels and all in pink. Clearly, the years of sparring with her mother had paid off.

After school, Jack printed out the photo of the building permit, and scanned the blueprints.

Although there was no numbered address, he compared the contours of the property to a map of the area. He found the scientist's compound on a bluff, in a notorious section known as *No Man's Land.* The permit listed the owner as Vocram, the name of the shell company that he had learned about from Winnifred Weaver. Grace was excited that they finally had found the location, but Jack worried about all the things that could go wrong if they tried to breach the property. The image of the microwave weapon sent shivers up his spine. He knew what that technology did to a frozen entrée.

CHAPTER NINETEEN

More Bad News

DR. MARCOV RECEIVED A PROMISING REPORT from his Canadian facility. The progress with the satellite fleet was ahead of schedule. To
celebrate, he decided to spend the day collapsing beehives. Bees pollinated
crops, and crops fed the nation. A food shortage would add that certain
something to his end of the world plans. Now that *he* had *his* escape route
to Sophia, he wanted to create a symphony of destruction, a crescendo of
attacks, that targeted everyone and everything, bees, bats, people, ice, air and
water. Fun, fun, fun!

* * *

That afternoon, Jack unlocked his front door and settled on the family room
sofa. Soon he was asleep and dreaming. It wasn't long before the ominous
hourglass appeared. Trapped inside, he felt the sand, pouring over his head,
burying him up to his neck. He gasped and sat up. His heart was racing.

Jack took a walk to shake off the smothering feeling that lingered. When
he reached Fountain Square in downtown Evanston, he was surprised
to find himself staring at a familiar glass cube. Shoppers were gathered

around, speculating this must be a new theater project. Jack found a bench and waited until the dinner hour approached. The crowd thinned out. Jack walked over to the cube, looked around to check that no one was watching, and opened the sliding panel. Max and Izzy casually jumped out. Grousing, the older boy complained.

"Man, I thought those shoppers would never go home. That's what I get for letting Izzy practice his parking skills. We were aiming for the lot behind Ryan Stadium."

But Izzy wasn't having it.

"You know he was nagging me. Firing off all these instructions. Turn here. Pull up now. Watch the wind meter. Talk about a backseat driver!"

Jack figured the boys did not ride around in the cube for no good reason. He asked what was up?

"OK, we'll tell you. But first, we're hungry?"

Jack led them over to a food truck parked around the corner. The boys ate a pizza each, and wiped sauce off their cheeks with paper napkins.

"So what have you been up to?" Jack asked.

Izzy whispered in Max's ear. Jack heard the words, *it's time* and *brother.*

Max turned away, and it seemed he was thinking, considering something.

Then he faced Jack.

"Uh, so there's something we haven't told you yet."

Jack felt his chest tighten, bracing for bad news.

"What is it? Is Charlie OK? I heard Izzy say *brother.*" Jack asked anxiously.

"No, no. It's not *your* brother that's the problem. See we think it's time for you to know the whole truth," said Max.

"What? What whole truth?" Jack's thoughts took off like a runaway roller coaster.

Max and Izzy sat him down on a bench. Max said

"The thing is, Vincent Marcov is sort of related to you."

"WHAT! WHAT! NO WAY!"

"The truth is, the rogue scientist and Joseph Spencer were brothers. Vincent's real name was Walden, and he was Joseph's closest relative, and so he felt *he* should have inherited Morningside. Which is odd, when you think about it, because the two hadn't spoken for decades."

Jack felt the blood drain from his head. Surely this was a nightmare, a terrible parallel universe. However, in his mind, on a giant billboard flashed the breaking news:

Vincent Marcov – Relative.

Jack's whole being protested . . . disgusted, betrayed, but also afraid.

Max continued.

"The brothers, just two years apart in age, were inseparable when they were young. Walden and Joseph had been about as close as two kids could be. Anyhow, they spent hours playing outside, climbing trees, and making boats they floated on a nearby stream. In their shared bedroom, the boys built forts and made all kinds of contraptions."

"But when Joseph was eight years old, everything changed when some kids on the playground teased Walden about his unusual name. The younger boy looked to Joseph for help, but his brother stood silent. Walden began to cry when he saw his brother look away. Joseph, his dearest mate, didn't seem to care about him. The other kids thought it was funny that his brother wasn't going to help. They taunted Walden all the more, calling him Waldo the Weirdo. When the tormenting continued, Joseph walked away, leaving Walden sobbing in a circle of sneering kids."

"Later Joseph felt guilty and said he was sorry, but his brother slammed the door in his face. Day after day Joseph apologized. Walden ignored him. After a while Walden seemed to grow a thick shell, so that he could not, or would not even listen to the apologies. The humiliation and Joseph's betrayal had wounded him to the core. Now, a twisting, grinding hatred festered within him. The parents tried to intervene, but eventually they had to separate the boys, putting them in different bedrooms. To make matters worse, Walden was envious of Joseph's serious green eyes. When the boys were introduced, everyone always commented on Joseph's unusual eye color."

"Walden began playing dirty tricks on his brother. In the beginning the pranks were harmless, but as the boys got older, he put Joseph in real danger. The family went to counseling, and things seemed to improve for a while. Then there would be a setback. Walden began to run with a bad crowd. As the years passed the police were involved on a number of occasions after Walden set fires. Finally, a judge sentenced Walden to a hospital facility for kids with severe behavior problems."

"Walden hated the place, blaming his brother, and vowing to get revenge. He made a string of bad choices, and his character seemed taken over by a darkness. Years passed and the boys seldom saw each other. Joseph earned a university scholarship. Walden dropped out of school, changed his name to Vincent Marcov, and began to study science for destructive purposes."

"Why the name *Vincent Marcov*?" asked Jack.

"Walden drew comic books and created a character in a graphic novel that sounded like a dangerous criminal." said Max.

"So you can see why Marcov would have it out for you, as you remind him of Joseph with your green eyes, and now as the heir to Morningside. But most of all it's your close relationship with Charlie. The way you take care of him. It's a trigger for reliving his own brother's betrayal. It's no wonder he attacked your little brother. He sees Charlie as your Achilles Heel."

Jack leaned against a tree, staring at a pile of dead leaves. Overwhelming shame seemed to shove him. From above, from below, from both sides. Because he knew that he had *not, in fact*, taken care of his brother. When it mattered. When the baby held the nanobot. Now Charlie limped. From brain damage. That likely would last a lifetime. Jack felt the under tow of his terrible family history. The knowledge that he had repeated a version of what Joseph had done to Walden all those years ago.

Then he noticed Izzy staring at him. The boy was reading his thoughts.

A tear rolled down the child's cheek.

Jack felt deep shame that this child now knew his darkest secret.

Suddenly, a high-pitched beeping sound rose from the cube's surface.

"Oh crap, said Max."

Izzy began to whimper.

"What's wrong?" Jack asked.

"That signal means the cube needs a re-charge. We're stuck here, for twenty-four hours. If Izzy hadn't messed up the driving directions, we would have had more than enough juice in the battery."

Izzy still sad, still processing Jack's betrayal, looked at his shoes. Then he approached Jack and gently took his hand, giving it an understanding squeeze. The touch felt like forgiveness.

Jack felt a rush of tears. But he choked them back.

It was clear Max was prepared to sleep in the cube, right in the middle of Evanston, on a cold October night.

"Come home with me. Stay in the guestroom. You guys can come to school with me tomorrow. We can say you're my cousins from Portland," said Jack.

Izzy looked hopefully at his brother.

"Ok, sure, Thanks," said Max. And they started walking.

"You can't leave the cube here," Jack said.

"Sure, we can."

And with that, Max slapped an official looking Apple Store decal on the glass cube.

"Hah, it looks totally like a pop-up kiosk," said Jack.

"Where do you think Steve Jobs got all those designs?" Max said.

"No way," said Jack.

"Way," said Max.

Jack laughed. He was relieved to have this distraction. He didn't want to think about what Izzy now knew about him. But the child had responded with empathy.

So Jack led the boys north on Orrington Avenue, bringing them inside the house to see his parents. They tossed their jackets on the bench and the boys eyed the pot cooking on the stove.

"Something smells good," said Max.

Jack was grateful that the meal was vegetarian. He knew serving chicken to these guys would likely cause a dust up. His parents welcomed the boys, remembering how valiantly they had fought when Charlie was attacked by the strangling mist.

The baby gave Max and Izzy a quizzical look, furrowing his brow, at the silver and green curls that resembled some of his more flamboyant stuffed animals. Then a dark cloud seemed to roll across his face as he recalled the night of the mist attack. He began wailing. Izzy gently touched Charlie's arm. In response, the baby smiled like the sun glowing after a sudden shower.

Then Izzy announced he needed to make a formal apology to the family.

"What can you possibly have done, dear?" Jack's mom asked, surprised.

"Well, you see, kids from Sophia play a game. When we visit your planet, we like to go into jewelry boxes and tangle chains. Sometimes we mess with phone cords, really anything long and twisty. Once in a while, we even mess with editing documents in a laptop."

"Well, that explains it. I've spent a lot of time untangling cords and chains over the years. And spell checking papers," said Jack's mom.

Then she considered what that might mean. These aliens had been visiting for decades.

"Sorry. Sophian kids just love to mess with them," said Izzy.

"If it's any consolation, we *do* get grounded for doing it," Max said.

Jack saw a look on his mom's face. She seemed confused about how to process this unexpected confession. Did visiting aliens always have benign intentions?

Izzy read her mind.

"Don't worry. It's just Sophians. We're good guys."

Jack defended them.

"Remember, Sophia is an advanced civilization. They can help us."

Jack's mom agreed and stepped back into her hostess role, bustling around to get dinner on the table.

Jack helped his parents set out the dishes and flatware, while they overheard the brothers' peculiar interactions with Charlie. The boys communicated in a strange language, their chatter sounding like a festive chicken coop, with the clicks and chirps.

After the meal, Jack told his parents the disturbing news about the identity of Joseph Spencer's brother. How the brothers had been close before the humiliation on the playground. How Vincent Marcov felt entitled to inherit Morningside as the closest relative. How Marcov wanted revenge on the planet.

"Bullying creates trauma that can last a lifetime," said his mom.

"I guess Joseph tried to apologize but Walden would not forgive him," said Jack.

"Deep hurts and family feuds sometimes continue for generations. Remember the Hatfields and the McCoys?"

Then they returned to the dining room, joining Max, Izzy, and Charlie.

At ten pm, they made up beds in the guestroom with fresh sheets and quilted blankets. Jack found some pajamas that he had outgrown years ago and that Charlie would wear in the future. He handed them to the boys. Dressed in the onesies, Max and Izzy looked like giant toddlers. The little guys from Sophia were tucked in bed, said their good nights. Through the door, the Abernaults overheard the boys reciting some form of prayer. It wasn't long before the house settled down.

The next morning Jack awoke early. The house was still quiet, so he stayed in bed. His thoughts turned to how many things in the world were getting better. Every night the news reported another corporation adopting green practices. Formerly flashy celebrities tweeted about a simpler lifestyle, and there was a big uptick in recycling. Even in Washington, green laws were fast tracked to roll back damage to the climate. The Council's mission to turn the tide seemed to be working. And all these changes were credited to the teachings from the Amanchara Text. Jack felt encouraged, however, always the skeptic, he hoped all this change was not too late.

Then Charlie called out. The day officially had begun.

After a breakfast of waffles, the three boys went to school. On the walk Max and Izzy admitted that the chefs on Sophia had not made any advances in the waffle department. Jack made a mental note to tell his mom.

As they approached the high school, Jack saw Grace and Mike waiting near the sophomore entrance. Jack noted that Max and Izzy's silver and moss green curls did not stand out, because several kids in the crowd sported pink and blue hair. The boys from Sophia looked cool, like a K pop band. But they would have to keep their mouths shut, pretending they didn't speak English. So, *visitors from Oslo* was the revised cover story. The clicks and chirps would have given them away. Even Portland, known for quirky people, wasn't *that* weird.

Max and Izzy went to classes with Jack and lunched with Mike and Grace. After school, the boys were unusually quiet, and Grace asked them if something was wrong.

"Well, since you asked, the classes were pretty boring and way, way too easy. On Sophia, we have avatars who work with each kid. Our teachers serve more as mentors, leading discussions about history, politics, art, literature, music, ethics, science, philosophy, law, and math."

"Well, you asked."

"No, no, I love that you're honest. Your school sounds amazing. I would love to have lessons like that."

Then Izzy responded, with a mischievous smile on his face.

"Well, maybe you will, sooner than you think."

Later that afternoon, Max, Izzy, Grace, and Jack walked to Fountain Square to the parked cube. However, as they approached, they saw something was very wrong.

A disgruntled crowd milled around the cube. Red paint was splashed on the glass, and it was clear someone had tried to break in. A line of yellow police tape had been set up around the structure.

"Uh oh," said Max.

"Do you think they damaged it?" asked Jack.

"Not likely, but this can't be good," said Max.

"I want to go home," said Izzy. The little boy looked anxious.

"We're going to have to resort to some special tactics so we can get out of here. We will say our goodbyes now," said Max.

"What do you mean? Shouldn't you come back with us? I can call Agent Bernstein for help," said Jack.

"No time for that. Hope you have some Tylenol. You'll be fine," said Max.

"What are you going to do?" asked Grace.

Max kissed her hand and pulled out a small device. He set some coordinates, and . . .

One minute later . . .

Jack and Grace looked around. They didn't remember how they had gotten to downtown Evanston. Other people also seemed confused, milling about, scratching their heads.

"What are we doing here? My head hurts," said Grace.

"Uh, no clue," said Jack.

"Let's go," said Grace.

They walked back to Jack's house. His parents asked if Max and Izzy had left.

"I think so. They're not around," said Jack.

Grace's brow was furrowed, she seemed to be retracing her steps.

Some vague memory remained. A splotch of red, angry voices, and a string of yellow crime tape flashed in his mind.

"My mind feels fuzzy," said Jack.

"Last night the boys explained how the cube's battery recharged by sapping up hydrogen and trace minerals, a carbon neutral process," said his dad.

Later that evening, Jack attempted to study. He knew his grades had dropped again because he had stopped cheating. Trying to focus, he sat at his desk. But fantasies of Grace kept pushing into his mind as he turned the pages of his notebook. And then there had been Max and Izzy's departure. That he couldn't remember. He started a math problem, but distractions sidetracked him.

These days, doing the next right thing for Jack, meant paying attention to whatever task was in front of him. But he was tired. His fatigue weighed on his shoulders like a giant sack of gravel. There would be moments of hope, signs that everything would turn out OK, and then *boom*, another attack on the ice cap.

Drained and depleted. Danger looming. He'd done all he could. After all, he'd followed the quest. He'd taken the heat after he'd disobeyed his parents and taught the Amanchara Text? He'd risked his safety and the security of his family and Charlie.

But would it be enough? The reports on the icecap were terrifying.

Then he recalled the final task from the Council. Jack tried to push aside this last demand

. . . *Neutralize Dr. Marcov.*

A bolt of fear shot through him.

* * *

The next day was Saturday. Jack and Grace lifted their bikes off the train at Lake Forest, and ten minutes later they rolled up to the entrance of Morningside. Deciding to swim first, they spent an hour in the pool. Time with

Grace offered a bright spot in his life, maybe because she always seemed full of hope. Full of courage.

After they finished the swim, they toweled off and dressed. Then they looked at the blueprints of the giant estate. Jack wanted to investigate a section built into the hillside that he had missed on earlier visits. They found the door leading to this lower mezzanine hidden behind a mural of a Persian garden. Jack slid open the pocket door and they stepped into a dark hall. The light switch failed, so Jack used his phone's flashlight to illuminate the steps. The two of them made their way down a stone staircase and found themselves standing in a large chamber with a high, vaulted ceiling.

Suddenly, the rotunda filled with designs that seemed to come from a hidden projector triggered by their movements. The two stood mesmerized, as they watched unfolding fractals, and intricately shifting snowflakes. Jack recognized Romanesco broccoli, a defrosting action, and other designs from nature. A flush of dahlias appeared above their heads. Then the most remarkable thing occurred. Holograms of tropical plants sprang up around them. Grace moved through the vines and blossoms, overcome with the Eden-like phenomenon.

Jack felt he was standing in the palm of a divine creator, sensing a tight lump hardening in his throat. Awash in these life forms, his eyes brimmed with tears, now feeling Grace's body next to him. His yearning for her came with a new intensity. A fresh awareness of their connectedness filled him. This experience of nature underlined what they were fighting for, the very stuff of creation. Humanity had been gifted with a tree of life that bloomed in all manner of creatures and flora. The diversity of the universe mirrored a divinely inclusive image, an incarnation of generosity and love.

Almost imperceptibly, the images and holograms faded, replaced by a soft light that surrounded them. A small ring of cushioned seats around a contemplation pool suggested this space must have served as the family chapel . . . the simplicity reflecting the Spencer's sense of stewardship. Lost in the moment, Jack felt centered, noticing his forehead, core and gut brighten and connect. He felt totally at peace.

The two sat there for some time, holding hands.

* * *

An hour later the two sat on the train heading south to Evanston. They didn't feel the need to talk, however Jack wondered what this girl was thinking. He knew he was deeply in love. She brought out the best in him. Making him courageous, helping him calm down. He could only hope she felt the same. Jack hesitated to tell her, to use the word *love*. Afterall they were only fifteen years old.

The spell was broken as the train neared the Evanston station when Jack's phone rang. Bernstein's voice brought him abruptly back to reality. The agent informed Jack they had arrested the owner of the copper-colored Nissan who had released the nanobots in the school auditorium.

"You're never going to guess who it is," Bernstein said.

But suddenly, Jack *did* know.

"It's Trip Grainger, isn't it?"

"How did you know?" asked the agent.

"When you said *copper colored Nissan*, it all just came back. I recall now seeing that car parked in the driveway when I visited the Grainger's house. I knew I'd seen that car someplace," said Jack.

The agent informed him that Trip Grainger and his father turned out to be major players in Marcov's web of collaborators. A laptop in the Grainger's house showed that the Masons, Tanya Stokes, Bernaski, and Lindy Simons, were involved.

"I can fill you in later but be careful. No telling who we can trust," said the agent.Jack was not surprised that the Masons and Tanya Stokes were bad actors. However, Lindy Simons had totally fooled him with the sweet-ness routine.

Jack wondered if the FBI knew about the family relationship between

Joseph Spencer and Walden?

"So, I just found out that Joseph and Vincent were brothers," said Jack.

After pausing a moment, Bernstein admitted that this was not new information.

"I knew about the connection, but we worried your family might be targeted."

"I should have been told," said Jack.

"All this devastation due to a bullying experience over Walden's unusual name. It's so ironic that Walden was named after Walden Pond, a serene lake known for the glory of untouched nature. I do know Joseph Spencer regretted to the day he died how he had deserted his brother to the bullies on that playground."

* * *

The following Saturday, Mike, Grace, and Jack returned to Morningside. Over dinner, they talked about the green technology that was popping up all over the place.

"The advancements in wind energy are amazing," said Mike.

"Speaking of advancements," Grace asked, "Have you seen Max and Izzy lately?"

Jack said he had not seen them since their puzzling exit from Fountain Square. Max had instructed him if they ever wanted to talk, they should point the giant telescope directly overhead. This would serve as their *bat signal.*

So, after dark, the friends put on their coats, hats and scarves and wheeled the telescope out on to the patio. Adjusting the telescope into position, they waited.

While they shivered in the cold, they wondered how this signal would work over such a great distance.

Then Jack saw an anomaly in the night sky, a bright star moving like a comet. Could that be the glass cube? The answer came a moment later when the space vehicle settled on the lawn next to the patio, and out slid Max and Izzy on an inflatable ramp.

"Our sensors on Sophia picked up your surveillance." said Max.

"Where did you go the other day?" asked Jack.

"Oh that. Emergency maneuvers . . . we induced amnesia with a frequency alternating disrupter and created a space time lapse. That event won't even show up on security cameras in the area." said Max.

"Woah, I keep thinking there's no more surprises from you guys. And then . . . *Boom,*" said Jack.

"Sorry," said Izzy. "Those people were getting riled up."

"They had read some conspiracy story on social media and thought they were being invaded," said Izzy.

Apparently, he had been mindreading again.

"I don't suppose you have any leftovers from dinner?" Max asked.

Jack ushered them into the kitchen, and after a few servings of pasta salad and fruit, Max stood at attention.

Then Izzy reached in his pocket.

"This is a special moment. Sophia wishes to reward your people for the planet's progress on raising its consciousness. As an advanced civilization, we want to acknowledge your population is ready to take the next step. We put all our formulas, organization policies, laws, and designs on this flash drive. Now you will know, what we know."

"Wow, That's amazing! Sophia is beautiful, a model of freedom, and we're grateful for your trust in us," said Jack.

"We feared this information would be exploited if your people remained undeveloped, but with all the growth in self-awareness and compassion, the Council feels the time is right. Although, some groups on earth still function from unhelpful beliefs," said Max.

"So sad. Keeps people destitute," said Mike.

"There's one more thing. We believe Marcov is working on a virus tailored for you Jack," said Max.

Jack said he suspected as much when his DNA was swabbed. Still, it was terrifying to hear his fears confirmed by the boys.

Jack called Agent Bernstein so he could take custody of the information treasure. He arrived within the hour, quickly made a copy, assuring Jack the data would be protected in a special vault. A team of politicians, psychologists, engineers, city planners, ethicists, artists, educators, bankers, and scientists would begin working on ways to implement the programs. The race to save the planet now seemed on an upswing. This influx of knowledge, like a booster rocket to earth's survival, filled Jack with hope. If only they had more time.

It was getting late. The boys fired up the cube and the teens headed for the train station.

The next morning, Mike called Jack.

"I was up all night. Made a breakthrough. Used game theory. A way to breach Vincent Marcov's compound. I'm positive his security system was made by the Aniketos and Alexiares Company. They were the Greek gods of defense. Marcov probably chose the firm because of the connection to the gods, with his overblown sense of entitlement."

"That sounds right. His building permit at Evanston's city hall listed a firm, *A & A*. Great job. I'd thought it was a contractor of some kind, but there're lots of companies with those initials."

"You know it seems the only way this information helps is if we hack into that company's security system," Mike said.

Jack realized his friend had been up all night. This was not the moment to get into this.

"Get some sleep. Let's meet this afternoon. And thanks, great work. Very Trip Grainger, dude," said Jack.

He texted Grace that they should meet up at three pm.

After Jack put down his phone, he considered his options.

Think this through. Grace and Mike and their gut intuition. Logic and reason, not their strength. Hacking was a bad idea. For so many reasons. When the three friends met up after school, Jack hedged, insisting he needed more time.

"What do you mean, *more* time?" said Grace outraged.

"We have the security system. The polar ice cap is melting, it's now or never," she said.

"Don't you think the FBI already tried hacking?" said Jack.

Mike grabbed Grace's hand, suggesting they take a walk, as he knew that when Jack dug in his heels, which was not that often, there was no point in pushing the issue. Despite his own frustration that all his research may have been a waste of time, Mike generally appreciated an opportunity to stand down.

When his friends left, Jack closed his eyes, clearing his mind. He took a deep breath, pushing away all thoughts of Grace's disapproval. All thoughts of Vincent Marcov.

It was time to go deeper.

Time to go under the level of security systems, and below the surface of what they knew about Dr. Marcov. Jack retreated to a quiet, empty space in his mind, drawing in a deep breath.

The image of a waterfall rushing over his mind, centered him, and quieted his thoughts.

Soon a parade of characters marched into his awareness.

The faces of Elinor and Joseph Spencer appeared. Jack let them pass, returning to his breath. Morningside's mural with the engineers flashed in his mind.

He breathed again.

Grace diving in the pool.

Gears inside the glass clocks ticked.

Another breath.

Max and Izzy floating under a pastel blue dome . . . Emptiness.

Silence.

Then flashing words, *Keep it simple*.

Suddenly, parked in his mind.

The image of his neighbor's dusty plumbing van.

Jack opened his eyes.

That was it.

The plumbing!

Maybe ... *maybe*, it was time to go *Old School*.

Grace and Mike walked in the door.

"Hey, I've got an idea. Hear me out."

"Marcov's security system likely is aimed at protecting incoming systems ... electric, water, gas, cable, but probably not at securing the outgoing system ... specifically, the sewer line," said Jack.

"And we know the scientist's compound sits on a bluff over the lake," he added.

"Interesting," said Mike.

"Go on," said Grace.

"We could tunnel through the waste pipe with a remote camera. My robot certainly has the capacity to carry one, and to perform simple tasks, like opening a cabinet. We can inflict a ton of damage. Basically, take out his lab if we keep our wits about us. No hacking necessary. Of course, there's still the issue of the microwaves, but it's unlikely the weapon is triggered by the sewer pipes. And we won't be inside the house. This will be a remote-controlled attack."

Grace and Mike considered Jack's plan. They couldn't deny he had made some good points. They all decided to sleep on it, and then meet up in the morning.

That night, Jack flopped around on his bed unable to settle down. Finally, he dropped into a deep sleep. Soon an assortment of utensils and tools floated into his dream. Animated with arms and legs the spoons, nuts and bolts, forks, and a corkscrew marched past, like in a movie theater advertisement for popcorn and drinks.

Finally, the golden whistle appeared. Instead of engraved numbers, an array of dancing letters arranged themselves on the golden surface . . . spelling a word . . . *HARMONICS.* This image, sinking in, bounced, and boomeranged from his unconscious to other parts of his dreaming brain, chiseling the word in a remote corner of his mind.

When he awoke the next morning, as hard as he tried, he could not recall the dream. Somehow, though, he sensed that the time was right to attack Marcov's compound.

After school, they finalized the plan, and signaled Max and Izzy to meet at Jack's house. They rushed around town with a list of items for their operation. Tomorrow was Thanksgiving, and they hoped the holiday would serve as a good cover for their covert mission.

The next day, the turkey dinners in all three homes were finished by 6:00 pm. After helping to wash the dishes, the teenagers bowed out of their gatherings, claiming they needed a walk after the heavy meal.

At 9:00 pm they met up with Max and Izzy at the harbor north of town. The area was deserted as most people now were in a food coma or parked in front of the television watching holiday specials. The kids descended the steps to the docks. Above them, the gorgeous white dome of the Bahai Temple glowed through the bare tree branches.

They were all dressed head to toe in slick black wetsuits, looking like well-oiled Doberman Pinschers. The bone chilling November weather whipped around them, but the extra layers they wore protected them from the elements. Max and Izzy looked like giant babies with their moss green and silver curls tucked in their hoods.

At the end of the pier, they boarded a motorized raft like those used by white water rafters. Jack did not ask how Max and Izzy had scored this boat, but the stenciled words, *Great Lakes Naval Station* provided a hint. Working quickly, they hauled their tools and Jack's robot into the watercraft. Fortunately, the wind off the Lake had died down making the waves more manageable.

Growling, the motor roared, and they headed north, hugging the shore of Lake Michigan. The boat created a sizable wake as the sleek craft cut through the dark water, sending up cold spray. A curtain of clouds veiled the moonlight as they approached the compound. When they saw the line of trees on the bluff, they knew they were close. Max flipped a switch, turning on a sound canceling device that masked the roar of the motor.

Soon the dark outline of Vincent Marcov's compound appeared, sending a shiver up Jack's spine. The imposing structure rose above them as the craft approached a formidable wall of stone. Behind this barrier of rock stood a veritable fortress. Shuddering, Jack saw the massive structure, and for a split second, he wondered if this venture amounted to pure folly. Then he saw the scientist's silhouette moving, oh so slowly, on the second floor of the estate. He hesitated, but pushing down his fear, he drew in a steadying breath.

Jack signaled the *go* sign. Pulling the raft quickly up on the beach, the five waited silently until, one by one, all the windows in the mansion darkened. He touched the chest pocket of his wetsuit, checking the golden whistle. Then the wind picked up again, and they smelled the stench of the sewer line.

It was show time. Mike located the sewer pipe jutting out from the wall of rock, above the lapping water. It was illegal to send raw waste into the Lake, however, Marcov, true to form, ignored the law. Izzy stepped forward with a canister from a Sophia environmental lab. He released a massive shot of a bacteria neutralizing foam into the pipe, flushing out the sewage. Then Max pulled out a rotor blade, produced from one of Sophia's newly discovered metals. It made short work of drilling, widening the pipe into a tunnel big enough to accommodate Jack's talented little robot.

Next, Jack released a plastic strip that unfurled into the tunnel. They had practiced sending the robot over the plastic path, adding treads to increase the traction. Now their preparation paid off as the robot disappeared into the passageway. In a few minutes, the camera transmitted an image of the compound's basement. They were in. And the little robot got to work. The five kids took turns operating it, sending it down hallways and careening into different rooms. As it traveled, it destroyed everything in sight with a compact laser gun. So far, they saw no sign of the refrigerator holding the virus meant for Jack. Max had outfitted the drill with a white noise apparatus so that the demolition remained almost silent, blending into the sound of crashing waves.

With one more floor to visit, Jack took the controls. In the second room he saw the two posters, one of Joseph Spencer and the other of him. The red X over Spencer's image sent a shiver up his spine. Jack saw the portrait of Cronos' menacing face glaring at him, the eyes glistening with pure evil.

Jack sent a blast from the laser, setting fire to the painting. Then, he turned the robot, sending him out into the hall. The monitor now showed a frosted glass door with *LABORATORY* etched into the surface. Jack pivoted the controls and rolled the robot inside. Spinning, to survey the walls, the camera rested on a refrigerator with a biohazard warning sticker. Jack fired up the laser, training it on the deadly target that housed the virus meant for him.

But then, the image went dark. In the same instant, the controls in Jack's hand fell slack.

His heart froze.

Suddenly Marcov's booming voice blasted over the roof from an outdoor PA system.

"Got you now! Alexa . . . turn on the microwave!"

A giant search beam now rotated wildly around the property, hunting for prey. The kids could hear the electromagnetic radiation weapon powering up with a growing hum.

Trapped, the five kids understood the impossibility of outrunning the microwaves that would cook them in minutes.

But in a flash of inspiration, Jack pulled out the golden whistle, blowing as hard as he could.

A tremendous woooosh emitted from the instrument . . . and the kids ran like crazy.

Max summoned the raft by remote control. They all jumped, just in time, because a powerful sound wave, a *harmonic*, hit the compound. In seconds, the entire fortress, walls, and towers, collapsed, crumbling the scientist's lair into a giant heap of rubble.

The force of the catastrophe shook the earth, producing a massive wave in the lake, as a black mountain of water rolled toward the shore.

The motor roaring, the raft sped away with the kids leaning into the wind. But outrunning the wave seemed impossible. A huge death wall of water headed directly toward them. No way they could survive this kind of force. Surely, they would perish in this watery grave.

Suddenly, a shaft of light from above appeared, calming the water's surface around the boat, holding back the black wall of water.

Max and Izzy shouted.

"The Council is helping us!"

They yelled joyfully. Jack quickly regained control of the craft, following the path illuminated in the water.

After twenty minutes of gripping the steering wheel, he saw the gleaming alabaster dome of the Bahai Temple. The boat pulled up alongside the dock. Climbing out of the rocking raft, the kids fell over themselves on to the pier, rolling with amazement at their success. Tears flowed from their eyes. They were not so alone.

The Council had finally intervened.

Jack and his friends knew they were lucky to be alive. At that last instant, the word HARMONIC in neon color, had flashed in his mind, saving the mission. Without the whistle sending out the massive vibration, the incoming microwave surely would have blasted them to bits.

Then the massive wall of water rolling toward them. The terror. Then rescue by the Council's power . . . Jack broke down again and wept. Grace held him as they rocked in an embrace. Max, Izzy, and Mike hugged. They had survived. The building complex was history.

But what about Vincent Marcov?

* * *

The next morning Jack couldn't dismiss the thought that maybe Marcov had escaped the harmonic because of his ability to go invisible. His suspicion was confirmed when later that day, a meme appeared on hundreds of millions of computer screens . . . the last grain of sand dropping in the hourglass.

Vincent Marcov, indeed, had escaped, going invisible at the last instant. While Jack's virus had burned up in the explosion, the fiend had transported himself to an abandoned railroad yard. Now homeless, and feeling outsmarted by those rotten kids, the rogue scientist fumed. Dressed in a charred cardigan, he berated himself that a harmonic weapon, and access through the sewer line had never even occurred to him. Hatred seared in his chest; from the place his heart should have been. He vowed to obliterate the green-eyed kid from the face of the earth. Marcov howled at the moon that was, even now, visible in the morning sky.

"I *still* have the ice cap. No more futzing around with the virus," he muttered to himself.

Then he pulled out his phone, checked for service bars and connected to his Canadian facility via a dark web link. The screen flickered for a moment and then zoomed into the remote location in Saskatchewan. The hundred or so individuals, dressed in maroon jumpsuits, saluted their leader, flashing a VM sign with their hands.

"As you were," said Dr. Marcov.

The team looked around. Tension on their faces. This was highly unusual for contact at this hour.

"It's time. Load the lasers on the entire fleet ASAP," ordered Dr. Marcov.

"Yes, sir," the team leader saluted.

The room cleared and for the next two hours Vincent Marcov watched his phone screen as his minions scrambled in the long hangar.

When the work was complete, the team lined up.

Marcov drew in a deep breath. It was time. Then he ordered them to open the large doors. A dozen of the team broke ranks and moved to push on the corrugated steel panels. The metal hinges let out a frightful screech and the frigid Canadian air rushed into the hangar. The satellites, lined up on a conveyor belt, began to move out to the launching pads.

Marcov, drew in a breath, trying to manage his overwhelming emotions.

Tears streamed down the craters in his old face.

"They will all *pay* now," he wailed.

The sun and moon hid their faces behind the clouds.

With trembling hands, he tapped in the code. In synchronized pairs his shiny new satellites, atop rocket boosters, blasted into the sky.

Flying in formation two hundred miles above the earth, they headed straight for the Arctic Circle.

Immediately, radar defense systems in a dozen countries in the northern hemisphere lit up as the rockets registered on military tracking screens. The United States Space Force scrambled to intercept, but the rogue scientist, activated thousands of decoys, his fingers moving furiously on his keyboard.

CHAPTER TWENTY

Armageddon

I N THE NORTHERN SKIES, A FULL-SCALE WAR erupted as Marcov's fleet of satellites raced into position. The Navy responded by firing missiles to disrupt the laser attacks. Torpedoes rode under the waves, seeking out targets that turned out to be decoys. Canada, the United States, and the European Union hoped the reinforced *iron dome* would shield the ice cap.

After hours of intense battle in the air and ocean, the radar screens at the Pentagon began to show Marcov's lasers disappearing with trails of light going dark. The Space Force and Navy Commanders hoped the tide had turned in their favor. Minutes passed.

Vincent Marcov smiled as he imagined his enemy's confusion. Drawing in a breath of anticipation, he counted, "One Mississippi, Two Mississippi . . ." until he reached ten.

Then he pushed a button. Flaps lifted on his satellites. Another tap on the keyboard, and tens of millions of tiny metal darts shot toward the arctic. The stiletto sharp blades hit the surface of the ice, hacking off a blast of glassy shards. Gigantic mountains of ice disintegrated into the sea.

Fast, cheap and out of control worked every time, Marcov rejoiced.

With the polar ice cap disappearing before their eyes, commanders at the Pentagon knew the iron dome was useless. It was clear the earth was losing the battle. The destruction came so fast, their screens shimmered, the images flickering, overwhelmed by the incoming data.

* * *

After early reports hit the news outlets, many people *still* dismissed the battle as just more conspiracy theories. On the streets of Chicago, London, New York, Sydney, Paris, and Hong Kong, most of the population went on as though everything was normal. People found it hard to imagine the possibility of losing the planet. It was easier to ignore the signs. They figured things must be OK as they saw airplanes flying, people shopping, and traffic lights still working. Maybe the climate issue was just another hype. If there was real danger, surely the government, or *somebody*, could handle it.

That evening, Jack's phone rattled on his nightstand. Seeing it was the FBI agent, a shot of fear hit him as he picked up the call.

"Are you watching TV?" said Bernstein.

"Why? What happened?" asked Jack.

"The entire polar ice disintegrated a half hour ago. It's over," said the agent, his voice cracking.

"No, **no**. There *must* be something we can do," said Jack.

"Spend time with your family. Stay off the streets. Once the president addresses the nation, there's sure to be rioting," said Bernstein.

The line disconnected. Jack put down the phone.

The realization hit him.

Vincent Marcov had won. The earth was on life support.

All the work, all the worry, all the danger had been for nothing . . . the damage to Charlie, his family targeted. And still . . . the planet would shrivel in the heat. New York under forty feet of water, Miami and New Orleans gone. Storms and fires would take out what was left. Crops would fail. Millions of people on the move, hungry, thirsty, trying to escape to higher ground. But there was *no higher ground*, nowhere to hide.

Jack turned on the television and the emergency broadcast channel flashed the message.

Environmental disaster. Stay calm. Stay home.

Still, he could not believe his eyes. Jack raised his phone to call Grace, but the device was dead now. He wondered where his parents were as they had taken Charlie for a doctor appointment. They should have been home hours ago. Then he heard the distinctive loud pop of an electrical power outage.

Jack walked outside and heard people running and shouting in the dark. Neighbors were loading up their cars with furniture. Maybe trying to escape to a cabin in the Northwoods? He couldn't believe his eyes. In a daze, he walked the few blocks to downtown where he saw people fighting in the street, trying to protect their bags of food and plastic water jugs. Broken glass covered the sidewalks, and Jack could hear rocks hitting store windows. Looting and gunshots in his town? It seemed impossible. A line of flashing lights from emergency vehicles blocked the street up ahead. Flames rose from a burned-out police car. Cracks of gunfire were getting closer.

Jack started to walk home, and as he approached his house, he saw candlelight flickering behind the shades. His parents must have made it home. Pushing open the door, however, he saw Grace sitting alone on the living room rug, hugging her knees.

"Oh my gosh, you're OK," he said.

He wrapped his arms around her.

"I didn't know what to do. I couldn't get home. The roads are blocked," she said. "I don't even know if my family is OK."

"Let me get the battery powered radio," said Jack.

A few minutes later he returned with the device. But before they could turn it on, loud banging on the front door startled them.

"Blow out the candle," he told Grace.

They heard heavy footsteps on the porch. An angry voice called out.

"Hey, get that guy before he makes it to his car."

Jack peeked behind the shade. A group of tough looking guys carried crow bars and a flare.

Grace and Jack heard the men go down the steps, and a moment later a shot rang out. From behind the shade, Jack saw his mild-mannered neighbor had gunned down one of the gang members. The body lay at the curb. Now the shooter was brandishing the weapon. The attackers ran off and the neighbor retreated into his house.

"We better hide. Bring the radio in the back. I'll grab some food and water," said Jack.

"Where do you think Charlie and your parents are?" Grace asked.

"I don't know," said Jack with tears filling his eyes. For the next twenty minutes they listened to the broadcast on the radio, but there was only the message to stay calm, and classical music intended to soothe the lost citizenry.

While sounds of mayhem wafted in the window, Jack and Grace held each other. There would be no graduations, no prom, no college, no travel, and no children. All their plans, hopes and dreams, crushed.

They ate some leftovers, crackers, and cheese, curled up in a big quilt. They pictured their families. Were they even alive?

Hours passed. Still no parents, no Charlie.

Exhausted, and defeated, their eyes closed.

* * *

The same evening, on Sophia, Izzy couldn't sleep. Something was wrong. He could *feel* it. Checking the news, he saw the alert about the Earth's polar cap. Even across the vast intergalactic span Izzy sensed Jack's despair. In his mind he could see the boy rolled up in the fetal position, under the quilt with Grace. Jack and his family had suffered terrible losses, and for what? The boy had fought valiantly, fulfilling his commitment to the Council, despite his fear and attacks from Marcov.

The worst had happened. The icecap was gone. Now the aftermath. Population migrations, revolutions, collapsing economies, famine, and drought. And Vincent Marcov would flee the gasping planet . . . to Sophia.

The child turned over these facts in his mind.

Now Izzy had turned eight years old the previous week, and as he blew out the candles on his cake, he felt a new sense of independence. Something was shifting inside him. He could feel it.

Max would be mad, of course. And he knew there would be hell to pay, but it was time to act.

Tiptoeing down the hall, he rounded a corner and went up the massive staircase. He counted the rooms as he passed the thresholds in the darkened hallway. One door, two doors, three doors. He took a deep breath, pushing open the forbidden door. The one no one had dared to open . . . not for millennia. The door with the letter *P* carved into the oak.

On a massive bed, slept great, great, great, etc.etc,. grandfather.

Izzy paused a moment.

For all of his eight years, he had been warned, under no condition, was he ever, *ever*, to enter this room.

But Izzy trusted his gut, moving quickly over to the bed. Knowing if he thought about this too long, he might back down.

Izzy saw the famous lyre at the bedside. This ancient instrument, according to the stories, was used by the old man to illustrate the psychic tension within people. In order to function in harmony, the strings should not be too slack or too tight.

Izzy drew in a deep breath.

"Psst . . . Time to get up, Grandpa," Izzy jiggled the bed.

The old man said, "Go away."

Izzy jiggled the bed again. This time with more force.

The old man let out a series of snorts.

Izzy now stood on the bed, jumping as high as he could.

"Hey, Grandpa, Wake Up!"

"Stop the boat," the old man yelled, disoriented.

Izzy stopped jumping and their eyes met.

Emerald-green irises fluttered under the heavy lids. The face, so wrinkled it looked like a mountain range.

"Who's that now?" asked the ancient figure, as he rolled over to see the child, who had slipped off the bed.

"It's Izzy. We haven't actually met. Well, how could we have? I'm eight years old. I've been told you've been sleeping for millennia. But, right now, *you* have to get up. There's an emergency. Everyone else has given up, it seems."

"What time is it?" the old man asked.

"Well, it's ten pm, past my bedtime, but when you hear what's going on, you'll understand."

Then Izzy handed him a tablet that showed the earth's polar section missing the ice.

"What's this?" the old man leaned out for support, trying to sit up.

"This is *terrible*." His eyebrows furrowed.

"I know, right?" said Izzy.

Izzy pulled the old man up, but it took several tries. Finally, the old guy sat on the edge of the bed. The child's eyes widened as he had never, ever seen a beard that long.

"Get me those slippers, and robe," the grandpa said.

Izzy complied, shaking the dust off the robe.

"You can't walk with that long beard. You'll trip for sure," said Izzy.

"I see what you mean," said the old grandpa, feeling the weight on his face.

"Maybe if we cut it down a bit."

Izzy found a pair of shears in the middle drawer, and he began cutting through the bristling tangle.

"That's better," he said finally.

Looking on the floor, Izzy saw a mass of hair that looked like a giant snowbank of white wires. A few mice jumped out, scurrying to find other shelter.

"Let's go," said the old man.

With Izzy's help, and a tall wooden staff, Grandpa Pythagoras descended the stairs. Picking up speed, he made his way into the Council's Chamber, throwing open the doors.

A gasp came from the assembly. The chairman looked stunned. And then scared.

Only Max's voice was heard.

"What have you done, Izzy?"

But Grandpa Pythagoras glared at the group.

"Izzy is the only one here with an ounce of sense. Why did you let me sleep so long?"

His voice boomed, shaking the glassware on the table.

"We couldn't find the wheel so we didn't think you could do anything if we *did* wake you up."

"Do you think I would leave that wheel laying around while I took a nap?" said Pythagoras.

No answer came from the incredulous council members.

Clearly there had been a *massive* breakdown in communication.

With that, Grandpa Pythagoras clapped his hands, and the engraved oak table began to spin. When it stopped, a wheel, shaped like the nine-pointed enneagon, floated above the table. It looked to be made of platinum.

A rumble of approval erupted from the room.

"So *that's* where you keep it?"

"Knock it off," Grandpa Pythagoras said, glaring at them.

Then the old man commanded.

"The Chain of Nine must be assembled."

A hush settled on the group. Immediately, the Council members filed out, leaving a core group.

Joseph Spencer, Izzy and Max remained among the designated few. Hildegard of Bingen, Tolstoy, DaVinci, and the tall red headed woman in pink silk also stood in the circle. Without needing a cue, Max and Izzy removed their blue contact lenses, exposing their dazzling green eyes.

"That's good," the grandpa said.

"Now, we just need that kid. What's his name?"

"Jack Abernault," said Izzy.

Max and Izzy moved fast.

Several hours later, they entered the house on Orrington. Moving quietly, they didn't want to wake Grace.

Minutes later, Jack, bleary eyed at this midnight voyage, sat in the cube. Max and Izzy had rushed him out of the house into the waiting glass vehicle before he could object. Stopping only to grab Jack's jacket. As soon as the cube passed through the time portal, Max explained what was going down.

"Pythagoras! The *real* Pythagoras?" Jack asked, clearly flummoxed at hearing the extraordinary events that had occurred that evening on Sophia.

Then Max and Izzy removed their sunglasses.

Jack saw the emerald-green eyes.

"You too?"

"Yes . . . us too," said Max.

"You see, we're actually cousins. To activate the wheel, a group must assemble. Only a tiny few of our relatives are part of the Chain of Nine. Seems we are genetically specific individuals. Sort of neurodivergent, but more encompassing."

"It has something to do with a mutated gene that provides a slightly altered electromagnetic chemical make-up. The special feature can skip many generations, and then it can pop up," said Max.

"Pythagoras says a naturally occurring algorithm seems to kick in, directing the incidence of this genetic mutation. But he agrees it's likely from a higher power," said Izzy.

"Bottom line, it's a mystery."

"Woah," said Jack. "That *is* crazy," he added.

"But why did you wear the blue contact lenses?" Jack asked.

"We wore the contacts because the focus group felt our green and silver curls *with* our emerald eyes would be off putting to Earthlings. The chirps and clicks in our speech pattern were already pretty odd," said Max.

When Sophia finally came into view, Jack's thoughts turned to the doctors on this planet who had saved Charlie's life. A sharp jab hit him as Jack wondered if his brother and parents were still alive.

Izzy nodded.

"They're back home. Two of our agents rescued them from the subway. When the traffic in the loop snarled, they abandoned the car."

Jack took in a breath of gratitude.

Then his thoughts were interrupted as the glass cube slowed, landing near the fountain. Making their way over to the Council's rotunda, Max and Izzy led Jack into the chamber. There, eating dinner, sat his ancient great grandfather.

"Oh, good you're here. Nice to make your acquaintance, Jack Abernault, I'm your great, great . . .etcetera, etcetera, grandpa."

Pythagoras lifted a cut crystal goblet in a toast. Wiping his mouth with a linen napkin, the old man rose.

Astounded that he was meeting Pythagoras, Jack looked around at the assembly, trying to get his bearings.

Max and Izzy had filled him in about the others with this gene mutation. The news that Tolstoy, DaVinci and Hildegard of Bingen were among his ancestors, just blew his mind.

Grandpa Pythagoras announced that the apple pie would have to wait, and he gestured the group to circle the platinum wheel.

"Extend your hands toward the center, like this," he said.

Obeying instructions, they assembled around the wheel, and lifted their arms. They were amazed to see a river of golden mist flow from their palms, and blend into a spinning disk.

A river of energy flowed, lighting up the paths and points on the circle, illuminating the enneagram pattern.

Pythagoras slowly lowered his arms, and the group followed, until the lighted paths merged with the platinum wheel.

"There we go," he said with satisfaction.

"Locked and loaded."

Then, the door to the chamber opened, and the entire Council took their places for this momentous occasion. Pythagoras rose.

"You may all sit down now. Prepare to be dazzled," he said, with twinkling green eyes.

CHAPTER TWENTY ONE

Integration

THE OVERHEAD LIGHTS DIMMED, AND a hush settled on the group. Pythagoras pushed a button on a console, and a large curtain of something resembling a panel of stardust appeared . . . creating a high-tech screen. The planet earth came into view. Growing larger, the image tipped and rotated, until the north pole rested in the center.

"Let me be clear. The wonders you will witness would be impossible without the inner work and focused action of Jack, Izzy, Max, and Joseph. They are the ones who prepared the Earth with technology and with teachings from the Anamchara Text. Millions of enlightened minds now function as an actual conductor. Like a radio channel, or morphogenic field, vibrating at a harmonious frequency."

Pythagoras blotted the tears from his eyes. Then he continued.

"Let me show you an infrared scan of the earth's consciousness two years ago, compared with how it looks today. This shift shows the change in how citizens view each other and the planet. Old caste systems are falling away as people gain dignity and respect. Resources reallocated."

On the split screen, the first image showed a dreary mist of red, and dark grey ominously hanging above the earth's atmosphere. The recent scan showed a soft glow of violet and pale blue now hovering above the earth. The contrast was stunning.

"Our efforts here this evening would be useless if the earth had remained in the dark. So, may we have an applause for our champions?"

The chamber erupted with enthusiastic whelps of,

"Here! Here!"

Jack choked back tears, as Izzy grabbed his hand. The significance of this gathering sank in as he awaited this intergalactic event.

Pythagorus rose, and placing his hands on the wheel, he began to turn it until a golden beam rested on the North Pole.

"Ok, let's get this system powered up. Prepare to encounter the wall where knowledge smashes into mystery."

Suddenly, Jack could hardly believe his eyes.

Superimposed on the globe was the sculpture he had seen in Lake Geneva. The one that had touched his soul. The one with the arms powering the gear shifts. Moving away from excess, shifting into balance. This piece of art captured his struggle, away from fear, into peace and courage. The move from point six to point nine!

Then the image of the sculpture faded away.

Like a maestro, conducting a symphony, Pythagoras, gripped the wheel, wailing to the universe,

"*Goodness, Kindness, Effectiveness, Creativity, Wisdom, Loyalty, Joy, Power, Peace.*"

Instantly, the virtues arose, manifesting as nine colors. Streaming in a ring that wrapped around the globe, sparks of energy flew from nine points of fire. The flashing traveled from point one, to seven, to five, to eight, to two, to four, and back to one. A brilliant pulsating triangle illuminated the enneagon's center.

"Come here, Izzy. You're the star this evening for listening to your heart, and for having the courage to wake me up."

Izzy stood up proudly, moving over to the wheel.

"Now!" his grandfather instructed.

Izzy pushed down on the wheel with all his strength, tipping it. A rush of silvery ice blasted out in a stream and began to coalesce on the North Pole.

The chamber erupted in applause and shouts of amazement, as they saw an immense island of fresh glistening ice cover the North Pole.

Then Grandpa Pythagoras beckoned Jack to take Izzy's place. Jack gripped the wheel, feeling an electric current pass through his arms and down into his shoes. Following instructions, he shifted his weight down on the wheel, and an emerald river blasted the Amazon, as forests magically rose on the South American continent. It reminded him of the holograms in Morningside's contemplation chamber.

The room exploded with happy shouts.

Jack wished Grace could have been there to see this.

Champaign was poured for the crowd. Dancing broke out, and the assembly sang the Sophian anthem. When the last note sounded, strains of Johann Sebastian Bach's *Joy* filled the air.

"It's way past midnight, Pythagoras announced.

"Go sleep now. We will let the weary earth adjust to the healing."

* * *

In a rundown motel, Dr. Vincent Marcov noticed his tablet dinging an alert.

Sitting down to check it out, he set his glass of cabernet on the desk. Tapping the keyboard, his eyes nearly popped out of his head when he saw the glistening, reconstituted polar ice cap on his screen.

He laughed.

"This must be a joke," as he rebooted the program.

A second ding, and the Amazon basin appeared, green and flourishing in areas Marcov aggressively had logged for decades. The rogue scientist checked the Wi-Fi signal, and his security settings to see if this was some trickster's hack. Because those images couldn't possibly be authentic.

But as the truth sunk in, the pulse of frantic, off the rails keyboard music began to build in his head. Louder and louder, it grew.

Joy by Apollo, the baroque pop version of Bach's 1723 composition, was now playing an ear-splitting soundtrack in his head . . . the musical score for the mental breakdown of Dr. Vincent Marcov.

Marcov felt his faculties fragmenting, his thoughts flying like shards of glass. Hadn't he totally obliterated the polar ice cap? How could this be? This was a living nightmare. Furiously, he grabbed the laptop, entering a code that launched a missile aimed at the hangar in Canada. Those idiots had failed him. Minutes later the blast took out his team. All that remained was a burned-out cavern.

He heard sirens in the distance . . . growing louder.

Vincent knew he needed to disappear. But the music was interfering.

He couldn't focus.

Images now intervened. The face of Joseph. Then Jack. And finally, the powerful sculpture in Lutetia's studio. The one with the living arms on gears. The art that had caused him to break out in hives . . . now overwhelmed him. The thing seemed to be dancing! It filled his field of vision. Wrestled him to the ground. Rolling on the floor, he closed his eyes to shut it out, but the sculpture was etched in his mind. No way he could muster the attention he needed to perform his disappearing trick.

The music now seemed to be blasting from the walls, and from the trees outside. Vincent felt warm blood began to flow from his ears. His auditory and visual faculties overwhelmed with incoming music and images of the sculpture.

Driving him mad, he collapsed.

After tracking Marcov's cell phone signal, the FBI broke down his door. Cowering in the corner, too disoriented to perform his disappearing trick, Vincent rocked and whimpered. The babbling doctor cut a pitiful figure.

Marched out in handcuffs and into an unmarked van, the neighbors looked from behind window shades, wondering what was going down. What they saw was a slender figure with wild eyes, begging his captors to turn down the music.

CHAPTER TWENTY TWO

The Future

For the next ten years, scientists, politicians, and educators worked on the flash drive information from Max and Izzy. The environment slowly recovered as new international cooperatives protected the polar ice cap and the Amazon-forest canopy. Green technology blossomed, but it was estimated that it would take decades for the air and water quality to return to preindustrial levels. Attitudes in the culture shifted, as kids all over the world sported tee shirts that read, *Conservation Is the New Black*. Meanwhile, Jack and his friends took part in a huge revolution in education.

Jack and Grace dated through high school; however, they chose colleges on opposite coasts. While they remained life-long friends, they understood they had admired qualities in each other that had attracted them in the first place. Over the years Grace picked up some of Jack's prudence, while Jack became more assertive, and peaceful. Mike studied diplomacy and eventually worked at the United Nations. Jack became a chemical engineer with an expertise in computational neuroscience. Grace joined Doctors Without Borders after medical school.

Max and Izzy continue to visit.

Note

THE ENNEAGRAM IS A MODEL OF PERSONALITY types based on nine gifts. The purpose of the system is to help an individual make a shift to balance the self. Breathwork, meditation, and trained teachers help with this process of individuation. The goal is to develop the "inner observer," and to "wear one's style more lightly." Twenty-seven subtypes further define variations in the nine patterns; however, no external description can ever capture an individual's uniqueness.

The system has ancient roots in many traditions, remaining mostly an oral tradition until the 1980's. Over the past forty years, three hundred books on the topic have been published.

Teens often benefit from journaling, interactive games, panels, and listening to stories about the styles of behavior. Mentors and workshops are available through the International Enneagram Association.

Dr. Jerome Wagner, Loyola University, created the WEPSS, a standardized, reliable, and valid Enneagram inventory for individuals, age 18 and older, reviewed in Buros's Mental Measurements Yearbook.

Anam Cara, or Anamchara, refers to a mentor or guide in the Celtic tradition.

Most of the green technology described in this book exists.

Children under the age of twelve generally lack the *capacity* to hold two concepts at the same time. As a result, it may be difficult to grasp that a **personality type** can **also** be **softened and lessened**. (Concrete Operations, Piaget. *either/or)*

However, by age twelve, a preteen often can understand that personality type can be balanced by making certain shifts in perspective and behavior. (Piaget, Formal Operations Stage, *both/ and)*

CPSIA information can be obtained
at www.ICGtesting.com
Printed in the USA
LVHW021449181121
703543LV00005B/25